Watchers of Kanah

Archangel Michael - The Young Years

Kevin L. Spinks

ISBN-13: 978-1-7374460-0-2 (paperback)

ISBN-13: 978-1-7374460-2-6 (hardcover)

ISBN-13: 978-1-7374460-1-9 (ebook)

Editor of first edition: Carol Gaskin, Editorial Alchemy

Editor of second edition: Melana Cassell

Book Cover by Deranged Doctor Design

Second edition published November 2023

Website: KevinSpinks.com

CONTENTS

1. SOMETIMES YOU LOSE 1
2. SOMETIMES YOU WIN 9
3. THE FIRST WALK 13
4. PAPEONS 19
5. THE DOOR 24
6. DANCE CLASS 27
7. THE NEXT DAY IN DANCE CLASS 33
8. THE WALK HOME 38
9. THE DOOR IN THE WOODS 44
10. CAVE FIGHT 52
11. THE GREAT ESCAPE 59
12. THE NEXT DAY 63
13. ANOTHER TRIP TO THE CAVE 69
14. PLANET EARTH 75
15. MICHAEL FOUND 79
16. AN EARTHLING AND A DOG 85
17. VINCE 95
18. GANG FIGHT 100

19. AURORAS 111
20. TIME TO LEAVE 118
21. ABDUCTED 121
22. DARKMAR 127
23. THE TOUR 132
24. RAMKRAD 145
25. VISIONS AND INVITATIONS 150
26. THE GALA 155
27. FIGHTING ON FLAVIUM 162
28. A PLEASANT EVENING 171
29. SHESLA AND GOLGA 178
30. TRAINING IN THE DUNGEON 184
31. THE PROMISE 190
32. BACKPACKED AND READY 195
33. BACK ON KANAH 200
34. GOLGA AND THE COUNCIL OF KANAH 204
35. MICHAEL'S TURN 211
36. BACK IN CLASS 217
37. SUITE MEETING 224
38. COUNTERFEIT FRUIT 226
39. CAUGHT 231
40. BACK TO DARKMAR 237
41. THE LIE 241
42. A WARRIOR IS BORN 245

43.	PENIELS IN THE PALACE	248
44.	A DUNGEON VISIT	254
45.	THE PLAN	258
46.	GABRIEL AND THE ARACHTOIDS	264
47.	GABRIEL IN RAMKRAD	269
48.	EXECUTE THE PLAN	273
49.	FUMBLING ON FLAVIUM	281
50.	A WEDDING CEREMONY – NOT	287
51.	THE ESCAPE	296
52.	THE REUNION	306
53.	THE DANCE COMPETITION	312
About Author		317
Acknowledgments		318

1

SOMETIMES YOU LOSE

Slam.

Michael fell to the mat.

All of the young angels in the warrior training class gasped.

Michael rose, gripped his sword tightly and continued sparring.

Slam. Oren threw him to the mat... again.

"Give it up, Michael," said sensei Caleb. "Watching you pains more than the pain you're feeling." The students laughed as Michael struggled to his feet again. All encircled the two fighters in a roda and cheered on their favorite... mostly for Oren.

"What's this pretend warrior doing here?" a classmate said loud enough for Michael to hear. "He's a puny runt. He'll never be a fighter. He's too small."

I can do this. Hang in there. Ignore him. Focus. He glanced at Gabriel, his only friend in the academy on Planet Kanah.

"But I can't take too many more of these fight sessions—every day," he whispered under his breath.

The little planet of Kanah was one of seven military outposts positioned invisibly around earth. Watchers were required to attend the academy of each outpost before graduating to the rank of angel. Some aspired to be warriors, while others chose a service role.

I'm going to defeat Oren this time.

The two went around and around on the mat punching and kicking one another.

"I'm bored!" Oren teased. "Fight me, watcher boy." Oren was one of the biggest watchers in the Academy. Everyone, including sensei Caleb, knew he was one of the best fighters in school.

"You're going down, Oren."

"Then what are you waiting for? Do it."

All watchers coveted the warrior's golden sword of fire awarded upon graduation. It signified mastery of fighting skills and warrior status. More importantly, graduates could join the king's army.

"Hang in there, Michael," Gabriel shouted from the edge of the mat.

Michael nodded. *At least one person supports me. Gabriel's a better fighter than me but even he refuses to spar with Oren.*

"One more time," Michael replied, pumping his sword.

A group of young female angels entered the huge auditorium of the academy.

"Look," shouted one of the warrior students—pointing. "Peniel watchers!"

Michael shifted his shoulder-length blonde hair as he turned to look. His blue eyes widened. "What's a peniel watcher?"

"Really?" Oren replied, lowering his sword. "A peniel is an angel created for beauty, dummy, and a watcher is a young angel," Orion shoved his red hair from his face with his left hand, purposely flexing his bicep. "Don't you know anything?"

"Of course I know what a watcher is but I've never heard of a peniel before." He glanced at Gabriel who was staring at the peniels along with the rest of the class.

All watched as the young angels whisked by.

Michael and Oren stood motionless in the middle of the mat as the others gawked from their sitting positions. Michael locked his eyes on one particular peniel, pulled in a breath, and slowly exhaled. *Hello pretty blonde.*

"Eyes forward," sensei Caleb ordered at the head of the class. He swung his long, white ponytail around to his other shoulder as he lifted his six-foot-five muscular frame from the floor. Everyone respected sensei as an honored warrior in the army of the king. He fixed his students with his piercing blue eyes. "Finish your match, warriors."

The class returned their attention to the two fighters as Michael reset his sights on Oren. He firmly grasped his sword again, inhaled deeply—reenergized at the sight of the peniels—and charged for sure victory.

Slam.

His newfound confidence was short-lived. He fell hard on his back, staring at the high ceiling, mourning the loss of his last bit of pride.

"Looks like you're the only one who's going down today, watcher boy," Oren said, draped above him.

Michael eyed a droplet of sweat forming on Oren's forehead. He quickly rolled away, in time to watch it spat on the mat.

"That's enough for today, young warriors—class is over," Master Caleb shouted. "See you tomorrow. Remember rule number one: Keep your sword with you at all times." He walked over to Michael and offered a hand. "Better luck next time, Michael. Keep practicing. Great warriors became great because they did what they had to when they had to and didn't do what they wanted to when they wanted to."

"Okay, Sensei," Michael said, rising from the mat. *I know he's trying to encourage me. It's not working.* Michael jogged away and headed towards the exit across the massive floor of the auditorium. *Another day only brings another opportunity to fail.*

Gabriel noticed him jogging away and excused himself from another classmate. "Hey, wait up, Michael." He jogged to catch up.

Michael slowed, turned his head but gave no response. He noticed the look of disappointment on Gabriel's face and knew it mirrored his own.

"Don't look so defeated," Gabriel said.

"Easy for you to say. I'm quitting the class. I'm too little, too weak, and too lousy of a fighter to ever become a real warrior. I'm going back to Krystar."

"Michael, we made a pact! We get through all the schools of the seven planets and graduate together as angel warriors. Remember?"

"I remember."

"You're not quitting. Someday you will defeat Oren."

"Gabriel, you're dreaming." He resumed jogging toward the exit at the front of the building.

Gabriel hurried to keep up. "Okay but listen. We're here to learn. So we're learning. Right?"

Michael gave a wry grin, barely turning his head. "Yes, but so is Oren and everyone else. And the problem is that I'm not keeping up. You are, but I'm not."

"Then we work harder and learn faster until we're at the front of the pack. 'Practice, practice, practice,' as Sensei Caleb says."

"We do practice... every day."

"Right. So keep your focus and don't quit," said Gabriel. "We knew this wouldn't be easy. We just have to earn the points."

"How can I earn points when I haven't won a match yet, Gabriel?"

"There are ways to earn points. Haven't you heard the prophecy?"

"I've heard of it."

'Hear, O hear, young watcher of Krystar, though you are least among warriors, you shall join the king as an archangel to defeat the enemies of the unseen realm on that day when the seven outposts align in the heavens. Your sword shall be as lightning and your wings as swift as the wind until the kingdom of peace is established on the new earth.' Perhaps you and I will become archangels someday. Whoever becomes archangel will receive extra supernatural powers and command legions of angels. That's what I want. Don't you?"

Michael stopped. "You never told me that you want to be an archangel." He resumed a slow jog.

"Who doesn't? Don't you want to become the most powerful angel in the universe and lead millions of angels in the army of the king? I do."

Michael noticed the peniels in their class and stopped. "You can accomplish the goal if that is what you desire, Gabriel, but not me. I don't have what it takes."

"I see you staring at the pretty peniels, Michael, but hear this. They say fiery angels appear in visions to those selected to become archangels. It's not your choice or my choice. The chosen are given tasks that must be completed to fulfill the prophecy. Many fail, few succeed."

"They're beautiful," Michael uttered. "What are they doing?"

Gabriel glanced at the peniels and their instructor. "It's a service class. No surprise. Most peniels formerly resided in the palace of the king on Krystar. They are here to study in the seven academies. Most wish to serve in some capacity upon graduation. Some will become guardian angels, some will teach, some will become messengers, others will become artists or appointed to transport human children from Earth to Krystar."

"They're writing, I think. Do peniels serve in the army?"

"All watchers are required to take at least one warrior class, including peniels. A few will attend the seven academies and join the army as warriors when they graduate the seven academies. Now, the tasks—"

"The tasks, missions, whatever they are, they're impossible to accomplish, or so I have heard." Michael glanced at Gabriel before returning his attention to the peniels.

"The king has created a new position called archangel who will be given extra supernatural powers and will be a prince over all other angels. The watcher who graduates with the most points in our graduating class or in one of the previous six will be given the role."

"You and I don't stand a chance, Gabriel. I doubt we'll be chosen, as you say. And if we are I'll be lucky to make it through all seven schools and graduate with any points."

"We have the same opportunity as the other students. If we're selected then we'll just have to find the best way to earn more than anyone else. Some tasks provide more points than others."

"But few are ever visited by the angelic fiery creatures, or so I hear," replied Michael.

"Don't know."

Michael swung his hair around so that it rested on his shoulders. "I hear we get extra points for capturing demons."

Gabriel started stretching. "So I hear, my friend. So I hear."

Michael started doing pushups. "But we don't get a chance to fight demons until we join the army. Right?"

Gabriel joined him in doing pushups until both stopped and sat on the floor. "I doubt we'll even see a demon before we graduate. Academy rules say we're not to engage them, but report them to the nearest angel warrior. Demon fighting is reserved for angel warriors. We have six more years before we will have that opportunity. Forget about demons. We'll have to find other ways to earn points."

"How will we know how many points we have?"

Gabriel placed his hand on Michael's shoulder. "We won't friend. The Council of Kanah keeps track of all points for those given tasks, but they keep them secret."

Michael stood up. "I probably already have negative points since I've lost all of my sparring matches."

"You're a funny one," Gabriel replied, getting up. "We'll figure it out if we're selected."

"You're dreaming again, Gabriel." Michael returned his gaze to the peniels. "Tell me more about the fiery visions."

"An angel warrior appears as bright as the sun and says something like, 'Hail, mighty warrior of the king.' Then he announces a mission of some sort. They disappear after saying something like, 'Let him who has ears hear what the spirit says,' and they disappear. I'm not sure if it's true."

"The visions are a myth."

"But some myths are true, Michael.

"A true myth. That's a new concept."

"I do wonder what they're studying?" Michael muttered

Gabriel turned to look. "We know it's not warrior training. Now stop staring and let's go."

"Wait here."

Michael approached the class where the peniels were. None of the classes on the arena floor had walls; only desks, chairs, and fighting mats for the warrior classes.

"Michael, what are you doing?" Gabriel whispered, following. "Come back."

Michael entered the classroom and sat down in a chair next to the peniel he had noticed while sparring. "I'm Michael. What's your name?"

The peniel glanced at him before letting blond hair fall, shielding her face.

She's shy. "What are you making?"

She remained silent, pulled her hair back, pressed her blue eyes toward the front of the class.

"What's your name?" he asked again.

Her silent green eyes met his. "Please go," she whispered. She leaned her head down toward the table and began painting.

"Young watcher," the instructor said after finally noticing him, "unless you wish to study landscape and sky designs, please wait outside."

He glanced at the peniel who was now frowning.

"Of course, you are welcome to join us if you would like to participate," the teacher added.

Michael jerked to a standing position, face reddening, and stared stiffly at the instructor.

"I—I think I'll wait outside," he muttered. "Forgive my intrusion." He hurried to rejoin his taller companion who rolled his eyes and quietly marched him toward the door of the arena.

Gabriel shifted his eyes toward Michael. "You blew it."

"I know."

2

SOMETIMES YOU WIN

A few days later some of Michael's classmates raced up behind him outside of the arena and knocked him to the ground. "Loser," one of them said. "Why don't you go back to Krystar," another shouted. love

Several other students witnessed the spectacle.

"Are you okay?" one of them asked, squatting next to him.

"I think so," Michael replied, lying face down. "But my ego isn't."

"Can you get up?"

He slowly rolled over. "Ouch." He blinked to focus on the young angel beside him. "You're the peniel. I almost didn't recognize you in those sunglasses."

"Who? Oh, it's you," she replied, standing up. "I didn't recognize you. You're the one who barged into our class. That was rude." She started walking away.

"Hang on." He drew his leg in and sighed.

She paused. "I only stopped to check on you because I thought you were hurt. I think you'll survive. I'm sure your ego will."

"I'm the class punching bag," Michael said as he struggled to sit up. "And it doesn't end when class is over." He pulled his other leg in and prepared to stand.

She hesitated. "Your classmates are not very nice. You should report them to your instructor. Are you sure you're okay?"

"I think so but perhaps I should sit still for a moment." He cupped his arms around his knees. *Please don't leave.* "So you're willing to talk to me now?"

"I just did." She turned to leave.

"Wait. Please. Please wait." He started to stand but sighed.

"She hesitated again, but didn't turn around.

He slowly stood, took a step, and winced. "Oh!"

She glanced at him and looked away impatiently.

"Please forgive me. I know I embarrassed you in your class. I embarrassed myself. I blew it. I was just trying to get over being dejected in my class. I lost a sparring match, again. I did a dumb thing. I'm not really like that."

"Yes, you did." She faced him. "A dumb thing."

"Can you forgive me? Please."

"I'll work on it but only because I feel sorry for you, a little."

"What's your name?"

She looked away as if looking for someone.

"May I know your name?" He eased into another step.

"Yofiel," she said, looking perturbed, avoiding eye contact. "My name is Yofiel."

He hobbled toward her. "Interesting name. I like it. They say practice makes perfect but it doesn't apply to me. I have yet to win a match." He caught her arm as he stumbled again. "But one never knows until they try."

"And in your case, keep trying," she added before stepping back and releasing her arm. "Perhaps you should change classes and find some better classmates."

"They're okay, really. They're competitive. Our teacher tells us to fight hard while in class but to be humble everywhere else. Getting beat up every day causes me to live in a state of humbleness."

"Are you trying to be funny?" she asked.

He gave a confused look. "Everything they say motivates me to try harder, or quit. By the way, what is your class about?"

"You heard our teacher, right? We're studying landscape and sky designs. We were designing and painting clouds for sunsets on earth the day you barged in. I was working with pink and white colors."

"I noticed."

She removed her sunglasses. "Pink is my favorite color."

"Like your sunglasses," he said as her eyes caught his. "Your eyes. They're like a kaleidoscope of golden sunshine mixed with light-green ocean waters on a summer day."

"My, we have a poet in Kanah. Maybe you should write instead of fight."

He held her gaze and then said, "They're stunning, as you are."

She put them back on and said, "Don't quit."

"What do you mean?"

"You said you may quit your class. Don't."

"I may stick around if I find a reason to." He smiled.

She looked away.

The two started slowly walking together on the crystal road as smooth as glass, observing the few buildings made of jasper. "I just didn't know school would be so difficult."

"Were you assigned to your warrior class, or did you choose it?"

"My guardian angel on Krystar knows my instructor, Sensei Caleb, and recommended him. So my friend Gabriel and I selected his class and here we are. Caleb is a highly decorated warrior."

"Most watchers—guys and girls—desire to become warriors, right?' He hesitated, remembering she was a peniel. "But peniels don't, I think." He looked at her awkwardly.

"I don't," she replied. "But some do. All angels wish to protect humans, just in different ways. We don't all have to fight demons."

"True but—"

"I'm glad planet Kanah is invisible so they can't see us," she said.

"Yea, thanks to the force-field." Michael rubbed his sore leg. "Our sensei said that most watchers will never see a demon until after we graduate, almost seven years from now."

Yofiel shifted her gaze down the street and pulled a few steps in front of him. "That's good news."

"Is this your last class for today, Yofiel?"

"Yes?"

"Me too. May I walk you to your place?" he asked, taking another step, wincing again.

She continued to walk away. "I have to go."

3

THE FIRST WALK

Michael stopped by Yofiel's class the next day and waited for it to end. "Hi, Yofiel," he said. He smiled when he noticed the blotches of paint scattered on her white, skin-tight yoga pants and T-shirt. "Looks like you had fun."

“Hi, Michael," she replied, matching his smile. "Yep, I did."

He smiled again when he noticed pink paint on the end of her nose.

"What?" she asked, matching his smile again.

He pointed to his own nose.

"Oh," she said, pulling a napkin from a pocket. "It's a casualty of the class." She glanced as his leg. "How’s your leg?”

“It’s better. But I still lost today. Four times.”

“They made you spar?” She stood there looking at him as she held her painting.

“My sensei didn’t know my leg was sore.“ He touched the sore spot and slightly grimaced. "Are you going anywhere now?”

“Not really.”

“May I walk with you to the castle? I assume you live there.”

“Doesn’t everyone?”

He nodded and caught sight of a painting in her hands. "May I see it?

"Sure. It's the skyline of Kanah with the castle front and center. It's my favorite building here—twenty-one stories of aqua-colored jasper and auroras in the sky."

"Nice. You're talented. So what do you say?"

She gave a confused look. "What? Oh. Thank you, but not today. I'm late." She turned to leave.

"Oh."

She paused.

"I just want to say again that I'm sorry for embarrassing you in your class."

"No worries." She hurried away.

Michael strolled by her class each day after his warrior class. Eventually, it became a ritual. Each day he asked if he could walk her to her place but each day she declined.

One day after asking her again, she said, "You can walk me to the door of the stadium. I'm meeting some friends in a little while."

Michael was momentarily shocked by her affirmative reply. *Yes!* He struggled to contain his excitement. "Oh, great." The door of the stadium looked like a spec from where they stood.

"So let me get this straight, Michael. You want to be a warrior. Right?"

"Yes, in a way. I think so."

She swung her hair around so that it landed on his shoulder.

"Oh, sorry."

"No worries." He grinned.

"Being a warrior in the army is a great service. It will be an honor to fight with the king. So why think of quitting? This may be your calling."

He looked away. "But I haven't won a single sparring match. So, it's an unrealistic dream."

"Keep practicing the way you have been. It will make a difference."

"I'm too small, too weak, too short to be a warrior, much less a leader." He stood straight to match her height. "I can't escape the facts. I'm the worst fighter in class. Really. Everyone picks me to spar because I'm easily defeated. I make everybody look good."

"Winners never quit, quitters never win," Yofiel quipped.

He felt her stare as if waiting for a response. "But sometimes it's wise to quit."

"Stay with the good, quit the bad," she whispered, still staring.

He turned and met her eyes. "Enough talk about me, Yofiel. Your friends are waiting." He pointed towards the front of the building.

"No, I have a few more minutes."

"Okay. Then let's talk about you. Why study painting when there are so many other choices?"

"I enjoy it. My friend, Tamor, and I are taking other courses, including warrior training. Tamor likes engineering and chemistry. She's into world-building and structural design. My passion is environmental design. You could say I'm artistic."

"Then why take painting when you can take more advanced design courses at the other academies?"

"It's a level-one course and the Academy of Kanah only has level one courses. Your warrior class is level one. Right?"

"Well, yes."

"I'll take level-two courses next year on planet Ascalon. This place is perfect for sky and environmental designs because it's like a garden."

"The city or the planet?"

"Both. The planet is small, smaller than earth's moon. There's much to see with mountains, streams of water, auroras in the sky, animals of all shapes and sizes, and miles and miles of flowers and trees that look like flowers. And the little town is charming with its jasper buildings, shops made of gemstones, colorful plants everywhere and crystal streets. It's beautiful."

“Like you,” he said.

“Are you listening, Michael?”

“I am and I agree with you. Kanah is a fine little planet. I like the military walls around the city, thirty feet wide, seventy feet tall made of crystal-clear chalcedony. They reflect the colors of the sky.”

“Yes, Michael, like our home planet, Krystar." She glanced around the huge covered stadium. "Oh, chairs. Let's go over there for a few minutes. Then I have to go."Sou

"Sure."

"Is it true, Michael, that watchers are not allowed to venture beyond the city without an escort?” Her long blonde hair swung around her shoulder.

Michael paused, trying not to stare.

“What?” she asked.

“Your eyes, do all peniels have big eyes? I like the color blue.”

"Yes, a characteristic of being a peniel angel."

“I know it’s cool for a guy not to compliment.”

“Who told you that? They’re wrong.”

“I don’t want to be a pushover.”

“What are you trying to say, Michael?”

He pulled closer. “That you're stunning.”

“Peniels were made for beauty, but we’re also created to be humble.”

“Your eyes are at least twice as big as mine.”

“So answer the question"

"What question?"

"About escorts.”

“Oh, yes. Watchers are encouraged to have an angel escort to exit the gates, but it’s not required. Keep in mind that Kanah is a military outpost, so caution should be observed. The army is here to protect humans on earth and sometimes the battles occur beyond earth. Space is enemy territory.”

"So why are all seven academies located on military outposts instead of the home-planet, Krystar?"

Michael faced her. "It's part of the experience, I guess. There's a contingent of angel warriors on each outpost in case there's a breach. I'm glad to be on an outpost. It adds to the academy experience because we get to do drills with the army. Each outpost provides the appropriate skill level for their resident academy."

She leaned in with a pensive look. "Have demons ever attacked Kanah?"

"No, thankfully. Not yet, anyway. You'll be safe with me." He flashed a look of fictitious confidence. "And besides, the forcefield protects the planet and makes us invisible."

Yofiel noticed her friends outside the door and waved. "They're here. Thank you for walking me to the door. Are you coming to dance lessons later?"

"Thanks for reminding me. Yes. Sensei Caleb said we have to if we expect to participate in our warrior class. Who's the instructor?"

"Hadessah, the queen of dance. She is short and stout for a dance instructor but everyone says she's a passionate teacher and a talented dance choreographer. Oh, I almost forgot. I'm bringing Tamor."

Michael noticed Gabriel coming their way and waved.

"I remember Tamor," Gabriel uttered while walking up to them.

Yofiel looked up to see who it was.

Michael beamed a smile. "Speaking of friends, this is Gabriel. Gabriel, this is Yofiel."

"It's a pleasure to meet you, Yofiel. Michael has told me about you. All good things, of course."

"It's a pleasure to me you also, Gabriel. So, you know Tamor?"

"We were in the same group when we arrived from Krystar. We talked. But I haven't seen her since. I'll be in class with Michael."

"Wonderful." She rose and started to leave. "We'll see you both this evening."

Michael and Gabriel watched as she walked away, her hair swaying back and forth like fields of wheat in a gentle morning breeze.

"She's as beautiful as you said and is super friendly," Gabriel said. "At least she's talking to you after pulling that stunt in her class. You two would make a good couple."

"Working on it."

4

PAPEONS

Yofiel arrived at her suite and began singing as she went from room to room.

Tamor knocked on the door and entered. "Yofiel, where are you?"

"Hi, Tamor. In here."

"How did your meet-up go with the blue-eyed blond guy?"

"Michael? Good. He walked me to the front door after class."

"To your suite?"

"No, the arena."

"He's a persistent one."

"He's not what I thought at first, though. He's nice, though a bit insecure. He keeps talking about quitting his warrior class and going back to Krystar. But I think I've talked him into staying. He and his friend are coming to dance class today. His friend knows you."

Tamor looked confused. "Who?"

"Gabriel. The guy who sat next to you on your trip from Krystar."

"Oh yes," Tamor said. "I remember him. I liked his long brown hair. They match his eyes. He's handsome."

"How about we get out of the city and take a walk?"

"That's exactly what I need after my classes."

"Let's go."

The two peniels exited the castle. "Look at all the angels and watchers flying in the sky," Yofiel said, stepping into the street outside the castle. "Do you want to join them?"

Tamor paused. "I'd rather walk. It's easier to talk."

"I agree." They strolled toward the east gate, their favorite point of exit for no particular reason other than habit.

"I love the coolness of the crystal streets on my bare feet," Tamor said. "Why wear shoes?"

"So right. The side streets with gems are prickly."

They arrived at the gate and joined a group heading out of the city. "The guard is glaring at us," Tamor said.

"He's just doing his job. Maybe he likes you."

"Funny."

The two separated from the group and walked into the surrounding field off the main path.

"I like how this field of flowers slopes toward the lake where the willow trees are," said Tamor. Some flowers were caught by the wind and spun through the air. "The smell is spectacular."

"The very reason we come this way."

"The auroras are purple and yellow on one side of the sky and green and lavender on the other side. Every day is like the first day on Kanah—there's always something new." Tamor took in a deep breath. "Smells like lavender, honeysuckle, and jasmine. I hope the other outposts are as beautiful as this place."

"We'll find out when we get there," Yofiel replied. Eventually, the two were out of sight.

Tamor paused. "Look. Dinosaurs."

"Tyrannosaurus rex. I count two."

"What do we do?

"Freeze," said Yofiel.

Rrroooaar! The sound shook the ground sending a shock wave through the acres of flowers like a rushing wind.

"They're coming this way," Tamor muttered. The faces of the little peniels shook with every step of the beasts. They paused in front of the girls, nudged them, exhaled loudly, and then strolled away.

"Whew," Yofiel whispered.

"They don't look tame," Tamor observed.

"Tameness doesn't belong with sharp teeth, scaly skin, and bad breath.

"True." They watched as the creatures ventured away. Yofiel cocked her head. "Do you hear something?"

Tamor exposed her wings and lifted off the ground. "I see movement. Something is coming this way, by Skylar's Pond." She floated back to the ground in the crop of white flowers.

"I hear it but don't see anything yet."

The girls ran toward the pond to get a closer look.

"Bzzzzz. BZZZZZ."

"It's getting louder," said Yofiel.

Airborne creatures swept down the grassy hill in their direction.

"Butterflies!" said Tamor.

"Papeons!" Yofiel replied. "I haven't seen any since we left Krystar months ago."

"I've never heard of papeons," Tamor said. "What are they?"

"They're small creatures, similar to butterflies. They sing and fly in swarms. Each has a tiny humanlike face and butterfly wings?"

"Interesting creatures, for sure."

"They are a continual chorus of song," Yofiel continued. "Their lilting voices are mesmerizing and their wings radiate colors like they're glowing."

Tamor gasped in delight. "There are thousands of them. Look how they fly in a helical swarm, round and round in perfect symmetry! They're sky dancing."

"Listen, Tamor. Their chants echo and fade as each word is repeated: "lovely, lovely, lovely, magnificent, magnificent, magnificent."

The song was interrupted occasionally by moments of laughter—as if they were giggling. But whether in song or laughter, the papeons continually smiled. Never still or stalled in motion, ever moving forward in flight, they circled objects of curiosity to spread their cheer, to look, or to simply offer greetings before flying away. The trailing edge of the creatures left sparkling sprinkles of colored dust. Each color wafted a unique fragrance like lavender, vanilla, or like freshly washed linen blowing on a clothesline.

"They're amazing, Yofiel." Tamor spread her arms out and began to spin in the surrounding garden of flowers.

The papeons swirled around the girls, imparting a hypnotic sense of celebration. The two raised their hands and joined the chorus in motion and song. The papeons appeared to cast a spell putting the girls in a trance that expressed itself in rapturous dance.

"We're dancing!" Tamor shouted. "I love this."

"Me too," replied Yofiel, turning around and around in sync with the papeons. The creatures lurched toward the forest in unison, like a waft of smoke caught by a sudden breeze. The girls continued dancing on the ground but then sprouted their wings and joined them in the air. Faster and faster the papeons flew. Deeper and deeper into the forest the peniels flew as they chased after the speeding kaleidoscope of colors.

After a few miles, a smaller group of papeons broke away from the main pack and dove toward an alternate path in the woods. The main pack continued in flight and song, unaffected by the break. The girls glanced at one another, pointed to the ground, and landed.

"Remember this spot by the tree with the large yellow flowers," Tamor shouted, as she chased after the breakaway pack.

"Looks like it's made of crystal."

"Hurry up, Yofiel. Keep up."

"I'm coming."

The breakaway pack flew as if spooked or in a hurry to get to their destination. The forest got darker and darker until the light of the sun drowned in the canopied trees.

"They're gone!" Tamor gasped, as she finally stopped dancing as if awakened from a dream. "Where are we?"

Yofiel steadied herself, breathless and dizzy. "Lost."

5

THE DOOR

"Yofiel, look," Tamor said as she stared at the pathway. "A door—a shiny white door."

"Why is a door in the middle of the path? And it's free-standing. Strange."

The two glanced at one another and then at the door. "Let's check it out," said Tamor.

The two peniels eased their way forward. Yofiel clutched Tamor's hand and reached for the door with the other. "It's cold. And it's made of a single white pearl, like the huge ones in the wall around Krystar." She turned to Tamor with a questioning look.

Tamor frowned. "I can understand pearl doors to the city of the king in Krystar but why here in the woods of Kanah?"

Yofiel shifted her eyes to the door. "Do you think anyone knows about this?"

"It's just a door. Perhaps someone left it and they're coming back for it." Tamor reached around Yofiel and placed the palm of her hand against the door. "Wow, you're right! It is cold—real cold."

"Tamor. The doorknob. It's a blue diamond." She glanced at Tamor again. "Turn it."

"But it's not connected to anything." Tamor backed away. "It could be a trap."

She considered the thought.

"Maybe we should leave," Tamor added. She slowly inhaled and exhaled as a soft breeze blew her long black hair across her face.

Yofiel caught the aroma of honeysuckles. "We can't just leave. We have to check this out. Maybe the papeons know something we don't." As soon as she touched the doorknob, a cave appeared on the other side. "What the…?" She jumped back into Tamor and both peniels landed on the ground.

"Where did that come from?" Tamor asked, staring at the cave around the door.

Yofiel arose and helped her up.

"Thank you."

"Look, Tamor. It's open. Perhaps the papeons are inside." She peered inside.

Tamor clasped Yofiel's waist. "What do you see?"

"Nothing yet. Come on."

"Are you sure?"

"We have to do this." The two stepped inside, squinting into the darkness.

"Are those stars I see at the other end?" Yofiel asked. She opened the palm of her hand forming a sparkling ball of light that rose and floated before them. The walls of the cave blushed a faint glow.

"There's nothing in here but rocks," said Tamor.

"It's too quiet. We're halfway there." They arrived at the other end. "Yes, those are stars. This is odd. It's never dark on planet Kanah, so what is this place?" A wind stirred.

Tamor clutched Yofiel's arm. "I hear something"

"I hear nothing."

"Look, Yofiel. A light glowing on the ledge. What is it?"

"I see it. It's a small whirlwind."

Tamor pulled on Yofiel's T-shirt. "It's getting brighter. Let's go back." The girls turned to leave.

Whoosh.

Yofiel clutched Tamor's T-Shirt and pulled her forward. "Fire! Run!" The girls dashed toward the white pearl door.

"I can't make it," Tamor shouted. "The wind's too strong."

Yofiel turned to look towards the ledge. "It's a tornado." The wind pulled them towards its spinning flames like invisible fingers that refused to let go. It grew stronger until both fell to the rocky surface. Tamor latched onto a boulder as Yofiel grabbed her by the waist.

"Hang on, Yofiel!" They could barely hear one another over the tumultuous winds. The sand whipping in the air stung like a thousand bees.

"I can't see," hollered Yofiel. "Where's the door?"

Tamor clutched at Yofiel as the two struggled to crawl forward. They had almost made it when the ground shook, causing Yofiel to lose her grip and slid towards the fiery tornado.

"Tamor, I'm sliding. Help!" *We're going to die!* She pressed her nails against the rocky floor of the cave to no avail.

"Hang on!"

The white pearl door pushed open against the wind as if someone forced it open and held it.

"Grab my hand," Tamor yelled. "The door's open."

Yofiel clutched her hand and the two peniels crawled through the opening.

Yofiel gasped for air and then muttered, "How did the door open?"

"I have no idea."

6

DANCE CLASS

Michael went to Gabriel's place and waited for him to get ready for the dance class. But it wasn't dancing they were interested in. While their attendance was mandatory, they had discovered two other compelling reasons to go: Yofiel and Tamor.

"I remember Tamor," Gabriel said, as he finished dressing. "She has kaleidoscope eyes as all the peniels do but hers are as green as emeralds."

"And long, black silky hair," Michael said.

"How did you know?"

"She's in Yofiel's class. I've seen her."

"Got it."

"What do you say we fly to the theater? We're late."

"Behind you, Michael." The two ran out of the castle, extended their wings their full ten feet, and leapt into the air.

Michael pulled even with him. "Flying is fun. But I can't wait to get real angel wings so we can fly faster."

"We only have seven more years to go. For now, student wings and student swords will have to do."

"I can dream," Michael replied as they glided over the crystal streets.

"At least we can fly," Gabriel uttered. The two landed near the little theater located between the castle and the Academy.

"Race you the rest of the way," Michael said. "I like to run. Especially since I'm faster than you."

"You think?"

The two raced along the street. Gabriel arrived ahead of Michael, opened the front door, and ran down the inclined aisle to the stage. Michael caught up to him and both fell at the edge of the stage, landing next to Hadessah. Some students cheered and laughed, while others rolled their eyes. The two grinned and stood to their feet.

"We're glad you could join us," Hadessah said, with a look of seriousness. Her light-green and rose-colored eyes stood out from her purple hair. "I hope you dance as well as you run. Are you ready to begin?"

"We are," Gabriel said.

"Absolutely," Michael added.

"Everyone has a partner already except for those two," she said, pointing at Yofiel and Tamor. She cocked a blank expression and held her eyes wide open. "Please join them on stage."

I'm glad they don't have partners yet. He saw Tamor whisper into Yofiel's ear and then giggle. The two jumped onto the stage without saying a word. Michael winked at Yofiel as he approached.

"All right, watchers," Hadessah said loudly, voice echoing over the silent rows of crystal chairs in the otherwise empty theater. "We have twelve months to learn the choreography, perfect the dance routines and turn you into a world-class, or rather, universe-class dance troupe." Her eyes pulled them in as all listened as if in a trance. "Dance is the greatest expression of joy. That's why I'm here doing what I do. That's why you're here.

"All of you will have the opportunity to dance at the Gala of Kanah. But only four couples will be selected to represent Team

Kanah in the Kingdom of Krystar Dance Competition. There are twenty-one couples here and each couple will compete for four spots.

"For those of you who have never attended a dance gala, they are festive events with incredible music, delicious food, colorful costumes, talented dancers, and spectacular dancing. Everyone always tries to outdo the previous Gala. It's all fun. You will be the youngest dancers since all of you are at the level-one academy here on Kanah. You will meet and mingle with watchers and angels from the other six outposts. Team Kanah will compete against six teams representing Ascalon, Gandara, Lagash, Macah, Ortona, and Pomaris. The difficulty will be choosing the winning team because there are so many."

Michael leaned over to Yofiel so Hadessah could not see him. "You'll be the most beautiful watcher in the competition," he whispered, tickling her ear.

She laughed.

"You are a—"

"Eyes on me please, everyone," Hadessah said as she glanced about. "We must move quickly to narrow the field from twenty-one couples to eight." She extended her wings and floated effortlessly over the stage as she spoke.

Michael caught himself staring at Hadessah. *She's an interesting lady.*

"My two dance instructors will assist in selecting the eight. We will look for efficiency in the execution of the routines, proficiency in characterization, accuracy of movement, synchronization, and overall pleasantness. One of the dance routines will be new to you."

The group moaned.

"You can do this, dear watchers. Each couple will perform two dance routines with a two-minute duration. Tomorrow, two members of the Council of Kanah will join us to help select the final four couples who will form Team Kanah. Training for the four couples will begin next week. I know this is quick but this is as it must be. Any questions?" She scanned the stage.

"The team who wins at the gala competition will dance for the king in Krystar, as will all dancers of the winning outpost. So everybody please watch the instructors. They will show you the first phrase of the new routine. Then you will take your positions as you see marked on the floor."

The watchers observed the instructors run through the steps and then all practiced in unison for several hours.

"We are so clumsy," Michael whispered to Yofiel.

"Everyone is," she replied. "We'll get it."

"Don't worry about mistakes," Hadessah shouted above the music. "Enjoy the process. It takes time to learn the art of dance and a lifetime to master it."

"She is known for her one-liners," Yofiel whispered to the others.

Michael thought of Hadessah's words and could not get them out of his head. He stood motionless on the stage and repeated her words but with a slight variation. *It takes time to learn the art of combat but a lifetime to master it.*

"Young watcher, young watcher, keep moving," Hadessah bellowed. "You'll not learn to dance standing still, dear one."

"Michael," Yofiel whispered. "Snap out of it." She spun about. "Michael!"

"Huh, what? I'm here."

"Dance," she muttered.

He started dancing.

"Time determines life, life determines legacy," Hadessah continued.

"This dance routine looks difficult," Gabriel whispered to Tamor. "My feet are too big to move quickly."

"It's simple," Tamor replied. "You're a warrior, aren't you? Then you can do this."

"If I do this and we're selected for the team, will you join me for a picnic—just the two of us?"

Tamor grinned. "Only if we win." She turned toward Yofiel and mouthed, "I like him."

Yofiel gave a slight smile.

Michael glance at Gabriel and Tamor. *Gabriel looks happy.* The two locked eyes and gave a thumbs up.

After several hours, the group managed to step through the whole dance routine without error.

"This is more like a workout than a dance," Yofiel said as she finished the last movement.

"I agree," Michael replied with a rueful smile. "We looked like we were doing fight katas."

"Funny."

"Good work, team," Hadessah said. "This is a complex dance routine but you got through it. That's all for today but don't leave. Take a break while we tally the scores. We'll report them shortly."

"I'm ready for a break," Gabriel said.

"Sounds good," Tamor said. "I'm going for a quick cold shower to cool down. Nothing beats a cold shower after a hot workout."

"Do you think it's good to mix hot with cold, Tamor?"

"Like you and me?" She said, smiling, as she walked away.

Gabriel stood motionless for a moment, thinking on her reply. "Wait, are you saying I'm cold?" he asked while trotting up behind her. "Or are you saying I'm hot?"

She turned and smirked before disappearing into the spa room.

"Whoa," Michael said. "What did you say to get that smile from Tamor?"

"Follow me," he replied. The two got a cold drink. "She likes me."

"A good thing," said Michael.

After the break, the students returned to the stage. "Okay everyone, we have selected the eight couples," Hadessah said. "The eight semifinalist couples are..."

Hadessah named four of the couples.

"Two more couples to go, Tamor," Gabriel said.

"I hope we make it," said Tamor.

"The last two couples are Gabriel and Tamor and Michael and Yofiel."

"Yay!" The four formed a group hug.

"We're in!" Tamor shouted and clasped Yofiel's hands.

"Congratulations!" the other couples said.

Yofiel extended her left arm toward them. "Join us."

The eight winning couples held hands and danced in a big circle.

The rest of the class joined them and all celebrated.

7

THE NEXT DAY IN DANCE CLASS

"There they are," Tamor said to Yofiel.

"I see them. They're early, as we are."

"Good morning, guys," the two peniels said.

"Good morning," Michael and Gabriel replied.

"We're delighted that we made the final eight," Yofiel said.

"I can't believe it," Michael replied. Michael opened the door to the theater. "I should quit the warrior class and concentrate on dancing"

"We discussed that already," Michael replied. "You're stuck with me until we graduate, buddy."

"We had this talk too," Yofiel added.

"Okay, okay, guys," Michael replied. "I'm just kidding."

The rest of the twenty-one couples began to arrive. Hadessah entered the theater and congratulated the eight couples again.

"To the stage, everyone," she said. "Let's go." They practiced the routines over the next three hours.

"Take a short break," Hadessah finally shouted.

"I'm tired," Michael said.

"We all are," replied Tamor, as she and Gabriel finished their last step.

Light entered through the front door as someone entered the theater. Hadessah turned as the door closed. All watched as the visitors walked the long aisle to the stage.

"Class," Hadessah said. "Here are our two special guests. Thank you, sirs, for joining us today."

The visitors waved. "Morning. It's our honor to be here."

"Thank you for having us," the other said.

"Class, this is Uriel. All of you should know by now that he is commander of Outpost Kanah and leads the three hundred warriors here. He is also Senior Council Representative for our outpost. Also joining us is Caleb, one of our twenty-four distinguished warrior instructors here on Kanah. He is also a member of the Council."

"They are handsome, aren't they?" Tamor whispered to Yofiel.

"You know it. There are some handsome angels on this little planet."

"Including the two little dance partners," Yofiel whispered back.

Tamor gave thumbs up.

"Please join us on stage and take your seats," Hadessah said to Uriel and Caleb. "You have accepted an invitation for a difficult assignment—selecting four couples among this outstanding troupe of eight to represent Team Kanah at the gala. We thank you."

"What is the name of the angel with the long silver hair again?" Tamor asked.

"Uriel. I thought every watcher on Kanah knew who he was."

"I do now. I love his silver eyes and his muscles."

"The other angel with the white ponytail and blue eyes is Sensei Caleb."

"Yes, I know. Thanks."

Yofiel turned toward Michael, "Did you know Hadessah has never won a gala dance competition in the seven years she's been here?"

"No," he whispered.

"Dancers, prepare to begin your routines," Hadessah shouted abruptly, causing Michael to jerk his eyes toward her. "Let's go, let's go, dancers."

Each couple lined up to perform their two-minute routines as they were called. Hadessah, her assistant instructors and special guests, watched, made notes of about each couple, and chatted back and forth.

"Thank you, everyone," she said as the last couple finished their routine. "We'll let you know the results the day after tomorrow. I have an all-day planning meeting with the instructors from the other outposts for most of the day tomorrow." She turned to Uriel, Caleb and her two assistants and began comparing notes.

"We must have some of Hadessah's lemonade before we leave, Michael," said Yofiel. "She makes the best."

"Sounds good. But are we permitted to stay while they're discussing the results?"

"Sure, lemonade is her signature item, other than her bodacious outfits. Tamor, Gabriel, let's get some lemonade?" Yofiel held a cup in each hand and then gave one to Michael. Some of the other students joined them while others left.

Hadessah looked up. "No flying in the house," she shouted after eyeing a few flying inside.

"This is good juice," Michael said after downing a cup.

"I'll take two, at least," Tamor muttered. Tamor gave a cup to Gabriel while drinking a second cup.

Tamor chugged two down, then flushed when she spotted Hadessah walking their way.

"Please, please do drink, enjoy. That's why it's here."

Tamor's cup refilled itself automatically as did all cups when held.

Hadessah gulped one down and started laughing as she placed it on the table. "I don't want to carry the lemonade back to my suite, or I'll drink it myself. I don't need the calories."

"But angel's can't gain weight I thought," Tamor replied.

Everyone laughed, including Caleb and Uriel, because they knew calories didn't affect angels. Uriel and the others joined them at the table.

"Hadessah," Yofiel said inquisitively, looking away before looking at her. "May Tamor and I share something with you?

"Please do." She beamed a smile.

"Tamor and I were walking in the fields yesterday when a hive of papeons flew by and began dancing in the air. They sang in unison and swarmed in perfectly symmetric patterns. They must have cast a hypnotic spell or mist because we felt a strong urge to join them. We started dancing and didn't stop for an hour or two, at least. The papeons flew toward the forest and we followed along. They sped up as they continued singing and dancing. We chased after them into the woods without regard to anything and were unaware of how far we had traveled until they disappeared into the woods. We had traveled a long way and realized we were lost."

"But the dance of the papeons was amazing," Tamor added. "Like nothing we've ever seen or experienced. May we show you."

"We think you will like it," Yofiel added.

"Yes, yes!"

One of the assistant teachers turned the music on as everyone remaining in the theater watched. The two began an interpretative dance to mimic the papeons and moved in elegant, sweeping, circular patterns. They floated at times, occasionally flew, as spun around in helical patterns.

"Look, Tamor," Yofiel said. "They like it. They're smiling."

All clapped when they finished.

"Interesting," Hadessah offered. "I haven't seen dancing like that before. Very compelling. This could change our strategy and choreography for the gala competition." She lowered her head as if deep in thought and then cocked a smile. "Will you ladies help if we do this?"

Tamor nodded in the affirmative.

"Count us in," Yofiel said.

8

THE WALK HOME

"Where are you going next, Yofiel?" Michael asked as the two left the stage.

"To my suite," she replied. She waved at Tamor and Gabriel who remained with Hadessah. "I want to tell you something."

"About the papeons?"

"About something that happened in the forest."

"Sure."

They headed outside and meandered through the streets enjoying each other's company.

"What is it you want more than anything else?" Yofiel asked, sounding more serious. "Down deep inside?" She asked the same question when they first met but was probing deeper now.

She is an inquisitive little lady. "You were going to tell me something."

"I will." She stopped walking, blinked slowly, and slowly curled her lips forming a smile.

He hesitated and blinked because she did. "I want what all of the watchers in my class want—to be a warrior and join the army of the king. I want to fight against Beelzebub and his horde of demons. This you know. So, what happened in the forest?"

"But why do you want to fight?" Yofiel asked.

I don't want to discuss it. "I don't know? What else would I do?"

She frowned.

She doesn't believe my answer. I don't either.

"Look," said Yofiel. "I love that little store. Let's go inside." The two walked across the street and went inside. "Oh, the fragrances are incredible—some sweet, some not so sweet and others in-between, if you know what I mean."

"I do, kind of, I guess," replied Michael—half listening. He was still thinking about her previous question, not being used to deep introspection.

"And the colors. We could remain here all day and see flowers we've never seen before." She fell silent, again. "Why," she finally asked, breaking the silence. "Why do you want to fight?"

Michael picked up a purple flower, slowly reached for it with his other hand, removed a petal, and watched it fall to the floor. He then removed the remaining petals, dropping each to the floor one at a time and then released the remaining stem. He squashed it with his foot, then watched for her reaction."

She frowned. "That's not good." She turned to leave.

"Exactly. People are like flowers. The demons remove the petals, watch them fall to the floor and then trample underfoot. That's why I want to fight. I want to keep the demons from trampling on humans. I want to be a part of something. I want to be the best at what I do." *Good answer, Michael.*

She remained expressionless and silent.

She didn't like what I said. "Look at the blue daffodils," he said, changing the subject.

"Let's go," she replied, walking outside. They walked along the street in silence. They reached the castle and went to her suite.

"Come on in while I change," she said as she opened the door and ran inside.

She must like me to ask me in. He walked through the rooms looking at the decorations. “You must like taking pictures,” he said loudly. “They’re everywhere.” Each picture was a hologram and revealed continuous motion.

Interesting! A pic of Yofiel with three peniels. They were standing in front of rainbows surrounded by bubbles and tiny flowers spinning in the air and releasing colorful mists. As the bubbles popped, they made funny sounds like water droplets falling in muddy puddles. The peniels were laughing hysterically as the bursting bubbles coated them like blushed rain.

Yofiel wore a blue dress in the picture. “Hey, I thought pink was your favorite color.” *Tamor’s in the red dress.* One of the girls had a white dress and another a green one. All were form-fitting and decorated with matching gemstones and glittering bling.

Yofiel entered the room wearing a fresh T-shirt and matching blue yoga pants. “Oh, that picture. That was fun.”

“Where was it taken?”

“We were celebrating with friends at a dance recital in Krystar a few years ago.”

“Nice." He looked around the room. "I like your place.”

“The floors are light-blue glowing sapphire and the walls are translucent crystal.”

“What are those creatures on the table?”

“This is my class design project. I'm using miniature holographic creatures: human children and white and black bears, jaguars, tigers, and various kinds of puppies. surrounded by snowy mountains in the distance.” She pointed as she identified them. “I call it ‘Pure Joy.’”

“The green grass surrounded by snowy mountains is creative. I like how trees change colore.” He paused and then pointed. “What’s that?”

"It's a rotating fountain of light that shoots lightning into the air. The lightning turns into wings that fly straight up before spinning down."

"I like it. Where did you get the idea?"

"I imagined it. I'm adding papeons and then it will be finished." She turned away. "Michael, something happened to Tamor and me today."

"Is this the something you wanted to tell me?"

"We found a door, a white pearl door, in the middle of the woods. It wasn't attached to anything. It was just there, freestanding."

"That's strange."

"It had a diamond doorknob, a blue one. When I started to turn it, a cave appeared on the other side."

"I heard a rumor about a secret cave from one of the older students at school."

"That's not all, Michael. We went inside and didn't see anything other than the inside of a rocky cave. It only took a minute to walk through it and then we went out onto a ledge. Stars were everywhere, brighter than I had ever seen.

"Then we noticed a light, a small whirlwind far away in space. But then it started coming towards us and turned into a blue tornado of fire. We ran through the cave to get away but didn't make it because of the wind. The sound was deafening. We fell to the ground and slid backward as if it was pulling us. We thought it was the end of us until the door at the front opened. But the strange thing about that it opened against the wind as if someone opened it."

"Did you see anyone at the door?"

"No."

"I'm glad you're safe, but I can't believe you discovered the door to the secret cave. Rumor is that the cave transforms into a blue spiraling fire which is what you must have experienced. Each outpost has at least one secret door if the rumor is true. You two must have been terrified."

"So you have heard of it?"

"Yes, but everyone thinks it's a rumor. It's works like a control center to allow angels to teleport through space from anywhere on Kanah. If the rumor is true, all seven outposts have one."

"Will we get into trouble for finding it?"

"Watchers are only allowed to portal when accompanied by an angel, but can only do so by going to the cave. I would like to see it. Can you find it again?"

"I don't want to."

"We don't have to go inside. We can just look at it. So you two didn't have an escort?"

Yofiel shrugged. "We tagged along with another group when we exited the gate, but then went our way when we reached the forest. That's when we found the papeons."

"Or they found you."

"Exactly."

"You two peniels went a long way by yourselves."

"We can handle it, Michael. Tamor and I intend to travel around the entire planet and camp along the way. We want to see all of the sights—the rivers, mountains, glaciers, geysers of fire, dinosaurs, the other animals and any other creatures we don't know about."

Michael smiled. "Sounds like fun. Now, will you please take me to the door in the forest?"

"Michael, did you hear what I said? I was frightened. It was scary."

"Please. I won't let anything happen to you."

"No, not today."

"All right. When?"

"Let's meet at the east gate when the morning auroras appear. That's when most watchers wake since it never gets dark here."

"True. See you then."

9

THE DOOR IN THE WOODS

The next day Michael hurried to the east gate, thinking he was too early until he spotted Yofiel at a sidewalk café across the street. He walked towards her. “Good morning." You are cute. "Are you rested?”

“Much. I’ll be ready as soon as I finish this.” She cast a warm smile. “Join me. A little breakfast will do us good.”

He sat down across from her at the little circular table. “I’ll have the same.” The order immediately appeared. “Excellent. Sweet fruit and fresh hot bread. Love this and the pancakes. Have you been here before?”

“First time.”

He began eating fast and then paused. “Forgive my manners.” He wiped his lips and studied the area before returning his gaze at her. “I don’t know what’s prettier: the flowers next-door, the gemstones in the walls of the café, or your eyes.” *Michael, you can do better than that.*

Yofiel blushed as she finished her last pancake. “I bet you say that to all of the peniels.” She turned away and glanced up the street.

“First time,” replied Michael, turning to see what she was looking at.

“Ha."

Michael glanced at her.

She pushed her plate toward the middle of the table until it disappeared and then peer up the street again as if looking at something in particular. “We should go soon so we can return before school starts.”

“We have time,” he said as he finished his pancakes.

Yofiel stood.."

“Wait. I have something for you.” He reached into the front pocket of his slim, straight-cut jeans and retrieved a small white box wrapped in a pink ribbon.

“What’s this?” She gave a puzzled look.

“A little gift to help you forget your experience at the cave yesterday.”

“This is not necessary, Michael, but thank you.” She untied the ribbon. “A pink silk scarf. Thoughtful.” She put it around her neck.

"You did say pink is your favorite color.”

Her eyes twinkled as she pressed her lips together.

She likes it. "Okay, ready to go?"

"Yes."

Michael was the first to rise from the table. "Let's follow that group. Looks like they're headed toward the east gate." The two followed behind and exited through the gates.

They walked several miles into the open fields of green grass. "Yofiel, let's separate from them and go our own way."

"Sure."

Do you want to walk or fly?”

She hesitated. “Let’s walk to the Meadow of Fate where I saw the papeons. Maybe they’ll reappear.”

Little twirling multicolored droplets of frost began raining from the clear blue sky, melting upon contact. They made humming sounds as they spun, dispensing a fresh ambrosial aroma. The rain ended by the time they reached the edge of the forest.

She took Michael by the hand, "Let's fly!" They extended their wings as if transforming before floating into the air.

"Race you," she shouted as she took off. She flushed him with a blast of air as she whipped her wings.

"You'll lose," he yelled, taking off after her. He flew hard, but couldn't catch her. He slowed when he saw that she had stopped and hovered in the air.

"I won!"

"You did," he replied, grinning. "Enjoy it. It's your last."

She pointed down. "The crystal tree I told you about. This is where the papeons separated. Come on." She floated to the ground as Michael followed. "Look at the mist spewing from the flowers—it makes a tiny rainbow."

"That's unique."

"The door is this way." She started running down the path.

"We're not racing again are we?" he said. He chased after her.

She stopped and looked back at him. "There it is."

"It's bigger than I thought," he replied, coming up beside her. "And it's one solid pearl—maybe ten feet tall. Awesome." He drew closer.

She reached for his shoulder. "Should we go tell someone?"

He shook his head. "We're here now. But yes, eventually."

"It's supposed to be a secret. Right?"

Michael nodded. "I want to see if what they say is true."

"What?"

"That it can transport travelers faster than light."

She stopped. "You can, but I'm not going inside again."

"I just want to look around."

Yofiel pointed at the doorknob as both cautiously approached.

"Whoa, it's a blue diamond." Michael placed his hand on the door. "And it's cold as you said."

"Open it," she said, "and the cave will appear."

He reached for the doorknob. The cave appeared as he touched it. "Whoa! Incredible."

"Told you."

"It's locked," Michael muttered. "Was it locked previously?"

"No."

"I'll get it open." He unsheathed his sword and set the blade in the seam.

The ground shook and a cold fog emanated from the door.

"Get back!" shouted Yofiel.

Michael jumped backward and pulled her with him. A face appeared in the upper half of the door and began to protrude through the icy surface. A piece of ice broke away from the door as the head of the image pushed forward. The image spewed snowy vapor at Michael and froze him like a lone statue in an icy cemetery on a winter day.

"What are you doing?" Yofiel shouted at the image. "Let him go," She charged the door and began beating on the image with her hands. It blew a cocoon of ice over its face and around its head, shielding it from her blows.

Tears of fright froze on her cheeks as she continued to strike. "Release him now. Let him go! Look what have you have done. He'll freeze, can't you see?" Yofiel twisted around to catch a glimpse of Michael before continuing her attack on the ice-covered bust. "Let him go. We came in peace." She finally grew weary and slid to the ground, pleas fading.

The shield of ice around the image began to melt, revealing its long, wavy, white hair, snowy skin, bulging red cheeks, a prominent nose, and dark blue eyes.

"Evil may not enter," it said in a gruff voice, spewing snow and ice from its mouth.

"He's not evil," Yofiel chided angrily. "His name is Michael. He's a student at the Academy of Kanah. Release him right now. You should be ashamed of yourself."

"I know who he is and I know you, Yofiel. But he drew his sword to attack."

"He did not attack. He was only trying to open the door. He's no threat."

"No one may force the door open. Only friends of the king may enter through me."

"He's a servant of the king. He'll put his sword away as soon as you release him."

"Very well." The figure blew a warm breeze and Michael thawed as quickly as he had frozen. She motioned for him to put his sword away, which he did and the two approached the door again. Yofiel rubbed his arms to warm him.

"Thank you," Yofiel said to the image. "Do you have a name?"

"My name is Sir Calidoore—Sentinel of the doors of Krystar. I watch, assess, and guard; I watch for activity around the door, assess friend or enemy, and open only for friends."

"Why were you locked to us?" Yofiel asked. "You were not locked earlier."

"The door was locked because another traveler was inside awaiting transport. He has now been transported."

"Why did you appear today and not the other day?" she asked.

"I appear as I will, little one."

"Where did the wind and the fire in the tunnel come from?" she asked.

"The wind and fire form a portal which is the blue spinning fire that you and Tamor witnessed."

"Strange," Michael muttered.

Yofiel took a step toward the door. "Sir Calidoore, may we enter?"

"Come." A cloud enveloped them and then dissipated.

"The image, it's gone," Yofiel muttered. "And the door's open. Let's go."

"I thought you weren't going inside."

"I changed my mind. Come on."

Michael started to draw his sword but instead placed his hand on the handle while gently pushing the door with his other hand.

Yofiel whisked inside. "It's darker than dark in here." She stared straight ahead into the darkness. The cave stared back in stony silence.

"It's so dark that I can almost feel it," said Michael. "No sign of a fire." He pulled ahead of her. "Do you want to continue?"

"Yes. I trust Sir Calidoore."

Michael noticed the curvaceous figure of the little penicl silhouetted against the light of the door. It slammed shut, causing both to jump into each other.

"Oh, I'm sorry," she said, clutching his T-shirt.

"For what?"

She pushed away and held her right arm out revealing a small dot of light in the palm of her hand that grew into a sparkling ball of light. It floated in front of her.

"How did you do that?"

"Magic." She blossomed a smile. They crept cautiously into the cave. "Look," she whispered. "The ledge is at the other end where the stars are. Let me show you"

"You're an adventurous one. Lead on." He reached for her hand and drew her close. *She has sweet hands.*

"I was scared during my first trip with Tamor but this is fun."

He gripped her hand. "Wait. Do you hear anything?"

"Nothing. Look at the stars." She tightened her grip and together they walked out on to the ledge.

Michael surveyed the area. “This is strange. The pearl door opens to a bright forest, while this end opens to dark space.”

She led him around the ledge as she gazed into the starry sky. “We could just step into space and float away.” She took a deep breath, held it, and slowly exhaled. “Look at all of the sparkling lights.”

“Look at them. Stars, stars, everywhere stars.”

“I count five shooting stars so far. How far does space go?”

“To the end.”

“Where’s that?”

“Where light, energy, time, and mass haven’t reached yet.”

“Is there such a place?”

“Yes, just beyond the human’s universe.”

“What’s after that?

“Loneliness, I guess,”

They sat and gazed into space, marveling at the beauty under the canopy of stars, picking out images in the glowing clusters across the oversized sky.

“They’re dazzling, as you are.” *That was awkward.*

“Another light.” She pointed. “Do you see? It’s slower than the others.”

“Where?”

She grasped his hand and pointed his finger. “There.”

“Probably a meteor. No worries.”

They continued watching as it moved across the night sky.

“Wait. It stopped. It’s coming toward us, I think—and getting bigger.”

Michael stood. “Time to leave.” He helped her up.

The sky ignited like an erupting volcano as surrounding stars turned red, like churning lava.

“Run!” Michael commanded.

The ledge vibrated causing both to stumble. "I got you," he muttered. They struggled across the ledge to the entrance. "Don't stop, Yofiel! Hurry!"

"Fire!" she shouted. "It's coming inside, Michael."

The two ran through the cave toward the pearl door that began to glow from the approaching fire. The tornado punched through the door from the ledge and blew a mighty wind that shook the cave.

"The door's stuck. Help me to open it." Both fell as the shaking intensified.

"I can't see the door anymore," Yofiel shouted. "Where is it?" Both grasped at the empty air where they thought the door was and then started to slide backward.

Michael clutched the diamond doorknob and tried to push the door open. "The wind is creating suction. I can't open it. We're trapped."

10

CAVE FIGHT

"A tornado," Yofiel shouted.

"Get behind the boulder," he yelled, still struggling with the door.

An explosion at the other end of the cave startled Michael. He turned. "I see something." The blue churning tornado of fire dissipated with the wind, leaving a red glowing mist in the cave. A fiery figure appeared near the doorway at the rear of the cave by the ledge. Unwelcome dampness filled the room.

"What is it, Michael?"

"I'm not sure, but I have an eerie vibe." He watched with bated breath. "Whatever it is appears to be about ten feet tall."

Fog followed the creature into the cave and crawled along the ground.

"Smells like sulfur," Yofiel whispered behind the rock.

"I smell it. And I see two glowing red eyes that aren't blinking—sure signs of a demon. It's coming," Michael drew his sword. Watchers were instructed to draw their sword at the sight of an unknown creature. "No matter what happens, stay out of sight." He shook uncontrollably. Fear exposed his façade of bravery as he started gasping for air.

"Michael, are you all right?"

"So far."

"I hear shuffling feet," she whispered in the quieting cave. "Sounds big."

"Ssshhh," he whispered, bringing a finger to his mouth.

The creature slowly approached and drew a sword that lit on fire as he raised it. It removed a black cloak and tossed it aside. Clods of molten lava slid down its frame that transformed into red-eyed snakes that hissed before scurrying into the dark crevices of the cave.

It's huge. It's a beast. "It has two circular horns pointing downward. What is this thing? It's no ordinary demon."

"What do you see?"

"Reddish-green scaly skin, muscular, a tail, leather straps around its chest, thighs and arms and small, pointy horns running the length of its arms, shoulders, and back." Michael attempted to open the door again. *Still locked.* He turned toward the beast. "Who are you?" No response. "Identify yourself."

Rroooaarrr!

The sound petrified Michael.

Yofiel peered at the creature. Rocks in the cave tumbled to the ground.

The beast snatched a roach from its face with its tongue causing Yofiel to almost vomit.

Shivers of fear covered Michael like a scratchy blanket. *How do we get out of here? I hope the beast doesn't find Yofiel.*

"My name is Beelzebub," the creature finally uttered, breathing fire. The voice was deep, like that of a giant. Smoke poured from its body and seemed to replace the steam in the cave. "I am Commander of the demons of darkness. Who might you be and what are you doing in the middle of space?"

Michael watched as the creature transformed into a humanlike form with long black hair. Its eyes changed to dazzling greenish red as the creature lowered its sword.

“I saw a bright blue spiraling light from space,” the beast continued. “I recognize it as one of the portals of Krystar. I want this portal."

"It's not mine to give."

"I'm not asking."

"Why do you want it?"

"Portals can transport my army of demons faster than light. It's a long way from heaven to hell. I know you call heaven, Krystar. I call my home Darkmar.” He gazed around the cave and smiled as he considered the possibilities before turning again toward Michael. “Don’t you know there are demons out here in space—like me? This is no place for a little watcher to be without an escort. Why are you alone?”

“My name is Michael,” he answered, sword still drawn. He saw that the creature looked at his sword, shaking in his hand. *Ignore his eyes. Ignore the sulfur. Ignore the snakes, the heat, the demon.* “I just found the cave today. I live here on Kanah—one of the seven outposts of Krystar.” *My eyes are burning. Please stay hidden, Yofiel.*

Beelzebub continued to gaze at his newfound catch. "So this is the portal of Kanah. I'm well aware of the seven outposts, little watcher."

“I must return,” Michael continued, shifting his weight from one leg to the other to reduce his shaking.

Yofiel snuck another peek at the creature. *It's rather handsome for a demon—not at all what I expected. I didn't know demons could transform.*

Michael rubbed his nose as the scent of the creature grew worse. He stared as the creature began walking randomly from one side of the cave to the other as though contemplating something. Spiders fell from the leg of the creature and crawled into another crevice in the cave.

Michael studied the demon. *He has the sword of a senior warrior demon—the flame flares as it senses a threat. The black blade outlined in gold and the images of lightning in the grip are cool. Truly this is Beelzebub! I'm dead. There's no escape.*

"You aren't in Kanah. I just arrived from space and here you are with me, in space." The flame of the demon's sword blazed brighter as the volume of his voice increased. "You're a long way from Kanah, or to any other outpost. Perhaps light-years away." The creature stilled his sword and set his red eyes on Michael.

"It's right through that door," Michael said, pointing behind him.

"Show me."

"I can't. It's locked."

"Your so-called king in Krystar claims he rules all space and all creatures. I beg to differ. He doesn't rule over me or my demons, or space, for that matter. I rule space! I rule millions of demons! I will rule all creatures! I am the king of darkness!"

Am I really standing in front of the king of demons? He glanced in Yofiel's direction as she remained unseen by the beast. "I speak the truth."

"What is truth?" Beelzebub retorted. The demon turned toward the ledge and peered into space before locking eyes with Michael again.

"You're in space—my space! I own the dark. Do you know what we do to trespassers and especially to warriors and to those who pretend to be warriors?" Beelzebub snorted derisively and then took note of Michael's sword. "You call that a sword, little soldier? Come to me. Show me what you've got." The demon pointed his long sword to challenge Michael.

No way can I beat this demon. Michael struggled to recall his training and knew he was ill-equipped for a fight. *I have no choice.* He raised his sword to eye level, centered it on the demon, and flaired his wings. Watchers and angels could transform to reveal their wings at will.

Beelzebub approached with a smirk. The two touched blades and glared at one another with no blinking.

Michael grew more nervous. *I can't hold on to my sword with this sweat*. I'm going to lose this fight. What will happen to Yofiel if this beast finds her? He remembered a few offensive maneuvers from class but nothing more. *I'm no match for the demon—he's too big, too strong and too experienced and I'm too little, too weak and too inexperienced. I'm the runt of my own class, the least of the fighters.*

"Why me?" he said, loud enough for the demon to hear.

"Why not you, runt?" Beelzebub replied as he lunged with his sword pointed toward Michael's throat. The demon twisted and opted to slap him in the face with the flat side of his blade.

He could have stabbed me. Why didn't he? He rubbed his face with his hand and looked to see if there was any blue blood. There was none, at least not yet. He lunged at the demon who effortlessly nudged his sword aside.

He's playing with me. He pointed his sword and charged straight at Beelzebub's heart. Again, the demon brushed it aside with his huge sword.

"Is this what they're teaching these days at your junior school?" Beelzebub yawned, getting bored.

"It's not a junior school," Michael retorted. "It's the Academy of Kanah. They teach how to fight."

"So, fight then!"

Michael attempted a roundhouse kick hoping to catch the demon off guard.

Beelzebub dodged the strike.

Michael turned himself completely around and tumbled onto his back. He felt humiliated as the demon laughed. *His laughter is hideous*.

The demon's smug expression faded into a cynical look of superiority. "Really? Is this the best you can do? Rise, little one. You can't fight on your back."

A chariot of fire pulled by two fiery dapple-gray horses stormed to the ledge from space, eyes aflame.

Beelzebub jerked to attention. "Strange. What's a chariot of fire doing here in the middle of space? What am I missing?" He paused to contemplate in his confusion. "Are you trying to trap me, watcher boy?" The horses reared and neighed as they sensed evil.

Michael scrambled to his feet and charged while the demon focused on the horses. Beelzebub backhanded him, sending him facedown to the rocky surface. He rolled back toward the demon and bit him on the leg.

"Ouch, you worthless piece of crud," the demon hissed as he twisted and kicked him in the face. He threw Michael's sword against the wall of the cave, breaking it into two pieces.

Michael fell to the ground and raised his hand to his face to check for blood. Seeing none, he rose to his knees and swung as the beast approached. The demon caught his arm, locked it and pushed him against the rocky wall of the cave.

Yofiel charged from her hiding place, pulled a dagger from her thigh and rammed it into the demon's back. "Leave him alone you evil beast!"

Beelzebub spun like a top, pulled the knife from his back, and backhanded her.

She fell to the floor, quickly rose, and unsheathed her sword hidden until now. She dodged a sudden thrust of his sword,, spun, and sliced his leg.

"Aarrgghh," Beelzebub yelled. His wound healed before their eyes. "Lucky for me, I heal quickly, children." He again thrust his sword towards her stomach. She attempted to block it but the demon parried, then struck her in the face with his left hand, almost knocking her unconscious. She fell to the ground, dazed. The demon pivoted and hurled a black flaming spear at Michael. He dodged a direct hit but was cut as it flew by and stuck in the wall.

The demon leapt forward and kicked the young cadet in the leg, almost breaking it. Michael spun in the air from the blow, clutching his leg. Beelzebub struck him in his side, slammed him into the wall, and watched as Michael slid to the ground. Michael hollered in pain, no longer able to stand.

Beelzebub grabbed him by the neck and lifted him off the ground. “Time for you to take a ride, little one.” The horses reared up and whinnied as the demon approached with his prey. The demon pulled him to his face and head-butted him. “If we ever meet again, little warrior, it won’t go well for you.” He threw him into the fiery chariot hoping he would burn in the flames. Michael hit his head at the end of the seat before falling to the floorboard.

Michael saw the demon lunged forward and electricuted upon contact with the chariot.

The demon ROARED. The jolt caused him to transform into the scaly-skinned, ten-foot drooling beast as he was when he arrived. The shout spooked the horses causing them to raise to their hind legs and neigh.

Michael was jerked backward into the seat of the chariot as the horses stampeded away. “Yooffiieel,” he cried into the blackness of space.

11

THE GREAT ESCAPE

Cursed watchers. Beelzebub remained motionless on the ledge, angrily observing his scorched hand. The burn mark slowly healed as he transformed back into his humanlike form. He heard a noise inside the cave, quickly turned and observed Yofiel sneaking toward the pearl door.

"Leaving so soon, my little dumpling?" he snarled loudly.

"I'm not your dumpling, you creep," she riposted just as loudly as she ran for the door.

The demon spread his batlike wings and flew toward the insolent peniel. He landed and chased after her, wings flapping.

The heavenly creature grasped the blue diamond doorknob and turned it.

Leaping into the air like a lizard, Beelzebub reached out with his long claws extended as she pushed the door open. The demon clutched the pink silk scarf around her neck as she escaped through his fingers. The door slammed in his face.

"Curses," the king of demons barked, followed by a barrage of choice words that echoed through the cave. Casting the scarf aside, he instinctively reached for the doorknob to give chase. But the doorknob flashed brightly upon contact, sending a pulsating shock of intense energy and knocking his arm backward.

The demon ROARED, though no one could hear. "Darned peniel. Who would have thought such a creature would be hiding in this God-forsaken cave?" *Her scarf wasn't tied, or it would have surely tightened around her sweet neck like a noose, dragging her right into my arms. No such luck, curse it. She was pretty enough to keep.* "To hell with the door and to hell with the watchers," he shouted, followed by a litany of curses.

The demonic king sat on a boulder contemplating. *This is no ordinary door to the portal.* "This is the door to Krystar and the seven outposts. There has to be a way to get in. I must find a way. But how?" His gaze fell to the pink scarf lying on the ground—a symbol of his failure to catch her. He retrieved it with his sword, sniffed it deeply, and wrapped it around his wrist. "How do I open this blasted door?" he hissed.

* * * * *

The chariot of fire sped through space faster than a falling star. Michael sat up in the seat of the chariot and watched the stars stretch out like rope lights. The horses sped along greater than the speed of light.

Where is this chariot taking me? I hope Yofiel escaped from the demon. She will not survive as his prisoner—he will do dreadful things to her. I'm a worthless fighter who failed to protect her. I am such a loser. Uriel and the rest of the Council of Kanah will hold me accountable for putting Yofiel and all of Kanah at risk, especially if Beelzebub opens the door and enters Kanah. What have I done?

* * * * * *

Yofiel turned her back against the door and slid down to a sitting position facing the forest. "That was close."

"I hope Michael is okay." She heard the faint screams of the demon behind the pearl door. "What if the demon gets through the door?" Fearful, she jumped to her feet and ran frantically through the forest, barely noticing the crystal tree and too terrified to look back. "If I fly, the demon may see me if he decides to fly." She ran and ran through the woods "Where am I?" She fell to her knees, overcome with the fear that the demon was pursuing her. She froze at a sound from the forest. "Papeons," she exclaimed, relieved at the sight. "They wouldn't be flying if there was a demon around."

The creatures flew over her in the direction of the city. She joined them in flight, no longer fearing the demon. She landed near the east gate and watched as the papeons disappeared over the horizon.

She ran through the east gate along the crystal streets, past the café where she and Michael had eaten breakfast that morning, past the flower shop, into the Castle of Kanah and straight to her Training, Advising and Counseling (TAC) angel. A TAC angel was assigned to every floor of the castle and served as a chaperone to the watchers

Knock, knock. She slammed the door open without waiting for a response. "Help, help," she shouted.

"What is it?" the TAC angel replied, running toward her. "What's the matter?"

"Beelzebub beat up my friend, Michael!"

"What are you talking about? Where? When?"

"Just now... in the forest. The demon showed up at the secret cave in the woods, from space. I hid at first and then stabbed him. He chased after me. I got away but my friend didn't."

"Whoa, slow down. Please take a seat."

She plopped down on a white couch that looked like a cloud.

"Tell me everything."

She conveyed the whole story to the TAC angel who recorded every detail.

"I will submit the report to our leadership for review."

"But my friend needs help right now! He's hurt."

"I will submit it right away."

"What do I do in the meantime?"

"Wait. I will let you know as soon as I hear."

She rose and slowly walked out of his office. *I hope he believes me.* She replayed the events in her mind: her time with Michael, their journey to the door, Sir Calidoore, the encounter with Beelzebub, Michael's fight, the chariot, and horses of fire and her escape. She had never seen a demon before that day, much less talked to one. Never had she smelled the scent of sulfur, or looked into the red eyes of a demon. Never had she witnessed violence, or heard words spoken with venom and evil. "What about Michael?" she blurted out to herself.

Can he walk after that awful beating? Did the horses take him to earth? Is he hurt? Is he lost? "Will I ever see him again?" She went straight to her suite and shut the door.

"Michael!" she yelled.

12

THE NEXT DAY

The next morning Yofiel jumped and awoke in her beanbag chair, remembering the dragon-like face of the beast in the cave. "I need to tell Tamor." She dashed to Tamor's suite, a short distance away in the castle.

Bang, bang, bang.

"Tamor, are you there?" She opened the door, for doors are never locked on Kanah.

"Tamor?" she shouted.

Tamor hurried from another room of her suite. "What is it, Yofiel? What's wrong?"

"Oh, Tamor. Michael is hurt."

"What do you mean he is hurt? What happened? Come sit with me."

"I took Michael to the cave in the forest—yesterday."

Tamor gasped. "Oh no. Was he swallowed by the tornado?"

"No."

"Oh, thank goodness."

"Worse. We met Beelzebub—the king of the demons."

"Okay, that's worse."

He arrived while we were there. Michael fought him and got beat up bad. The demon threw him into the chariot and it sped away."

"Where is he now?"T

"I think the chariot went to earth. Michael's hurt. He needs our help." She teared up.

"Did the demon see you?"

"It chased me, but I escaped and slammed the door behind me. I don't know where it is now. It could be here on Kanah."

"You're breathing to heavy. Calm down. You need your your favorite drink, coconut mixed with mango. Just speak the order and it will appear on the table."

"No, I like making it myself."

"No, just relax and catch your breath." Tamor returned a few minutes later.

"Mmm, this is good," Yofiel said after the first sip. "I feel better already. Thank you."

"Now tell me the whole story. I want to hear the details."

Yofiel related the events of their encounter with Beelzebub. "I also reported the story to my TAC angel and he said he would get back to me as soon as he hears something. I'm still waiting."

"Good. So hopefully that will be soon."

"It could take days, Tamor. We need to go to earth and find Michael ourselves. I know he's hurt."

"That's risky, Yofiel. We can't go by ourselves. First, it's dangerous—the demon could be waiting for you. Second, we need an escort. Let's wait and see what your TAC angel says first. Perhaps you'll hear today."

"We should also tell our teacher," said Yofiel.

"Agree. But let's tell Gabriel first and see what he says."

Yofiel nodded. "I think he's in his warrior class now. Which reminds me. Our class will start soon. I won't be able to concentrate knowing Michael is in pain somewhere on earth."

"If we leave now, then we should be able to catch Gabriel before he leaves the arena."

The two girls hurried to the academy.

* * * * *

Gabriel and his classmates conversed while removing their protective armor at the end of their class.

"Where was Michael today?" a student asked Gabriel.

"Did he quit?" another asked.

"I heard him say that he wanted to return to Krystar," replied a third student.

"He's probably embarrassed about losing all of his matches," another student commented.

"I don't think he's warrior material and he finally figured it out," piped another.

"No, you guys are wrong," Gabriel replied, shaking his head. "There's more to it. He would tell me if he was not coming to class. Think about it. He's never missed class before. None of us have." *Where are you, friend?*

"Valid point, Gabriel," replied a classmate. The others agreed.

"Hey guys," one of the students pointed. "Look at the peniel watchers coming this way.

All looked.

"I recognize them," Gabriel said. "They're coming for me."

"Yeah, dream on," one student said.

"Time out, Gabriel," another said in jest. "We think they are here to admire us and ask for our autographs."

"They want to invite us to the donut shop across the street and feed us the candied ones that we love to munch on," added another.

"You wish, guys," replied Gabriel.

"There are two of them and one of you, Gabriel. Don't be greedy. Introduce us."

"Not this time. Something's awry. They may have news about Michael." He watched as the peniels ran between the students scattered in the arena and left the group to meet them in private. "Is everything okay?

"We need to talk," Tamor said, bumping into him.

"What's going on?"

"Somewhere more private, please." The three exited the stadium.

"What's wrong?" he asked.

"Michael fought with a demon while he and Yofiel were exploring a cave in the woods. Yofiel and I found a portal door in the forest and she took Michael to see it."

"You guys found a magic cave in the woods and a demon showed up?"

Yofiel took a deep breath. "Exactly. The demon said he was Beelzebub, king of the demons. It hurt Michael and then threw him into a chariot of fire. The chariot took off to earth, we think."

"And Michael is hurt," Tamor said.

Yofiel pulled on Gabriel's arm. "And lost. We have to find him."

"Whoa, hang on, ladies" Gabriel replied. "Time out. This is too much to digest. I'm confused. Let's go to the park across the street and discuss it further."

The three found a bench under a bright red tree. Yofiel told Gabriel the story while Tamor assisted with the facts as if she had witnessed the whole thing.

Gabriel inhaled deeply while leaning forward on the bench. "We should tell our leaders and let them address this."

"No," Tamor said. "You know they will not allow us to go to earth and search for him. We need to go as soon as we can."

Gabriel sat up and leaned back between them. "But Tamor, we have to tell senior leadership. We must trust our leaders."

The girls nodded.

"I told my TAC angel last night," Yofiel said.

"Okay, that's good," Gabriel replied. "What did he say?"

"Nothing yet. I'm waiting for him to get back with me."

"Look," said Gabriel. "There's Caleb talking with Uriel at the door of the arena. Let's tell them about this and see what they have to say. Okay." He looked at both of them as they nodded and then the three crossed the street.

Caleb and Uriel turned toward them as they approached. "Hello, watchers," Caleb replied. "Are you coming for us?"

"Yes sir," Gabriel replied. "Yofiel has something to tell both of you if you have a few minutes."

"Of course," both replied.

Yofiel explained everything that happened in the cave. "Please, oh please, help."

"I was wondering where Michael was today," Caleb said. "It's not like him to miss class. Gabriel, were you aware of this?"

"No, sir. I just heard the news a few minutes ago."

"What do you think?" Caleb asked, turning toward Uriel.

"We have seen several cases similar to this over the years. There is a precedent for such matters. Our policy is to give watchers several days to return. If they do not return in that time, then we send a search team. In all previous cases, missing watchers have returned within a week and most returned within three days or two."

"But sir, Michael is hurt." Yofiel cried. "He is in pain and probably needs assistance."

"Yofiel," Gabriel said. "Respect the decision of your leaders."

"Forgive me. I'm just concerned."

"I'm certain he will return soon, on his own." Uriel replied.

"Yes, sir, thank-you," Yofiel said. The three left.

Uriel turned to Caleb. "Issue lightbands to all watchers. We must be able to track them in cases like this."

"Will do."

"One more thing, Caleb. Send a scan team to the cave in the forest to see if Beelzebub left anything behind. Also, check the program to verify that the chariot flew to Earth."

"Right away, Uriel."

13

ANOTHER TRIP TO THE CAVE

The next day Gabriel, Tamor, and Yofiel wandered around the town, talking about Michael. They happened by Café de Kanah where Michael and Yofiel had breakfast the previous morning.

"Let's take a break," Gabriel said, pointing at the cafe.

"Let's," Tamor replied.

Yofiel sighed. *We don't have time for this.*

"What's wrong, Yofiel?" Gabriel asked.

"We have to do something, friends," replied Yofiel.

"We will, soon," Gabriel replied. "What would you Peniels like to order?"

"Panna cottagape, replied Yofiel. "It's similar to baklava, durian, and bananas cooked with honey-coconut ice cream." The dessert appeared on the table before her. "The best dessert on the planet."

"Yvonavita," Tamor replied. It appeared a moment later. "I love the mango and strawberry puree mixed with durian.

"That's different," Gabriel observed.

"It's the best," she replied. "Order a slice."

"I'm already full," said Gabriel, leaning forward. "But if it's as good as you say..." He picked up a fork. "May I."

"Please do." She replied.

He stuck her fork into it and took a bite. "It is good. Thank you."

"I knew our leadership wouldn't respond immediately," Tamor said. "They need to act now."

Yofiel stared into her dessert and stuck her fork into it.

Gabriel caught the body language. "What is it?"

"I wish we knew where Michael is."

"I thought he went to earth?" he replied.

"The figure in the door—Sir Calidoore—said the default destination is earth. So I think he did."

"I thought the cave was just a wild rumor," he replied. "I say we go to the cave and find a way to get to earth."

"Really?" replied Yofiel, lifting the first piece of her desert to her mouth.

"Why not?" he replied. "We could bring Michael back in an hour or two, so no one would know we left."

"But the escort has to be an angel and you're a fourteen-year-old watcher," said Tamor. "You're four years too young, as we all are."

"She's right, Gabriel. We need an angel escort."

"Do you know what could happen if we're caught?" Tamor asked. "This could mean suspension from the academy, or expulsion at worst."

"I know," he said, shrugging it off. "But I'm concerned for Michael as you are. As I said, we'll be back without anyone knowing."

Yofiel shoved her half-eaten desert away and pushed back from the table. "Okay then. Let's go."

Tamor took another bite and stood from the table. "If we're going to do this, then let's go."

"Let's fly," added Tamor.

"We can't," replied Gabriel. "Watchers must check out through the gate."

"I forgot that only angels can fly in and out of the city," Yofiel replied.

The three hopped into the street and proceeded to the east gate. When they cleared the wall, they took to the air, eventually landing by the crystal tree.

The peniels took off running down the path.

"I'm not racing," Gabriel shouted, though he started jogging after them. "They're like children." They were already standing by the door when he arrived.

"Who would ever believe a secret door is unattended like this?" He glanced at the two. "Ladies first."

"I don't think so," Tamor replied, nudging him in the side.

Yofiel eyed him. "She's the cautious one. I'll go first."

Gabriel tilted his head and squinted "After what happened yesterday?"

Yofiel stepped up to the doorknob and gave them a glance. "Exactly. I want to do this."

Gabriel nodded. "I'll be behind you." He turned to Tamor who nodded in the affirmative.

"Sir Calidoore, are you there?" Yofiel asked. No response. "He doesn't always appear."

"We don't present any risk, I suppose," said Gabriel.

"Remember, the chariot of fire will take us to earth," Yofiel said. "I don't know if the fire and wind will show up. Here goes..." She turned the doorknob and pressed her ear in the opening. "All is quiet." She pushed the door all the way open and entered.

Tamor went around Gabriel and followed. "What do you see?"

"Darkness."

Gabriel stepped inside. "I see nothing, hear nothing, smell nothing, feel nothing."

Tamor pinched him.

"Ouch."

"Feel something now?"

He chuckled. "Stay here and hold the door."

"Okay," she said, gripping the diamond doorknob. "Watch Yofiel."

"I will."

"Look at the stars at the other end," Yofiel said, reaching for his hand.

"Tamor, too much light is coming inside," he said. "Could you close it a little more please?"

"I can't see anything yet," said Yofiel. She opened her hand and the sparkling ball of light appeared again. She tossed it into the air and it floated before them.

"I won't ask you how you did that."

She turned to Michael. "Magic."

Gabriel followed her to the ledge. "Magnificent view. We do seem to be in space on this end of the cave. I don't understand it."

"I could come here every day just for the view."

"He returned to the entrance. "Tamor, you have to see this. Come on."

Tamor stepped inside.

"Don't let the door shut," Yofiel shouted.

Slam.

"Sorry." She checked the door. "It's unlocked."

"Follow my voice, Tamor. There's nothing in the way to trip you. Come on."

She opened her hand and a sparkling ball appeared as it had for Yofiel.

"That helps," Gabriel said.

She walked through the cave and onto the ledge. "Unbelievable."

Yofiel gazed up at the night sky. "So as long as there are no demons around, we're okay. But if there is any sign of one, I'm running. Watch for any moving light, except for shooting stars, of course."

Gabriel paused. "You are freaking me out with this demon talk."

Tamor nudged him. "Focus on the stars."

"Right," he replied. They lay down on the ledge and watched the sky. "This is a natural high."

"What's a natural high?" asked Tamor.

"Some astronomers told me about it during a mission trip to earth. You find a secluded spot to focus on the night sky. As you stare into space, it appears that the stars begin to move and you feel like you're floating above the sky among them."

"Let's do it," Yofiel said.

"Get a natural high?" Tamor asked.

"No. Go on mission trips to earth." Yofiel drew silent and pointed. "I see something—a moving light. It's probably the chariot. We'll have to move out of the way."

"I see it," said Gabriel.

"It could be a shooting star or a meteor," Tamor added.

Yofiel sat up. "It's coming toward us. Maybe the chariot is bringing Michael back."

Tamor sat up beside her. "But it could also be the demon again."

"You could be right," Gabriel replied, getting to his feet. "We should go." The sound grew, like the approaching hoofbeats of stampeding horses.

"But we came here to go to earth," Yofiel said. "We can't just leave."

"Yofiel, you already had one encounter with Beelzebub," Gabriel said. "Do you want to risk another encounter? I say let's go." Gabriel hurried off the ledge with Tamor following. The ledge and the face of the cave began to glow in the light of the approaching object.

Yofiel lingered on the ledge. "It has to be the chariot."

"Get out of the way, Yofiel!" Gabriel shouted. "It's coming right at you."

"Yofiel!" shouted Tamor.

14

PLANET EARTH

"The Chariot of Fire!" Yofiel shouted at Gabriel and Tamor who had perched themselves at the entrance of the cave. "It's coming!"

The chariot with the two horses of fire stormed the ledge, almost running her over. Their eyes of the horses burned as bright as the sun. She froze at the sight. A blue fire spun in the rear, blowing a strong wind.

"Yofiel, get out of there," Gabriel shouted. He shifted to Tamor. "I may have to get her."

The two horses reared up and neighed, causing Yofiel to fall to the ledge. She rose and began fighting against the wind to reach the chariot. She turned and motioned for the two to come.

"There's no sign of a demon, Tamor?" Gabriel said. "We need to get to the chariot."

"It's too risky," Tamor shouted.

"It's our way to earth. We have to." He grabbed her by the hand as she nodded in agreement. The two shielded their eyes from the shearing wind.

"Any sign of Michael?" Gabriel shouted to Yofiel as they approached.

“No. Let’s get in.” She climbed in and sat on the single bench seat.

“Are we sure about this?” Tamor shouted.

“None of us are,” Gabriel replied. “We could wind up anywhere.”

Yofiel squinted in the wind, waiting for them. “Hurry. Get in. The horses are going to leave.”

Gabriel jumped inside and sat next to Yofiel.

“No,” Tamor shouted. “It’s too risky.”

“We need you, Tamor,” Yofiel shouted. “I need you.”

Yofiel hesitated and then hopped into the chariot.

Gabriel reached for her hand and pulled her close. “No venture, no victory.” He held the hands of both girls and braced for takeoff.

“The fire—it doesn’t burn or give off heat,” said Yofiel, placing her free hand on the side of the chariot.

Tamor put her face down towards her knees, bracing for takeoff.

The horses reared up again. Gabriel clutched the peniels tightly. “Hang on.” The chariot stormed away in a streak of fire.

Tamor peeked up. “Have we left?”

“Look how fast we’re going,” Yofiel exclaimed. “Look at the stars and the objects in the sky around us?” Objects closer to them whizzed by.

“I can tell we’re going fast but I didn’t feel any acceleration. I didn’t think we had left the cave yet.”

“L o o k a t t h e b l u e s p i n n i n g c o n t r a i l s b e h i n d t h e c h a r i o t,” Gabriel said.

“W h a t‘s w r o n g w i t h y o u r s p e e c h?” Yofiel asked.

“O u r w o r d s a r e s l o w i n g d o w n!” Gabriel said. “W e a r e a p p r o a c h i n g t h e s p e e d o f l i g h t.” Suddenly, there was a bright flash.

"The flash!" Tamor said. "I think we just blew past the speed of light." Particles of light began flowing through the three like dust in the wind.

Gabriel held out his arms. "Look at us." Light is flowing inside of us. Contrails of light particles lagged the movement of his arms and we waved them back and forth.

"We're beings of light!" Yofiel said. "Look. We're transparent. I can see through you."

"Look at the stars," said Tamor, pointing. "They're turning into strings of light like they're being stretched."

"That's new," said Yofiel.

"Look," Gabriel said, pointing. "Earth." The chariot slowed with no feeling of deceleration.

"Look," Tamor said. "The strings of light are growing shorter." There was another flash of light.

"We're slowing down," Gabriel said. "There it is."

"There's what?" asked Tamor.

"The cave to earth. Do you see the blue spinning light floating in space?" He pointed to a blue haze of light in the direction they were heading.

"Really?" said Yofiel. "The cave spins?"

"Yes," Gabriel replied. "All of the portals look like a bright spinning blue fire so the horses can find them."

"I guess it makes sense," Yofiel said. The chariot screeched to a halt on the ledge and the three exited. The tornado of wind formed behind the chariot as usual but then dissipated. As they entered the cave, the horses reared up, neighed, and took off into space.

The three watched them as they looked like a tiny dot. Tamor was the first to reach the entrance to the cave. "The pearl door is glowing on the other side of the cave. Why is that?"

"Probably so travelers can find their way through the cave," replied Yofiel.

The three proceeded into the cave, opened the pearl door, and stepped into the woods.

"Here we are, peniels, somewhere on planet earth," Gabriel said as he studied the surroundings. Ducks splashed around in a nearby pond, birds flew about, bees hovered over some purple flowers, and trees swayed in a humid breeze.

Tamor took a deep breath. "We're here."

Yofiel watched the bumblebees. "Neat critter. This place looks just like the pictures we've seen of earth."

Gabriel sneezed. "Yes, this is definitely earth."

"We need to remember this spot so we can find the door when we return," said Yofiel.

"How can we?" Tamor asked. "We are surrounded by trees."

"These three palm trees mark this spot," replied Gabriel.

"And that pond marks the area," Yofiel added.

"How did you know those were palm trees?" Tamor asked.

"I studied earth's habitat. All watchers have to take courses about earth." He turned all the way around, surveying the area. "Let's spread out and look for Michael. He should be nearby since he is likely hurt." They spread out and searched the area.

"How do we know he was even here in this location on earth?"

"We don't but what else do we do?" he replied.

"Yiiii," Yofiel screamed as she neared the pond. "What are those long green things with all those teeth?"

"Alligators," Gabriel said. "Avoid them."

"And what are those?" Tamor asked.

"Rabbits. They don't bite."

A fury cub ran out of some bushes toward Yofiel. "Look, everyone." She kneeled and picked it up.

Tamor ran up to her. "She's adorable."

A huge bear arose behind some bushes.

"Yofiel!" Gabriel shouted. "Get rid of it!"

15

MICHAEL FOUND

Gabriel drew his sword, jumped forward, and stood in the gap between the bear and Yofiel. *Today you die, bear.*

Yofiel put the cub on the ground,

The huge bear charged through the bushes straight towards them.

Yofiel held the palm of her hand out toward the big bear as if signaling it to stop. Lightning flashed from her hand with the sound of thunder. The motion of the bear halted in mid-stride as if time had stopped. A single burning ember from the lightning bolt floated slowly but purposely toward the bear and then popped in its face. The forward motion of the bear continued. But its face changed from one of rage to a look of calmness during its approached as if recognizing Yofiel. It slowed and then bowed in front of her.

"I beg your pardon, most beautiful lady of the stars," the bear said. "I see my cub has found comfort in your presence. I hope she was no bother."

"Of course not," Yofiel replied. "She's a delight. What's her name?"

"Her name is Yazhi Nakasi. We call her Nakasi. She was lost and now is found."

Turning to the cub, Yofiel said, “Dear Nakasi, you must return to your mother. I enjoyed our visit together.” The little brown cub cooed as it scurried away.

“Thank you, lady of the stars. We must return from where we came—deep within the forest.” The bears waved goodbye and then turned and disappeared into the woods.

“So that is one of the biting ones?” asked Tamor, half smiling.

“Definitely,” Gabriel replied. “But apparently that’s not a problem for you peniels. What just happened?”

Yofiel smiled. “Let’s just say we’re full of surprises.”

Tamor rolled her eyes at Gabriel.

He raised his arms to show his confusion. “Okay, let’s get back to searching for Michael. Spread out.”

The three searched for hours. Every once in a while they called out to each other.

“Yofiel,” Tamor called.

Yofiel stopped. “Over here.” She scanned the area and saw movement in some bushes. She ran toward the area and stopped short. “Michael, is that you?”

He waved. “Over here.”

She knelt by the bushes and moved the branches to find him. “Michael!”

“I knew you guys would come.”

She hurried around the bushes. “How badly are you hurt?”

“Bad enough. It hurts to move.”

“Let me call the others.”

“Who’s with you?”

“Gabriel and Tamor.”

She helped him to sit up and then walked away to call. “Gabriel, Tamor, I found him!”

“That demon did a number on me.”

"You're lucky that this is all he did to you, Michael." She paused, staring at him.

"There you are," Tamor said as she ran up to them.

Gabriel arrived minutes later and kneeled next to them. "Michael. How bad are you hurt?"

"My side and my leg are throbbing." He pulled back some of his torn clothes. "See?"

"It looks like a bad bruise," said Yofiel.

"Thanks for coming for me," he said as he covered the sores.

Gabriel threw his hands up. "We're family. Oh, I brought another sword for you. I heard yours was broken when you met Beelzebub."

"Thank you for that," Michel replied.

"Yay, yay, yay!" Yofiel exclaimed. "We found you."

"We weren't sure that we would," Tamor added.

"Can you get up?" Yofiel asked.

"I'll try. Ouch!"

"We'll help you," Gabriel said. "You can't spell 'pay attention' without p a i and n."

"It has my attention and I paid the price for it," Michael replied.

"That's why some watchers don't pay attention," Tamor added. "It pains them too much." She swung her long black hair over her shoulder.

"Good one, Tamor," Gabriel said. "For a serious girl, you can be funny."

"Who doesn't pay attention?" asked Michael.

"You don't," Tamor replied. "Yofiel told you she didn't want to go to the cave, but you took her anyway."

"I had to see it for myself," Michael replied, struggling to sit up.

"That's my point," she countered.

"Let's focus on the here and now, shall we?" Gabriel interjected. "We need to get back to Kanah before we're missed. Remember?"

"How?"

"Through the cave," he replied.

"No way," Michael quipped. "I just had the worst experience of my life in that cave. I'm not returning to it." He glanced at the peniels. "Not yet."

"Some warrior you are," Tamor said.

He frowned and attempted to get up.

"Michael, we need to get back to Kanah soon, or they'll notice our absence. We were not approved to come here."

"Then you three return without me. I just can't do it now. I'm sorry."

"Let's see where this path leads," Yofiel said, changing the subject. She glanced at Tamor and the latched on to his arms.

"Sounds good," Michael said. He stood up with their help and slowly put weight on his leg. "Ouch. It's my left leg."

"Don't rush it," Gabriel said. "You fought Beelzebub and survived." He said that to make Michael feel better. "We'll do the walking for you. But tomorrow, we must return."

"Okay," Michael replied.

"We're missing our classes, Yofiel," said Tamor.

"All of us are," replied Gabriel. "We'll return as soon as Michael is ready."

Gabriel led the group down the sandy path in the woods. "The pond is over there but we don't know where this direction will take us."

"We'll find out," Yofiel said. "Let's go."

"I'm with you guys," Tamor added.

Gabriel stepped aside as the ladies flanked Michael and passed him by.

"All right," Gabriel replied. "Let's do this."

"Okay, okay, slow down," Michael said—pain evident on his face. "You are handling sensitive cargo."

"Poor thing," Yofiel said.

"Thanks again to all of you for coming," he replied in a serious tone. "I thought a search party would come."

"We're it," Tamor replied.

"That demon got a lucky kick, for sure," Michael said, recalling the fight.

"You're lucky he didn't slice you in half," said Gabriel. "Think about it. You fought a real warrior demon—a foe fiercer than Oren and probably all of the angels on Kanah. And it was no sparring match. It was a real fight. You could have been destroyed."

"Does Sensei Caleb know?" Michael asked.

"We spoke with him and Uriel. We requested a search party to come for you but they told us that Kanah policy is to wait a week. The three of us decided not to wait." He motioned to Yofiel. "Let me take your spot."

"I got him." She glanced at Michael. "We're lucky the chariot brought us to the same spot. Otherwise, we may not have found you."

"I wonder why the chariot brought us to the same location?" Gabriel asked.

"We didn't change the destination in the program from its previous departure," answered Yofiel. "So I guess that's why."

Michael glanced at Gabriel. "Will you get in trouble for coming?"

"I hope not," he replied. "The only rule I'm aware of is that an escort is required for a watcher to travel from Kanah. Technically, I'm the escort."

"But you're not an angel yet, Gabriel," Michael replied. "At least not until you graduate. You know this. I don't want to see you get in trouble for coming here."

Gabriel shook his head. "I was hoping we would find you and then return without anyone knowing we left. We'll see what happens."

"They'll know we left," Tamor said.

Gabriel turned to Michael. "Are you sure you can't go back today?"

"I can't do it," Michael replied. "I am still freaked out from my encounter with Beelzebub. I just can't do it; not until I heal. You guys go."

"That's not going to happen," Gabriel replied. "He looked at Yofiel and Tamor. "You two can return now if you like."

"We're not leaving, or I'm not," Yofiel replied, glancing at Yofiel.

"I'm staying with you guys," she replied.

"We'll need to find a place to rest for a while," said Gabriel. "Can you fly if we carry you, Michael?"

"No, it will hurt. Walking is easier."

The three took turns assisting Michael.

"Did you guys travel through the cave on your prior trips to earth?" Yofiel asked.

"We traveled with angels but they didn't use caves." He turned to Yofiel. "A portal—a blue ring of fire—appears at will for angels. So we followed them into the portal wherever it appeared. There was no cave."

The sun crossed the sky above the trees during their trip through the woods.

"How much further?" Michael asked.

Yofiel pointed. "A human!"

16

AN EARTHLING AND A DOG

"A girl!" Gabriel said.

"And houses," said Michael. *We're out of the woods.*

Yofiel nodded. "She looks our age, maybe a little older." They watched as she went into her backyard.

"Our first human!" Tamor exclaimed. "She looks like us."

"She does," replied Yofiel.

"What next?" Michael asked.

"We need to find a place to stay for a while," said Yofiel. She scanned the row of houses lining the forest.

"The girl's house?" Tamor asked.

"That's the best scenario at the moment," Gabriel replied. "Michael could use some rest. What better place than a house?"

A hairy little creature ran toward the four and began to bark.

"Is that a dog?" asked Yofiel.

"Yes," Michael replied. "They come in all shapes and sizes."

"Cute," she said. "Love the red and white fur."

"Is it a biting animal?" Tamor asked.

"Some do, some don't," replied Gabriel. "I'm not sure about this one."

Yofiel smiled and squatted down. "She's wagging her tail."

"It means it's friendly," Michael said. "I learned that in my animal science class."

"Rosie. Rosie," called the girl, returning to her porch.

Yofiel stood up. "The dog is a she. The human is as tall as you are, Tamor."

"I like her jean shorts and red T-shirt—and she's barefooted," Tamor replied. "I like her already."

"Rosie, come here," the girl shouted.

The little dog ran back to the porch. The girl had no sooner petted the animal than it took off running in the direction of the watchers.

Michael sprouted his wings.

"Rosie, Rosie," the girl shouted louder than before while chasing after her.

"What do we do?" Tamor asked.

"We need a place to stay," Michael said. "This may be our opportunity."

"I agree," Gabriel said.

"Hide your wings, Gabriel," Michael whispered. "Humans aren't supposed to see them."

"Okay. Done. And our swords."

"I forgot," Michael replied. "Done."

I wanted to see what the dog would do when it saw my wings."

"Girls, change your eyes so they look human," said Michael

"Done," they replied in unison.

"We need earth clothes," Gabriel said.

They clicked their fingers and their clothes immediately changed into shorts and T-shirts. Yofiel's outfit had blue and white colors, Tamor's was black and white. Both had tennis shoes. The guys transitioned into regular jeans, T-shirts, and sandals.

The dog walked around to where they were standing. The human swung her long, dark-blonde hair away from her face as she looked behind the bushes. She stopped and gave a blank stare when she saw them. The four returned her stare.

"Hello. You have a cute puppy," said Yofiel.

"Oh," the girl replied. "I didn't see you guys."

Michael observed her. *She's nervous.* "We didn't mean to startle you."

Yofiel approached and held out her hand. "We were just admiring your dog. I'm Yofiel. This is Tamor and Gabriel and this is Michael."

"Hello," they said.

Tamor squatted down. "What kind of dog is she?"

"Australian Cattle Dog."

It cautiously approached. Tamor petted it.

"May we ask your name?" Michael asked.

"Oh, I'm sorry. My name is Leah." Her golden eyes opened wide. My dog's name is Rosie—she has a red spot on her back that looks like a rose. My brother named her." She looked down at the dog and then glanced at Michael. "What are the four of you doing out here, if I may ask?"

"We were hiking in the woods," Yofiel replied. "We're not from around here."

Michael held out his leg. "I got hurt."

"And we don't know where to go," Tamor added. "He needs a bandage."

Leah looked at his leg and then stared at him. "Have we met? You look like a guy who visited my mother in the hospital a few years ago. May I tell you the story?"

"Please," Michael replied, a look of embarrassment crossed his face.

"She said she was in much pain and was depressed when another patient she liked was released to go home. She wished the same for herself but realized she would never go home again. The next day a boy wandered into her room and said that she would have a grand homecoming soon. The room began to glow and the pain she experienced left her that moment. I arrived just in time see as he was leaving and her room did appear to be glowing. We didn't know what to think. My mom was joyful for the next three days and then she passed away in complete peace. I never saw the boy again and no one knew who he was. I could never forget him. He looked like you."

"Interesting story," Michael said, nervously looking away. He pressed his fingers together and sprung them open toward Leah—time stopped. Sparklingly crystal snowflakes formed in front of his hand and began spinning like a miniature whirlwind of snow.

"What are you doing?" Tamor asked after Leah and Rosie froze in place like statues.

"I stopped time to infuse peace in her. She was shaking in fear. Couldn't you tell?"

"Of course," said Yofiel said.

"Who could blame her?" Tamor asked.

"It's a good idea," Gabriel added. "Otherwise, there's no way she would invite us into her house. She still may not."

The snowflakes formed a sparkling halo and floated above Leah's head and then popped. Sparkling snow dust sprinkled around her and then time restarted.

Leah took a deep breath and stopped shaking. She beamed a big smile as if nothing had happened. "I have bandages. You are all welcome to come inside. My brother won't be home until later tonight. He won't mind. Please come." They headed toward the porch. She looked at Rosie. "You sure got quiet, girl."

Yofiel and Tamor assisted Michael to the porch.

"What happened to you?" Leah asked.

"Let's just say I was on the wrong end of a demon's foot."

Tamor nudged him and gave him a sharp look.

"He must have been an evil guy."

"He's at the top of the list," he replied.

"Come in, everyone. Welcome to my home. This is our den." All entered.

"You have a pretty house," Yofiel said. "I like the wood floors."

"Thank you."

"I like this fluffy chair," Gabriel said as he placed his hand on it. "May I?"

"Please do." She then motioned to everyone and said, "Follow me." She helped assisted Michael to the bathroom as the rest followed.

The team tended to Michael's wounds and cleaned him up and then helped him back to the den.

"Thank you, Leah and team," Michael said.

"Sure, you're welcome," she responded.

"Thank you, Yofiel and Tamor."

They nodded.

Gabriel rose from the chair. "We need to go."

Leah gave a surprised look as did the others. "You just arrived. Where will you go?"

"I have no idea," Michael said.

"You're all welcome to stay here. We have a third bedroom. Only my brother and I live here."

"That's nice of you but—" Tamor said.

"Please, I insist."

"Thank you," Yofiel said. "We'll stay." She eyed the guys until they nodded.

Michael smiled. *Yofiel is an assertive little peniel.*

"Super," Leah declared. "Follow me." The peniels followed while the Gabriel waited in the den with Michael.

"You may share this bedroom," Leah said. The light-green room contained a double-size bed and a tan pull-out couch. "My bedroom is next door and my brother's room is across the hall."

Gabriel entered the room. "What's your brother's name?"

"Vince."

"Are you sure he won't mind us being in your home?" Yofiel asked.

"He'll be fine. He is in the eleventh grade at Chiles High School. It's been two years since our mom died. He tries to put on a good face but some days I can tell he misses her."

Yofiel noticed the portrait on the wall. "Whose picture is this?"

"It's my mother when she was eighteen years old—the same age I am now."

"She's lovely. You resemble, with your olive complexion."

"Thank you." She left and returned to the den. The others followed.

"Is that a picture of Vince?" Tamor asked.

"Yes, it is."

"He looks like he could be Gabriel's younger brother," Tamor said. "Both have brown hair but Vince has green eyes instead of brown."

"Vince is shorter, too," Leah added.

"I like the picture of the fox hunt," Gabriel said, interrupting.

"Gabriel, you or Michael may have to sleep on the floor since the couch is small. Or you could sleep here in the den. We have blankets for everyone."

"I'll be fine with the others," Michael replied.

"The floor is okay with me," Gabriel said in a jovial manner. "I'm glad to have a nice place to stay."

"I think there's a sleeping bag in Vince's room. I'll get it."

"What's a sleeping bag?" Tamor whispered after Leah walked out. They looked baffled and began to laugh.

"What's so funny?" Leah asked, sleeping bag in hand.

"We don't know what a sleeping bag is," Tamor said.

"Really? Here it is. You guys have never been camping?"

"Is it that obvious?" Gabriel asked, in jest.

"Too bad," she replied. "Camping is fun. You sleep in the woods under the stars. Everyone roasts marshmallows around a campfire and tell scary stories."

"Tamor and I plan to go soon," replied Yofiel.

"All of us must try it sometime," Gabriel said.

"I will cook something to eat while you guys wash up," Leah said. "Follow me." The peniels and Gabriel followed.

"Here are the knobs and this is how to use them." She gave them soap, shampoo, and towels. "Okay, that should do it. I'll see you in the kitchen when all of you are ready."

The three entered the shower stall fully dressed, turned on the cold water, and began laughing as the water soaked them.

Upon hearing the laughter, Leah returned to the bathroom. "What are you guys doing?"

They looked at each other and then at Leah.

"Where are you guys from? You're supposed to take showers alone, with your clothes off, and everyone leave until it's your turn."

"Water where we come from is used for enjoyment and artistic expression, though we do occasionally wash," Tamor said. "We have incredible fountains, pools, spas, and water rides that go high—miles high—into the sky where we come from. But there are no single showers dedicated for cleaning purposes. We rarely get dirty."

"Where are you guys from?" she asked.

"You could say we're from out of this world," replied Tamor.

Leah gave a dubious look. "It sounds like it. Let me get some dry clothes for you guys to wear."

"May I go first?" Gabriel asked.

"Sure," replied Leah.

The sound of the shower knobbed squeak as he turned it on. He soon finished his shower, dried off, and got dressed.

"Gabriel," Leah said, observing from the kitchen. "You forgot to wash the soap out of your hair."

A few minutes later, Gabriel returned with the soap washed out of his nicely brushed hair, though it was still damp. "Next in line."

Tamor showered next followed by Yofiel. Both enjoyed cold showers.

"Dinner is ready, everyone," Leah finally called from the kitchen. "Michael, I'll bring a tray to you so you don't have to get up."

"Okay, thank you."

Yofiel brought the tray to him moments later.

"I can get used to this, you know," he said with a teasing look.

"Wishful thinking. Sorry to leave you by yourself."

"Okay, thanks for this."

"I hope everyone has an appetite for shrimp and grits," Leah said with a smile. "I used an old family recipe from my grandmother."

"They're good," Gabriel said. "Never had this before. They're creamy and smooth."

"You got that right," Michael said from the den. "Delicious." All agreed.

"My water glass is broken," Yofiel said, holding it up.

"Let me see," Leah said, reaching for it. "It's just a smudge mark, perhaps from your lipstick."

Yofiel grabbed her lips as if something was wrong with them. "What's lipstick?"

"Where are you from, girl?" Leah asked. "You've never heard of lipstick? It's makeup. It's used to color the lips. I'll show you." She pulled some out of her purse and put some on."

"It's like paint," replied Yofiel. "I enjoy painting, but I've never used lipstick."

"Neither have I," Tamor added. "We don't wear makeup where we come from."

"You girls are natural beauties? Are you sure you're not wearing makeup?"

Yofiel took her napkin and rubbed it against her face and lips and held it out. "See. Nothing there."

"I believe you," Leah replied. "Now, back to your glass. It looks okay to me."

"It doesn't refill itself," Yofiel said. "It's empty."

"Oh, there's a pitcher of tea," Leah said. "Just refill your glass."

"Oh, so it doesn't refill itself?" Yofiel asked.

Tamor, Gabriel, and Michael laughed as Yofiel poured a refill.

Leah gave a confused look. "I get it. It's a joke."

After dinner, they spent the next couple of hours talking around the table. Later that night, everyone went to their rooms.

"So this is different," Yofiel said as she peered out the bedroom window. "A dark sky—no lights. How do humans see at night?"

"Humans require sleep every day and most sleep in the night," Gabriel said. "Earth has one moon that makes the night sky glow."

"What should we do while Leah sleeps?" Tamor asked.

"Talk," Michael replied. The four talked for hours.

Knock, knock, knock. "Are you awake?" Leah called.

"Yes," they responded in unison. "Come in, Leah."

Leah was surprised to see all of them wide awake. "I can't sleep. You either, I see." They talked into the early morning hours until Leah began to yawn.

"Here I am yawning every other sentence and you guys haven't yawned once," Leah said. "You must be night owls. I think I'm finally ready to fall asleep now. Goodnight."

"Goodnight," they replied.

"Why do humans say goodnight?" Tamor asked.

"Humans are steeped in tradition," Gabriel said. "By goodnight, they mean for you to sleep restfully."

The next morning, the aroma of eggs, bacon, and coffee filled the air.

"I smell something good," Tamor said.

"Let's go see what's cooking," Michael said. He sighed, forgetting his pain until it reminded him.

Gabriel reached out to him. "Let us help you, soldier." Gabriel and Tamor helped him to the kitchen.

"Good morning," Leah said, acting as if she knew them for more than a day.

"Good morning," they replied, unsure what else to say for a morning greeting.

"What can we do to help?" Yofiel asked.

"Get your plates and glasses and dig in. I'm a morning person. Breakfast is my specialty and I love to cook."

"We love to eat," Michael replied. The peniels rolled their eyes. Everyone filled their plate and enjoyed their first breakfast on earth.

"You are skilled at cooking, Leah," Yofiel commented. "Did you take classes?"

"Oh, no," Leah replied. "My mom and grandmother taught me. Cooking and preparing food in creative ways is my passion. Someone has to look after this family. Oh, I hear Vince."

17

VINCE

Vincent shuffled into the kitchen half-asleep, squinting into the lights. He walked directly to the refrigerator, found some pulpless orange juice, and poured a glass. He stopped when he noticed the strangers.

Yofiel caught his eye. *What the—?*

"Good morning, sleepyhead," Leah said. "These are my friends Michael, Gabriel, Yofiel, and Tamor. They're staying with us for a few days." She turned to the four. "This is my brother, Vince, everyone." They exchanged hellos. Vince gave a silent, half-wave.

As his eyes adjusted to the light, he took a second look at the peniels seated at the table and started to blush. "Oh, my God, they're amazing."

Yofiel read his heart rate from her place at the table and knew it was racing. She smiled at Tamor knowing she was also aware.

"You must have come home late last night, Vince," Leah said. "I didn't hear you come in. Are you feeling well? Your face is red."

"Too many questions," he muttered. He sat in the only available chair at the table, which was between the peniels. He stared down at his plate without looking up.

Leah added some hot bacon to his plate. "Yofiel said you look as if you could be Gabriel's brother, Vince. What do you think?"

He glanced at Vince, shrugged his shoulders, and presented a faint smile. He stood and stumbled to the floor.

"Vince, what's the matter?" Leah wailed, running to him.

"He's conscious," Gabriel said, running to assist. The two helped him back into his chair.

He coughed.

"Here, drink your water," Leah said. "I'll get a cold pack. You need food. That's the problem. You've starved yourself since yesterday." She glanced at the others. "He's never fainted."

"Give him a slice of bacon," Gabriel suggested. "He needs a boost."

Yofiel handed him a slice from his plate.

Leah placed the cold pack on the back of his neck. He flinched and started to let out an expletive but refrained.

She slid it around. "Sorry, I know it's cold."

He sipped ice water and ate the bacon. The sweating subsided and the redness dissipated.

"When did you eat last?" Leah asked.

"I feel fine now."

"You have to take care of yourself. School called and requested a written excuse for missing your math class yesterday."

He made eye contact with her and said nothing. Then he finished another slice of bacon, removed the cold pack, and stood to leave. "I have to go," he said before heading to the front door.

Yofiel sensed the hurt in Leah as she carried dishes to the sink, watching Vince through the window. *I see your pain. I feel it too.*

"Are you going to school too?" Gabriel asked.

"No, I take classes at the college and I also work part-time. Today is Saturday, so there's no school. And I'm off this weekend."

Yofiel went to the sink and helped with the dishes without saying a word. Finally, she broke the silence and said, "Thank you for breakfast, Leah. It was good."

Leah nodded as she continued washing dishes, looking stoically into the sink. The others remained silent as they finished eating.

The doorbell rang and Leah proceeded to the door as she dried her hands with a dishcloth. The four thought the doorbell tune was a song.

"Only two notes in the song?" Tamor asked with a confused look on her face. She joined Yofiel. They waved their hands at the dirty dishes and kitchen and the dishes immediately became clean and stacked in the cabinets. The food containers flew into the refrigerator. The counters and kitchen table appeared spontaneously clean. The kitchen was spotless.

"Hey," Gabriel said. "I wasn't finished with my plate."

"Sorry," Tamor said.

"Vince just left," Leah told Vince's friend at the door. "If you hurry, you will catch him." She closed the door and returned to the kitchen.

"Ladies, how did you clean up already?" Leah asked in astonishment. "I was only away a few minutes. The whole kitchen is clean!"

The two peniels smiled. "We work fast."

Everyone took a break and relaxed at the kitchen table. "Thank you for breakfast, Leah," Tamor said. "Everything was very so good."

"You should be a chef," Gabriel suggested.

"I'm glad you enjoyed it."

"And Vince is very handsome," Tamor added.

Leah grew silent and lowered her head. "I dislike the friends he hangs with these days. I don't know what to do. Mom would be disheartened if she were here but she always believed in him. His friends are not a good influence. I fear he's changing for the worse. He's lonely and wants to be a part of something. We don't talk as much as we used to." A lone tear drifted down her cheek.

The guys exchanged seats so the girls could be closer. Yofiel and Tamor gave her a collective hug and remained quiet.

"Why don't we go into the den where you will be more comfortable?" Tamor finally suggested.

"Okay," she muttered.

They spent the next few hours conversing. Leah poured her heart out and mentioned a letter from her doctor. "He said I need to have more tests to determine the cause of my headaches."

The telephone rang and Leah hurried to her bedroom to take the call. The four were confused when they saw her running through the house. Gabriel went to check on her but stopped short when he heard her talking.

"That was a telephone call from a girlfriend of mine," Leah said, returning to the den. "She said there's a rumor of a street fight tonight. That darn gang. I am concerned he may not come home some night."

"What time and where's the fight?" Gabriel asked. The peniels glanced at him.

"Eleven p.m. downtown at the old railroad station," replied Leah. "It's an isolated area near the narrow section of the river in town." She paused. "I cannot expect you guys to get involved in our issues but I appreciate having someone to talk to. You have all been so nice in the short time you've been here. I'm glad we met."

"We feel the same way, trust me," Michael said. He followed Gabriel into the kitchen.

"I got this," Gabriel muttered. He glanced at Leah.

"What do you mean?" Michael asked. "You've got that look about you—pure mischief."

Gabriel looked away as if deep in thought. "Seriously, I think there's a reason we came to this house. If we can help, then we should. Angels are sent on special assignments to watch, help, comfort, deliver a message, to save a life, or to comfort and carry a soul to the king in Krystar. Sometimes we ‘re meant to be seen by humans on Earthwa, sometimes not.”

“We’re not on an assigned mission and we’re not angels yet.”

“But we’re supposed to be here, now, to help this family. I know it. Shouldn’t we do good when we can?”

“Okay, okay. But I’m coming with you to the gang fight.”

“Have you forgotten your injuries?”

“I know but I’m not missing this. I’ll just watch.”

“That’s all you can do.”

“Okay. It’s settled. I’m coming.”

18

GANG FIGHT

"Timeout," Leah said as she walked into the kitchen with the peniels following. "What's this talk of angels?"

"Leah, we are watchers—young angels," Gabriel said.

"What? I think you guys should leave... now."

The four watchers began to glow until they shined as bright as a bolt of lightning. Leah fell to her knees in worship.

"Please stand, Leah," Yofiel said. "Don't worship us. We're created beings as you are."

Leah rose to her feet. "You are angels? How can this be?"

"We're watchers," replied Tamor. "Young angels from Krystar."

"Is that why you're used to drinking glasses filling themselves, how you cleaned the kitchen so quickly, why you didn't know about the shower and why you never heard of a sleeping bag or lipstick? Are you guys real? I can't believe this is happening."

"I told you we were from out of town," Michael said, chuckling.

"But out of this world is not quite the same as being from out of town. I've heard stories about angel visitations. I never believed it until now. This is unreal. I have questions. No one will believe this. Where are you from? Who made you? How long do you angels live? Do angels die? Do they marry? Do they have wings? What do you do for fun?"

"Whoa, slowdown, Leah!" Tamor said.

"Let's go to the porch," Yofiel said. The three went outside. "We'll answer your questions best we can. We're from Krystar—the headquarters of the universe where the king and most angels live. All watchers and angels were created by the king. We live forever but our bodies can get hurt and even destroyed. If that happens then we're remade—but we can live without bodies just like demons can. Our spirit never dies. No, angels don't marry. Yes, most angels have wings, though they're usually hidden until needed."

"Yes, we have fun," Tamor added. "Out-of-this-world fun. It will take too long to tell you the things we do, the places we go, and the celebrations we attend, especially in Krystar, our home planet."

"Amazing," Leah said. "Please, I have another question."

"One more," Tamor said.

"How old are angels?"

"Watchers are made to be like a fourteen-year-old upon their creation," Yofiel said. "All of us are sixteen now. We'll graduate to the rank of angel when we turn nineteen. We continue to grow physically until the age of thirty and we live forever. That's enough for now."

* * * * *

Later that evening, Gabriel and Michael stashed their swords under the bed and left the house.

"How will they know where to go?" Leah asked, as soon as they left.

"Oh, they'll find it," replied Tamor.

"I don't want them to get hurt," said Leah. "Michael is already in pain." Leah touched her head. "Oh, my head—it hurts."

"What's wrong?" Yofiel asked. *She looks pale.*

Leah started crying. "The doctors told me that I have a brain tumor and things don't look good. If something happens to me, then what will become of Vince? He will be alone in the world."

"Take a seat, Leah, please," Yofiel said. Yofiel and Tamor placed their hands on Leah's head. The two watchers lowered their heads and closed their eyes in silence. Moments later, they began to glow and a shower of sparkling light rose from their hands. The two backed away to watch.

Leah opened her eyes and observed the sparkling light, now spinning above her in the air. "What is it?"

"The answer," Yofiel responded.

The sparkling light began raining down upon Leah.

"What do you feel, Leah?" Yofiel asked.

"I feel like it's snowing on my head and ice crystals are sliding down my face. My brain is tingling." Tears flooded her eyes and raced down her cheeks. The three embraced her.

"You're not going to have any more of those headaches, Leah," Yofiel whispered.

* * * * *

"Gabriel, I'm too sore to fly on my own," Michael said.

"Hang on to my t-shirt."

Gabriel exposed his wings and he began to glow. The two took off vertically, like a balloon. They headed toward the site and soon located the place. They landed undetected in a dark area away from the dull streetlights—one blinking on and off continuously. A damp fog lapped the streets. Muggy air lingered like smoke after a forest fire. The smell of wet garbage escaped from nearby dumpsters. A black cat scurried down the street—enticed by the echoes of a distant catfight.

"So far, no sign of anyone," Michael said. *Maybe they won't show.*

"I was hoping to arrive first. Look, guys are coming this way."

"That would be his gang."

"I see Vince. He's one of the smallest kids in the group," Gabriel observed.

"Look at the hardware they're carrying. This looks bad. What's the plan?"

"To watch and stay hidden."

"But what if Vince gets hurt?"

"We're supposed to remain unseen, Michael. You know the rules."

"The rules change with the mission and this is not a Krystar-directed mission."

Gabriel floated up and hovered over the street. "We'll have to see how this goes. Look. Here comes the other gang."

Michael joined him in the air. Guys of all shapes and sizes came out of the dark corners of the train station. The moon played hide-and-seek behind clouds skipping across the sky. In the jovial side of town, busy weekenders scurried about, oblivious to the foreboding storm of youthful ignorance.

"Vince's gang is outnumbered, Gabriel. This is not going to end well."

"They've spotted each other," said Gabriel. Like insects flying into spiderwebs in the dark, it's a destiny of disaster where dreams turn into nightmares.

"Ignorance meets ignorance," Michael muttered.

"The cup of evil never satisfies," Gabriel observed. "It fills the mouth with gravel and leaves a soul with twice the hell."

"Look," Gabriel said. "The bigger gang members are located at the front of their packs."

"Vince is in the rear. I sense his fear."

"He's thinking about Leah. He's a ball of twisted emotion headed down the road of misery. He secretly wants to go home, like half of these guys do."

Michael let go of Gabriel and attempted to float to the ground by himself.

"Where are you going?"

"They're a gang of kids. I'm going in."

"Are you ready for this?"

"Not quite." He winced as he landed harder than expected.

"Yeah, you're right about that."

The two gangs stopped about twenty feet from one another.

"Boys should never come to a man's fight," someone shouted from the other gang.

"We're men, so what does that make you?" Vince's gang retorted.

A guy from the other gang charged with a ball and chain in hand and plunged it into the head of the person on the front line of Vince's gang. The guy dropped hard to the unforgiving street and lay motionless. The rest of the gang rushed forward with weapons held high. The gangs collided like two trains on the same track—metal against metal and flesh against flesh. The fight quickly turned into a chaotic mass of hate. Michael made himself invisible and walked into the middle of the chaos. He incapacitated some of the brawlers by touching them on the shoulder.

The leader of the other gang fought his way forward. He was about six-foot-six and muscular. He was the toughest, strongest fighter on the street. He swung a metal rod widely—striking everyone in the way.

Within minutes, most gang members were cut, bruised, or lying on the street in pain, bleeding, or unconscious. Vince continued to hang near the rear of the pack trying to avoid fighting, as did his young cohorts.

One of the fighters in the other gang started to run away. Michael pointed his finger at him and the boy froze in place and floated upward. The guy kicked the air and struggled like a kid lost in a blanket. "Help, help!" he yelled. No one could see or hear him.

Michael floated to him. "What's your name?"

"Chau," he said. "What's happening?"

"Never mind. Why are you in the gang?"

"My friends, they're in the gang," he said. "They won't let me out."

"Some friends. Why won't they let you get out?"

"You don't understand. They don't let anyone out. You have to die or move, or maybe get married and have kids, before they will allow it. I want out."

"Are you willing to leave the city?"

"Yes, I have no family here."

"I can make it happen, this very moment. But there's no turning back. I will snap my fingers and you will appear on the steps of a big house somewhere far away. All you have to do is knock on the front door and tell them Michael sent you. They know me there. You will be accepted and they will give you a new life. But there is no coming back. Agree?"

"Who are you?"

"That's not important. Just have faith. Now do you agree or not?"

"I agree."

"You must be certain. Are you really willing to leave your life behind and go there tonight?"

"I am, but would you tell me who you are?"

"You don't need to know." *Click*. The boy vanished.

Gabriel spotted the other gang leader moving through Vince's gang and saw that he had his sights on Vince. Vince—unaware of the pending strike—was barely going through the motions of fighting. The gang leader wound back 180 degrees for a full-power strike. He unwound like a corkscrew. He turned toward him when the rod was halfway through the swing.

Gabriel dropped from the sky at the sound of a thunderclap and landed between Vince and the gang leader. He grabbed the guy's arm in mid-swing. The momentum of the rod continued unabated—at full force—into Gabriel's head. The impact would have crushed a human's skull.

The gang leader stumbled to the ground at the sound of the thunder and the appearance of Gabriel. He stared at Gabriel, expecting him to collapse from the blow. Those still fighting stopped to observe.

Gabriel—who had transformed into the biggest guy there—grabbed the guys arm, silently and calmly stared at the muscular, shirtless guy and began tightening his grip.

The gang leader squirmed as Gabriel's grip tightened. The guy fell to his knees, crying in agony. "Please stop!. Please stop!" Gang members on both sides began fleeing as a second peal of thunder sounded with another flash. Gabriel's eyes began to glow like white fire.

Michael approached, sensing Gabriel's rising anger. "Gabriel, stop. Stop it, now." He squeezed Gabriel's other arm. "Vince is fine," he said in a lower tone. "Let go."

Gabriel slowly loosened his grip and released the guy. The gang leader's arm was crushed and he fainted from the pain.

"What just happened?" Vince asked as he approached the two. "Who are you guys? How did you take that hit, Gabriel? You should be dead."

Gabriel turned to him with eyes still afire. "We're from another world." His voice sounded like rushing waters.

"Whoa, your eyes..." cried Vince, turning pale. He tried to speak but fell to his knees.

Michael held him up. "Fear not, Vince. We are watchers—young angels. We are not of this world."

"Yeah, right," he finally replied. "Druggies say the same things."

Gabriel balled his fist and held his right arm up. A third peal of lightning shot between the sky and his fist. Vince fell to the ground in shock. The remaining stragglers fled. Only Gabriel, Michael, and Vince were left under the blinking streetlight.

"Fear not," Gabriel repeated, rousing Vince. He helped him to stand. He and Michael held him and floated upward into the misty moonlight.

Vince panicked and started kicking his legs around in the air.

"Stop, Vince," Gabriel ordered. "Relax, look at me, and breathe."

Vince slowly stopped kicking and focused on Gabriel as a strange sense of calm came over him.

"Vince, we care about you and your sister, Leah. We're from Kanah, a planet smaller than your earth moon. It's one of seven military outposts stationed around earth."

"We're servants of the king of Krystar," Michael added.

"My mom used to tell me stories about such a king," Vince said. "But then she died. This king—if he were real—didn't keep my mom from dying. My dad, when he was around, left us after she died. I don't know what to believe, or what is real anymore. Does Leah know about you two? I assume your girlfriends are watchers too."

"Yes, and Leah knows," Gabriel replied.

Vince alternated between staring at the ground and the two watchers. "I, I can barely see the ground."

"Why are you in a gang?" asked Michael. *One cannot avoid a question from someone who has their life in their hands.*

"I want to be a part of something and the gang is all I have, besides Leah. My mom was taken from me, my dad left us years ago—God knows where he is. I have no interest in school; the teachers don't care. My friends are in my gang. They are my people. They got my back. Schools cater to the better students while the rest of us struggle and fall behind. Even churches frown on me because they think I'm a bad influence on other kids—and they're right. We're a problem no one wants to solve."

"Vince, people care," Gabriel said. "I know Leah does. One's perspective influences life. It determines vision—what they see, what they don't see, what they hear, what they don't hear. Change a perspective, change a life."

"I know some people care," he said. "Occasionally I find a teacher who seems to. And I do better with them for a time. But those individuals are the minority. Everyone is busy, life gets in the way, people don't want to be bothered. It's never convenient. I get it."

"Vince, I understand life on earth can be hard," Michael said. "People care and so do demons—but in a different way."

"So, demons are real?"

"Yes, they're quite real," Gabriel continued. "They want you to lose at life, to experience the negative, to hate, to want the wrong stuff, and to believe you're not good enough. I've seen demons—they're real. Michael is hurt now because of a recent fight with one."

"I don't believe in demons," Vince said. "I only believe in my gang. I know my sister cares but she gives me lots of grief. Too many people have hurt me, disappointed me, and left me. I don't care anymore. My purpose is my gang."

"You have a purpose on earth that only you can fulfill, Vince," Michael said. "And when your life on this earth is finished, your spirit leaves your body and immediately goes to Krystar."

"He's right, Vince," Gabriel said. "You will be given rewards for the good things you do on earth. You will be introduced to your family who is everyone in Krystar—we're talking about millions of family members."

"What rewards?"

Michael wondered if Vince heard what Gabriel said after mentioning rewards. "You get a mansion made just for you, a new body that never grows old and you live forever. How's that?"

"Sounds great."

"And no more tears, no pain of any kind and you never have to sleep if you don't want to," Michael continued. "That makes six."

"I kinda like to sleep," he replied.

"Many things," Michael said. "You get to see the king. You get to live in his kingdom. You live in a city made of gold. You will know everyone there and everyone will be like your best friend."

"You will be able to fly," Gabriel added. "You'll get treasures much greater than anything on earth. The colors of the world are incredible. You will get land and even planets, and you will get to design the landscapes, and put animals and creatures on them—even dinosaurs."

"Will I meet girls like Yofiel and Tamor?"

"Yes," said Gabriel. "And friends like Michael and myself."

"The food and drinks are better than anything on earth," Michael said. "Every child who goes there has family to take care of them. Young children will have candy trees in their yard and pets that talk. You simply think of what you would like to drink and your glass refills itself until you've had enough to drink.

"You will find no trash or mean animals there. The whole universe is our backyard. Banquets and parties are everyday events—there is no night, though there will be on other planets.

"There will be sports and adventures of many kinds. You will have the opportunity to work, design, and build things, and even create living creatures. I've already told you more than I should—much more than humans are supposed to know.

"You will attend fabulous parties, galas, and festivals. You will enjoy phenomenal music, concerts with light shows, and dancing.

There are spectacular waterparks and spas. I could go on, but I must n ot.

"That's enough," Gabriel said. "He must focus on earth now."

"When do I get to go to Krystar?" Vince asked, eyes still locked on Michael.

"You must fulfill your destiny on Earth first," Michael replied.

"Take me there now. Please."

19

AURORAS

"Are you listening, Vince?" Gabriel asked. "You're not done on earth."

Michael pulled him close. "Didn't you say you want to be a part of something?"

"Yes."

"Then join us."

Vince looked away.

Michael glanced at Gabriel.

"Look at the people," Gabriel said as the three floated downtown. "We can identify people by their auroras."

"By what?"

"We'll show you," Michael replied. They flew to a busy section of the city and hovered out-of-sight over the busy sidewalks. Michael clenched his fists and then opened them revealing a blue spinning ball in each hand. He started to place them over Vince's eyes.

"Will it hurt?"

"No," Michael replied. The fireballs floated toward Vince and then turned into sparkling dust as it blew into his eyes causing Vince to blink. "Open your eyes now."

Vince opened his eyes and his pupils glowed a bright blue. He looked downward. "Unbelievable! Some people have a blue aurora glowing above their heads and in their eyes and chests. Wow! I can see inside of them. Some of them have a black aurora. Others have a white aurora. Amazing. What does it mean?"

"Humans with the blue aurora are followers of the king and are therefore part of the kingdom," Gabriel said. "Those with the black aurora belong to Beelzebub and his demons and are part of the kingdom of darkness. We call them vipers. Those with white auroras haven't made a choice yet. They're the undecided."

Michael put his arm around Vince. "Our mission, Vince, and yours if you join us, is to support humans with blue aurora and protect them from the kingdom of darkness and to impact those with white auroras so they join the kingdom of the king. Those with blue aurora get rewards for kingdom service. The angels of Krystar constantly watch over them."

"I've never seen a demon and don't want to," Vince said.

"Angels and demons fight over humans," Gabriel continued. "That's why we have seven outposts close to earth. Demons earn rank by how many humans in their territory gets the black aurora. They also get rewarded for driving humans to do evil things."

"I heard about angels and demons when I used to go to church," Vince said. "But how do I know angels and demons and Krystar are real? How do I know if anything in the unseen world is real?"

"Really?" Michael asked. "We're watchers, young angels, and you see us. Demons and their world are invisible to humans because it would terrify you to see them. Like them, we live in other dimensions. Everything you see and don't see was created. There would be no animals, humans, air, water, light, planets, or stars. There would only be a dark, massless, empty space without life. There would be nothing to go bang in the dark. Things don't come from nothing." The three floated down to the ground.

"That makes sense, I think," Vince replied. "But the reason I joined a gang is to be a part of something. But it's hopeless as well. I want out."

"Vince, this story may help you," Michael said. "A boy dreamed he was trapped with many others in a bottomless pit far below the surface of a rocky mountain. It was a dark and smoky place lit only by glowing lava and torches of fire. Every day the people would gather before a large boulder to worship a dragon they called Modeerf. Over and over they would chant his name and dance around a fire at the base of the great rock inscribed with his name.

"The elders, as they were called, oversaw a bowl that contained seven golden coins. It was a known fact that a single coin would be given to anyone willing to leave the bottomless pit to journey to the surface of the earth. There was a single iron door that blocked the only passageway to the surface and the traveler was required to put the coin in a slot of the door for it to open. But the passageway beyond the door led through the territory of Modeerf and it was believed to have killed all previous travelers.

"One day the boy informed the elders that he wished to go. After much ceremony, he was ordained as a traveler and given a single gold coin. He entered the narrow passage in the boulder with a few people who were chosen to follow a short distance. They followed him through the boulder to the beginning of a rope bridge overlooking a mighty river of lava miles below. He traversed the rope and reached the door on the other side. They watched as he took the golden coin and placed it through the slot in the door.

"The great door opened. The boy entered through the door and then watched as it slowly locked behind him. A bluish, glowing fog enveloped the passageway. He walked for hours and came upon another iron door but this one was much larger. He panicked because he didn't have a coin for the second door. He searched the rocky surface for another coin but only found a large mallet.

"Finally, he stood up, raised the mallet, and slammed it against the door as if it were a gong. The sound echoed through the passageway behind him and beyond the door. He waited but nothing happened. Finally, the door opened. Several people from a local village stood on the other side. He explained who he was and why he had come.

"They told him about opening the door with a key passed down by their ancestors, and about a prophecy where someone would one day sound the door from the inside of the mountain and cause the mountains to sing. The singing of the mountains were the echoes he had heard. They also said their ancestors had escaped from a giant who had lived there. The giant lived at the great boulder and forbade the villagers from being there. The villagers tricked him by telling him they wanted to honor him with the title of Modeerf who was a great god and convinced him to allow them to carve his name on the boulder. He agreed and so while some worked on the inscription, others worked on a passageway to escape. When the inscription was done, they had a big celebration and got the giant drunk. They escaped through the passageway when he fell asleep. The giant awoke and chased after them but fell into the lava pits where he perished. The real reason they chose the name Modeerf was so that any future prisoners would understand the coded word. It was the word 'freedom' spelled backwards. The encryption in the rock was intended to identify the passageway to freedom."

"Okay, so what does it mean to me?" Vince asked.

"You are blind to the path to a better life because you lost your faith."

"What do you mean?"

"You lost your faith in people, in yourself, in Leah, and in the king of the universe."

"I have faith that you're here right in front of me."

"Anyone can believe what they can see. Faith believes in things unseen."

"If you could see as we see, you would know the unseen is more real than your world," said Gabriel. "But it's all real."

Vince looked away. "I've been wrong. I want to follow the king."

"That is all you need to say," replied Michael.

A bright blue transparent cloudlike vapor appeared inside Vince and he began to glow—the blue haze also hovered over his head. His body became transparent blue.

"Amazing," Vince said. "This is unbelievable. Will I always look this way?"

"No, we're allowing you to see this," Michael said.

"Welcome, follower," Gabriel said, as he and gave him a bear hug. "You're a warrior now."

"Wait. Where did the blue aurora go? Where's my sword?"

"They're invisible to you, but they're there."

"I want to do great things for the king."

"You will," Gabriel said. "But do not discount the little things. There would be no beach without each pebble of sand."

"Interesting," Vince replied. "Never thought about it that way. May I ask one more question?"

"Okay but we need to go," Gabriel replied.

"How do you kill a demon?"

"That's some question," Gabriel replied. "Demons cannot be killed because they are invisible spirits—like ghosts. But when they possess a body, then that body can be killed. When that happens, the demon spirit must find another body to possess, or it fizzles into a black frothy tar substance and flies to their abode—planet Darkmar—until they locate another available body."

"Will I become an angel one day?"

"That's two questions. No, angels are different than humans."

* * * * *

Leah was asleep when the guys arrived after midnight. She rose early in the morning to prepare breakfast. Tamor and Yofiel joined her in the kitchen.

"Good morning, ladies," Leah said. "Awake already??

"Oh, before we forget, we have something for you, Leah." Yofiel presented a small purple bottle with a white ribbon.

"Thank you, girls," Leah said. "What a pretty bottle."

"It contains water from Kanah," Tamor said. "The water was touched by an angel and has healing properties."

"Use it if you ever need it, Leah."

"Thank you. I will. Now breakfast—."

"We want to help," said Yofiel.

"We have recipes," Tamor added.

"By all means," Leah replied.

They showed her a special way to make pancakes. Yofiel added a secret ingredient—it gave the pancakes a sweet taste. The finished product glittered. Toppings included tiny bits of strawberries and mango fruit.

"Look," said Leah as she sat down. "The pancakes are glowing. What did you put on them?"

"An old secret family recipe," Yofiel said with a smile. "We call them manna cakes."

"They're excellent." She chewed slowly and swallowed as a smile emerged. "The taste is still in my mouth as if I just took another bite. How long does it last?"

"A while," Tamor replied.

Michael and Gabriel walked into the kitchen, followed by Vince, who wore a smile rarely present on his face—especially in the morning. He gestured toward the pancakes. "That's different."

"Tamor and Yofiel made them," Leah said, smiling back at Vince.

"Michael and Gabriel saved my life last night," Vince said. "They really did—I mean it. I'm a follower now."

Leah could not restrain her excitement as she shouted and danced around the kitchen before embracing him."

"Okay, that will do," he said. All celebrated as they enjoyed the pancakes.

Later that morning Leah approached Gabriel. "Thank you," she said as tears swelled in her eyes. "I don't know what happened, or what you said. I don't need to know. I will never forget this."

They two hugged until he pulled away. "We have to leave."

20

TIME TO LEAVE

"Sir! Planet sensors detected the departure of three watchers to earth yesterday," a guard reported. "And they're still on earth."

"Who are they?" Uriel asked.

"Gabriel, Yofiel and Tamor, sir."

"Okay. Thank you for the update. They can call on their lightbands if they need us. I see no reason to send a search team."

"Yes sir." The angel left.

* * * * *

The following morning, the four hugged Leah. Vince was still asleep in bed.

"We'll miss you, Leah," Yofiel said.

"Will I see you again?" she asked.

"Someday," Tamor replied.

"Here," Leah said. "It's not much but I want you two to have it."

"What is it?" Yofiel asked. "It's mercy water. It's water from the Pool of Bethesda. They say it was touched by an angel and has magical healing properties. I know you guys don't need it but I want to give you something that means a lot to me."

"You could have used this for yourself, Leah," Tamor replied.

"I know, but I was waiting for the right time. And now I don't need it, thanks to you guys. Please take it."

"I love the purple bottle," Yofiel said. "I adore it. Thank you." The three hugged. After Yofiel and Tamor petted Rosie and the four said their final goodbyes, they flew away.

"How do we know the door will be there?" Yofiel asked.

"We don't," Gabriel said. "But something tells me it will appear at the right time."

Michael stared over the horizon of the woods. *It better be there.*

"There's the pond," Tamor shouted. The four floated down to the sandy path. "I see our tracks from yesterday,"

"So the door should be close by," Gabriel muttered.

Yofiel retracted her wings and pointed ahead. "The three palm trees."

"Let's go," said Gabriel. He jogged to the palms followed by Tamor.

Yofiel remained with Michael. "How's your leg, Michael?"

"Surprisingly better. Thanks for asking. I remember the cave was in this area. This is the spot where I crawled out of the cave."

Gabriel placed his hand on one of the palm trees. "The cave should appear shortly, I hope." They huddled as they surveyed the area.

"Where did they go?" a strange voice shouted in the distance.

"Take out the guys and get the girls," another said.

Tamor glanced at Michael. "Who's that?"

"Three men," Michael said. *I got this.*

Bang.

Gabriel hunched over. "I'm hit."

"Gabriel!" Tamor shouted.

"The bullet went through his chest," said Yofiel. She placed her hand over the wound and the bullet popped out into her hand. The wound healed itself within seconds as they watched.

Michael turned to the shooter and shot lasers from his eyes, hitting the stranger in the shoulder.

The hunter fell to his knees. "I'm hit."

Yofiel raised her right hand toward the sky and as she did, a whirlwind formed above them and began breaking branches in the area.

"Tornado!" one of the men yelled. "It's coming toward us. Take cover."

The blue spinning tornado grew in size and the tip of it reached the ground. A light flashed and the white pearl door appeared where the tip of the tornado had touched the ground.

"The door!" Michael shouted. "Go, go, go!"

"There they are," one of the hunters yelled. "Shoot!"

Sir Calidoore appeared and blew a shield ice in front of the cave absorbing the bullets.

The cave appeared behind the door as soon as Yofiel turned the blue-diamond doorknob. She was the first to enter the cave. The tornado transformed into a blue spinning portal of fire above the cave. It disappeared as soon as Michael closed the door. The wind quickly dissipated leaving no trace of the tornado except for the downed branches in the area.

"Did you see that?" one of the men exclaimed.

"Where did it go?" another asked as they all stared at the area by the three palms.

"Nothing happened here," a third replied. "We didn't see it. All of you! You got that?"

"Got it," they repeated.

21

ABDUCTED

"Aaahhh," Tamor yelled as she fell to the floor of the cave.

"Tamor, are you okay?" Gabriel asked.

"I'm glad we got away from those creeps," she replied.

"They were after you girls," said Michael.

"I don't know about, Michael," Gabriel replied. "Some of the gang members may have been stalking us."

"These guys were too old," Michael said.

"You may be right," he replied again.

A ball of sparkling light grew in the palm of Yofiel's hand. She launched it into the air before them. "Let's get to the ledge." She proceeded through the cave with the light floating ahead of her.

Tamor stood up. "Wait for me. I'm coming."

"This place holds memories for me," Michael said snidely. "Bad ones."

"You're alive," Gabriel said, slapping his arm around Michael's shoulders. "That's what matters."

"Agree."

"Hey, peniels," Gabriel called. "Wait up." They followed the peniels.

All followed Yofiel to the ledge. "Oh, the sky. It's as beautiful as ever."

"I see a fireball, like a meteor," Tamor said.

"The chariot!" Gabriel answered. "Time to go."

"Kanah, here we come," said Tamor. "Wait, where did it go? It disappeared!"

Michael whispered to Gabriel. "That's weird. The stars are disappearing in the sky." *What's happening?*

The group peered into the oversized sky space.

"Smells like gaseous sulfur..., like the day I fought the demon," Michael said. "I think we should leave."

"Get to the door everyone!" Gabriel shouted. He and Michael pulled their swords from their sheath and followed the girls.

Twenty demons flew inside the cave, knocking everyone down.

Oh no, not Beelzebub again. Michael sliced at one of the dark creatures but missed.

The cave lit up with fire.

"Demons!" Yofiel shouted.

The demons were humanoid with faces similar to apes, lizards, and wasps. Most walked on two legs and had red eyes but a few appeared as black shadows and floated about like rotten sheets in a wind.

"These things stink," Tamor said. "Get away from me!"

"Go away," Yofiel shouted. "Don't touch me."

Some of the creatures had long, sharp claws and tails like a lizard. Some had the skin of frogs while others had a jellyfish covering. Others were covered in fur, or had the scaly skin of a reptile. They attacked Michael and Gabriel, while others taunted and grabbed at the peniels with mouths drooling.

The girls transformed into semi-transparent figures outlined in a thin line of blue fire. A whip of fire appeared in their right hand and a sickle in their left as a halo of fire ignited over their heads. Their eyes turned to white fire that matched their halo.

The guys were stunned by their appearance. Even the demons paused in wonderment.

The demons began attacking the peniels two at a time as the others encircled them.

The two peniels ripped their fire whips—slapping and striking the demons. Those struck transformed into black mush and scurried away like snakes. One demon jumped Yofiel from behind. He wrapped himself around her. She couldn't dislodge him, much to the amusement of the other demons. She reached for the dagger bound to her thigh and sliced his neck. All laughing ceased as the clingy demon slid to the floor.

Tamor reached for her twin daggers and planted the blades into the eyes of another demon. She pulled the daggers out and dropped them in the air. They flew to her thighs like magnets.

"Did you know they could fight like that, Michael?" Gabriel asked.

"Not a clue."

Beelzebub watched the action from the ledge and finally entered the cave. "Uuurrrrr," he growled. The ensuing shockwave dazed the girls, causing them to stagger. The demons quickly tied them and took their weapons.

The demons turned their collective attention to the guys. One managed to knock the sword out of Michael's hand, while others took turns punching Gabriel. The two were pushed, spit-on, and knocked back and forth within the circle.

A large demon came forward as the others made way. Michael saw him and mustered the energy to strike at his neck. The demon caught his sword between his rotten teeth and flung it against the wall. The demon opened its mouth revealing a snake. It lunged at Michael but was too short to reach.

Michael saw his sword lying on the ground by the wall of the cave. *It didn't break—good.* He pretended to fall to the ground and rolled toward it. But another demon kicked it away. Michael clutched a rock before rising.

Gabriel charged the demon from behind but was backhanded. He fell to the ground, dazed.

Michael charged the demon, striking it in the head with the rock. All watched to see if the big demon would fall. They cheered, quietly at first but began yelling louder as it became clear the demon was unaffected by the strike. The demon retrieved Michael's sword and bit it in half while staring at him. It laughed like a hyena—the other demons joined the chorus.

The big demon suddenly jumped and twisted in midair like a corkscrew, striking Michael in the head with his elbow. Michael flew into the wall face-first. The girls screamed as he fell backward to the rocky floor, unconscious. All of the demons hissed and cheered.

Another demon picked up a rock and hurled it at Gabriel, striking him in the head. He fell to the ground. The demons tied them.

"Cut their lightbands off," Beelzebub commanded. Two of the demons cut the lightbands on Gabriel, Tamor, and Yofiel and tossed them into the side of the cave.

Tamor ran toward them but grabbed her by the hair and pulled back.

Yofiel slapped him. He retaliated by striking her to the ground.

Beelzebub smiled as he entered the circle. The demons cowered in his presence. He slowly scanned the room, eyeballing everyone. "Even demons have rules," he roared, voice reverberating against the walls of stone. "And rules must not be broken." He lifted his sword and it lit on fire. The demons cheered and drew quickly silent. "But there is one rule every demon must honor. He must never, never, NEVER —" he said with increasing volume as he swung and sliced through the neck of the offending demon, "... strike a peniel.

A peniel is the most beautiful creature in the universe. Please, my fellow demons, handle with care."

The headless demon fell to the ground, melted into black slurry, and slithered out of the cave. The others chanted, "King, king, king."

Beelzebub approached Michael who was lying unconscious. He then eyed the demons standing closest to Michael. They twitched nervously and then pulled Michael to his feet. One of them slapped him to arouse him, unsure if he was still alive

"Michael," Yofiel shouted. He cocked his head toward her and then at Beelzebub, trying to maintain consciousness.

"Didn't I tell you, little warrior, that bad things would happen if we met again?" Beelzebub turned to his demons for a response. They hissed in approval. "When I give my word, then it is a guarantee because I'm Lord of the darkness, ruler of demons, king of the universe."

The demons began chanting again, "king, king, king."

Beelzebub raised his hand to silence them. "But you just can't stay away, little soldier. What should we do?" He paused, turned to Yofiel, and smiled. "I know," he said gleefully. "All of you will be guests in my home." He backhanded Michael, knocking him to the ground again. "Take them to Darkmar." He left the cave with some of the larger demons in tow.

One of the demons confiscated Gabriel's sword and threw it against the cave, breaking it in half. Another demon confiscated the peniel's daggers. The four were led to the ledge, where Tamor and Yofiel tied securely to a demon for the trip to Darkmar.

"Get your nasty, scaly, sweaty hands off of me," Yofiel barked. She slapped one of them.

The demon yanked her but didn't hit her out of fear of his master.

The demonic entourage flew into space with their prisoners in tow headed for Darkmar—the abode of demons. The pained stars fled the night like minnows escaping along the shore.

"I see it" Michael replied.

The planet was encapsulated in raw dark matter mixed with black fog that veiled the planet from detection like a fly buried in black molasses.

Tamor's eyes widened. "Oh, no."

22

DARKMAR

They exited the wide-open, star-filled night and entered the murky atmosphere of planet Darkmar—headquarters of Beelzebub. Thousands upon thousands of demons took to the air through ventholes scattered around the landscape, like endless bubbles rushing madly to the surface of the ocean, like wasps stirred from their nests. They filled the sky to welcome the return of their master.

"Behold, my demons," Beelzebub roared from the head of the pack, a look of glee pasted on his face.

"This place looks like a nightmare come true," Tamor shouted in the choking air.

"It's muggy, stinky, and ugly," Yofiel replied. "I can hardly breathe."

The red-orange-brown-black magma-colored planet—three thousand miles across—was composed of black and brown sand, gray sludge and rocky, mountainous terrain that crisscrossed like cobwebs over rivers and seas of glowing lava. The sky was gray and red with reddish-orange and blue noctilucent clouds of molten lava crystals. It rained hot sulfuric water droplets that smelled like rotten eggs. Tornados were a daily occurrence. Vegetation was absent except for leafless trees, cactus bushes, and some black kudzu-looking plants. Demon work crews scattered on the surface looked like columns of ants. They carried huge rocks and black sludge to and fro. Large black birds flew in the skies while spider-looking creatures ran among the rocks.

"That volcano looks to be over ten miles high," Michael said as he pointed in the distance.

"It's sixteen miles high—one of the tallest in the universe," Beelzebub shouted so all would hear. "It's the capstone to my home."

The pack descended toward the entrance located in the steeple of the volcano, high above the surface of the planet. Lava flowed intermittently into the desolate valley from various openings in the mountain as pellets of molten fire shot high into the sky. Giant black spiders and roach-like creatures skittered around on the sides of the mountain. A rocky road wrapped around the mountain like a coiled snake.

Huge iron gates covered the entrance. Fire emanated through the vents while thick black smoke poured into the sky. An image of a red dragon was centered on both gates while images of demons and human beings lined the perimeter.

The word, "DARKMAR," was engraved in a semi-circular pattern over the gates, running the entire length of the entrance—each letter glowed from the lava flowing inside.

Beelzebub looked at the watchers and pointed at two beasts standing in front of the gates. "My guards!"

Michael glanced at Gabriel. "They're huge."

"Crocdor and Magnon. They're tyrannosapiens, similar to the Tyrannosaurus rex that roamed Earth. But these have humanlike legs and arms, stand erect, and don't have tails."

The entourage landed on the ledge and released the four watchers. Several glowing images approached from the gates.

"They're called lookers," Beelzebub said. "They're two-dimensional demons that look like glowing blankets.

The lookers approached and placed light chains around the ankles of the four watchers.

"Take them off," Yofiel demanded.

Beelzebub glanced at the lookers. "Lightbands for the girls."

The lookers removed the lightchains from the peniels and placed lightbands on their wrists.

"The lightchains and lightbands will ensure you remain in designated areas," Beelzebub said. "If you stray too far, they'll heat up and turn to fire in minutes. My demons also wear lightbands but theirs are not the same. They protect them from abaddonite inside the mountain so it doesn't weaken them. They are also star-positioning systems, so they are can navigate the universe. Yours limit your powers and restrict your territory. Now about Darkmar. It is a prison. No one may enter and no one may leave unless I, or one of my commanders, approves it.

"If you ask a senior demon, he would tell you Darkmar is the most glorious planet in the universe. It's an awesome military world with the prime objective of training demons to be warriors. They learn the skills that will enable them to attack and conquer the army of your king and to one-day take over Krystar and your seven military outposts. We will also take over earth and rule over humans. We will rule the whole universe. Hallelujah! Though I hate the word, thinking about it makes me ecstatic.

"My demons already serve as secret agents. They influence humans to do evil and self-destructive things. And they're darn good at it. Why should my demons kill humans when we can get humans to do it? Humans are such easy targets. Especially the stupid ones and most are quite stupid. They'll do anything for happiness and self-actualization. And the blind fools never suspect that we're the real culprits of their destruction—and they never will. They think they're free and independent. Makes our job easier."

"Some humans successfully resist demons," Michael said. "Your demons flee when that happens."

A demon slapped him to the ground. Beelzebub acted as if he didn't notice.

"Why did he hit me?" Michael asked, surprised.

"Haven't you heard, little watcher?" Beelzebub charged. "Wide are the gates of destruction, and, oh, the fun the blind fools think they're having along the way. Behold the wide gates to the tunnel that leads to my home, as you see before you.

"Now, where was I before I was interrupted? Oh, yes. My demons. Demons seek rank and it takes many years for demons to work through the ranks. Our maniacal, lower-ranked demons and monsters reside far beneath the surface in a place called Ramkrad—the lowest level near the lake of fire in the middle of the planet. Residents of Ramkrad are wild and constantly fight and destroy. They must be beaten into submission. The stronger ones take advantage of the weaker creatures for the joy of inflicting pain.

"The further toward the center of our planet one travels, the more fire and tar pits and beasts of darkness there are. The smarter demons work hard to earn rank so they can leave Ramkrad. The higher the rank they achieve after leaving, the closer to the surface they are allowed to reside. Our most senior demons live in the steeple of this volcano that rises high into the sky, as you see. So that's a synopsis of Darkmar. Welcome, watchers, to my home."

"Rrroooaaarrr." The sound emanated from a mountain across the valley. Everyone froze in place.

"Fierian the Dragon!" Beelzebub roared. "Run, or be annihilated."

The huge dragon leapt into the air from a mountain cliff and flew straight toward them.

All of the demons stampeded for the gates leaving the watchers behind.

"Let's fly!" Gabriel shouted to the three. He attempted to fly but couldn't.

"It's our light chains, Gabriel," Michael shouted. "It's making us weak."

"The gates are closing!" Tamor yelled.

The four ran for the entrance.

The dragon dove toward them and prepared to torch them.

"Dive!" Gabriel yelled.

23

THE TOUR

The tyrannosapiens struggled to pull the chains attached to the wheels of the two gates.

"Hurry!" Michael yelled, "They're almost closed."

The dragon drew close as the four watchers leapt through the closing gates and blew fire through the opening. Several were scorched. Fierian slammed into the gates causing rocks to fall around the entrance and into the valley. the Tunnel of Ekron.

"I should call fire from the sky and fry that dragon," Beelzebub muttered. "But I like him."

A gorilla beast scorched from the blast stumbled forward in agony and then fell unconscious. Beelzebub spit into his hands and then placed them over the burned area of the beast. The burnt skin healed before their eyes and the beast came to. Freed from his pain, the beast rose to his knees and bowed to Beelzebub and said, "Glory to the king of Darkmar."

Beelzebub looked at the four watchers who witnessed the event and said, "I'm a miracle worker. You too will learn to worship me."

"Never!" Yofiel replied.

Several demons approached intending to do her harm but then glanced at Beelzebub and bowed away.

Beelzebub approached the peniels. “We shall see about that.” He turned to the demons in the area. “Let’s go.”

Gabriel put his arms around the girls. “Are you okay?”

“We’re fine,” Tamor replied. “It will take a lot more to get to us.”

“I didn’t know you two could run so fast,” Michael said.

“We didn’t either,” replied Yofiel. “We tried to fly but couldn’t.”

“The abaddonite inside my light band made me weak,” Gabriel added. “It’s all over the planet.”

“I’m glad we’re together and everyone is okay... so far,” said Yofiel. She smiled.

Beelzebub approached the four. “Fierian is the guardian of Darkmar. He comes out when he detects movement in the sky—he detected us when we entered the atmosphere. We have his mate, Poquim. She’s the guardian of the lake of fire in the underworld. Best you avoid her. Those two are the largest dragons on our planet.”

The trouped proceeded into the cave.

Michael stopped and look back at the gates. “Ramkrad,” he said. “I thought this was Darkmar.”

The other three read the sign.

“It’s Darkmar, you fool,” a demon hissed. “Turn around and keep going. All of you.” Several demons pointed their spears at them.

Fierian suddenly appeared on the inside of the gates and screeched. All of the demons in the pack fled deeper into the Tunnel of Ekron leaving the watchers with Beelzebub.

“There’s nowhere to run or hide,” Michael shouted as he searched for a way of escape.

“Get back here, you idiots,” Beelzebub yelled at his demons. “It’s only a statue.” He turned to the four. “Some of my demons are dumb.” He rolled his eyes at their cowardice.

“But it’s Fierian, the dragon,” Michael replied. “Is it not?”

"It is," Gabriel replied. "It moves and blows fire. And those red eyes look real."

"The fire is real," Tamor said. "So why the statue?" She gave an inquisitive look.

"To command respect," he snapped. "It's not the real Fierian. It's a scarecrow. It guards this side of the gates and will annihilate any creature who ventures this way without permission." The pack of demons who ran away returned and bowed low to him.

Beelzebub nodded at them and they bowed away.

"Seems real to me," Yofiel said.

"Me too," Tamor chimed.

Beelzebub laughed abruptly, catching the girls off-guard, causing them to jump. "My statues are easier to control than some of my demons."

"Aaahhh!" Yofiel yelled. "What are those creatures hanging on the walls?"

"No need to fear them, dearie," Beelzebub replied. "They're demons who have failed me and are paying the ultimate price. They're nailed into the mountain." He laughed, spread his wings, and floated towards her. "Now let's go to my palace shall we?" Several demons latched on to the four and carried them through the Tunnel of Ekron. Firepits lined the walls the rest of the way, casting a glow to the legions of crucified and dying demons.

The group landed at the edge of a hole that was larger than the opening of the Tunnel of Ekron. "This is Demon's Hole," Beelzebub said. "It's like an atrium with many rooms above and below us. It runs from the top of the steeple to the middle-world of Darkmar. The middle-world of Darkmar sits on top of the underworld of Ramkrad which is located around the lake of fire at the center of our planet. Now look over there. Notice that the stairs spiral along the walls of the hole. Demons rarely use them since they fly."

"I can't see the bottom," Gabriel said. "Of course not," he quipped. "I just said it goes all the way to the middle of the planet, or almost."

"I hear screams," Michael said, glancing at Yofiel.

"And it smells awful," said Tamor.

The demon eyed them sternly. "Guys, this is Darkmar and the screams you hear are the creatures of the underworld. What did you expect? This is not the Garden of Eden."

The four stared into the black hole.

"Darkmar is my headquarters, children," Beelzebub continued. "Ah, the sweet smell of my millions of demons."

Michael leaned forward. "I can't see the bottom either."

Four demons flew above the hole extending their arms, palms facing toward the watchers, and shot a beam of light forming a rope. They jerked Yofiel, Tamor, Michael, and Gabriel forward so they floated in their direction.

"Your lightbands and lightchains enable them to do this," Beelzebub said. "No worries. Just go with it."

"This should be interesting," Michael muttered to Gabriel. The four floated above the hole, unaffected by gravity.

"I thought we were going to freefall," Yofiel said.

Beelzebub joined them in flight.

"This is one big hole for the lava," Michael said. "Must be half a mile wide."

"Close," Beelzebub replied, continuing his self-appointed role as tour guide. "We diverted the flow of lava through channels inside the walls of the mountain. This allows us to use Demon's Hole as an atrium for travel within the planet."

The group flew two levels up into the steeple of the volcano. "Signs designate the names of the levels within Darkmar from the bottom of Demon's Hole to the top of the steeple in the volcano,"

Beelzebub said. "The letters glow in molten lava. This is level Casa de Lues as you see. The next is Altus."

"Look at the bull-like demons stationed around the hole, Michael," said Gabriel.

"Flaming spears—impressive," replied Michael.

"My palace is on this level, friends," the king of demons continued "Only my most trusted senior demons and special guests are allowed here. In case you're wondering, the grunt demons who live in Ramkrad—those who are civilized and sensible enough to earn rank—spend their time making gun powder, digging tunnels, monitoring human souls, and making weapons in anticipation of that Great Day."

"What great day?" Michael asked.

The group landed on the ledge of Altus. "Don't you know anything?" Beelzebub snarled. "The Great Day is the day we attack Krystar and defeat your king. My single goal—my eternal desire—is to sit on the throne, ruling the universe from high on the mountain of Krystar. After all, it was your king and his angels who threw me out of Krystar many eons ago when I and my loyal clan of angels attempted a coup. But we were not as prepared as we should have been. No. There was no master plan then. But we have one now," he hissed with glee. "I will be numero uno!"

The group walked through a gate and entered a circular hallway that looped around Demon's Hole.

Yofiel rubbed her arms as if she were cold.

Beelzebub paused, looking her up and down and then said, "The red, white, and black refractory ceramic is special," he continued. "I built my palace out of it. It repels the constant heat for our volcanic home and cools the place." The group entered a large room with a sign over the door that read *The Throne Room of the King.*

"Ah, my favorite place in all of Darkmar."

Countless numbers of senior demons fell to the floor as did many lifelike statues of lifelike dragons inside the large circular room. "Hail to the king, hail to the king. You alone are worthy to rule Darkmar."

They rose to their knees and shouted, "Glory to the king, glory to the king, glory to the king." The firepits along the great circular wall jerked in unison to the cacophonous cries. The watchers covered their ears.

Beelzebub held up his hand and the chanting slowly subsided. Turning to the four, he said, "Spectacular, isn't it? They love me."

Michael observed both glee and fear in the faces of the demons.

"Look, my throne," the king of demons said. The phrase *king of kings* was engraved over a throne that sat atop the elevated platform. Two large animated statues of dragons made of a red spinel gem were positioned in front of the steps. Both had red eyes and fire protruded from their mouths. Statues of lions and demonic horned characters lined the forty steps to his throne.

"My throne is made of a single carved black spinel gem on a raised silver floor. I attached the red spinel gems to it myself."

"I wondered what his throne would look like," Michael whispered to the three.

"Spectacular," Gabriel replied. "I would like to have one like it."

Beelzebub overheard the comment. "That can be arranged, my friend."

Gabriel smiled but looked away, pretending to gaze around the room.

Michael frowned. "Be careful, Gabriel. You don't want him to think you empathize with him."

The king of demons started up the steps, stopped, and turned toward the four. "Please join me." The eyes of all demons in the room were riveted on their master while the entourage traversed the steps.

"Let me introduce the four creatures around my throne. They are my humanoid archdemons: Gog, Magog, Endor, and Legion. They are seven feet tall in their regular, untransformed state and twenty feet in their transformed state. The flames of their spears are never extinguished.

"Endor is the muscular white gorilla with two horns and the tail of a scorpion; Magog is the green humanoid ox covered in horns with red lizard-like eyes, Gog is the black humanoid panther with horns with an extended neck like a snake and Legion is the black, tailless dragon. All have wings, glowing red eyes as you can see and razor-sharp teeth and claws." He paused until the watcher caught up to him. "Look around." He turned and traversed the remaining twenty steps. "Enjoy yourselves." The demon king sat down and inhaled deeply. "This place makes one feel powerful, doesn't it?" He grinned.

The four watchers gazed about the room, taking in the sights.

"Look at the lava waterfall," Tamor said. "Now that's an awesome sight."

Yofiel looked at one of the dragons positioned along the circular wall. Each blew a plume one at a time in succession so that a plume of fire was also being blown in the room.

"Join me for the rest of the tour," Beelzebub said, before standing and proceeding to descend the steps.

The four glanced at one another and followed.

Beelzebub turned to face them halfway down the steps. "As permanent guests of Darkmar, there are things you need to know about your new home."

"Kanah is our home," said Yofiel. "We want to go home. Now!"

"There now, little dumpling. You will see I'm a most gracious host—assuming you follow the rules and show respect."

"Never!"

A demon approached from behind, raised his arm to strike but held back, recalling Beelzebub's directive. The demon then lowered his arm, bowed toward Beelzebub, and shuffled up the steps. Yofiel winced but peeked when nothing happened. Beelzebub proceeded down the remaining steps and headed out of the throne room with the envoy in tow.

"Be careful, Yofiel," Michael whispered. "Don't want to rile him."

Beelzebub paused and pointed at the dragons along the wall. "You would be mistaken if you think the statues of the dragons are lifeless," Beelzebub said, continuing his presentation. "I assure you they're alive."

"They look scary," Tamor said.

"I trust none of these creatures, Tamor," Yofiel whispered. "Demons, wasp creatures, ape creatures, tyrannosapiens, lookers, spider creatures, gorilla creatures, dragons."

"Interesting how the carvings in the walls depict victories of your demons over the angels," Michael said. "Were they actual battles?"

A demon punched Michael in the stomach and walked away. Beelzebub continued onward. They walked by a large banquet hall with a sign over the entrance that read *Café de Erotica*. Two demons that looked like large gorillas stood guard at the entrance. They stood upright and had a long single horn like that of a rhinoceros on top of their heads.

The four watchers glanced inside.

"The room is almost as large as the arena of our academy on Kanah," Yofiel said. "I can't see even see how high the ceiling is."

"There's a party going on," Gabriel spouted. "Look. Demons and demonesses everywhere."

"Whoa, some are scantily clad," Michael added.

"This is a sensuality festival," Beelzebub said with the same enthusiasm he espoused when he described his throne. "It's a cornucopia of pleasures to indulge the lustful hunger of the citizens of Darkmar. Beings have a right to pleasure. We have no prohibitions or inhibitions here."

Many of the partiers were lying around, some were standing and a few were flying about or chasing others. Jollification was in full bloom. Provocative humanlike female demonesses enticed other creatures one-on-one and others were in display cages scattered about the room—all voluptuous and appealing to the senses and imagination. Some swung on high swings, while others swam in floating, see-through swimming pools. Merry-go-rounds were scattered about as were water fountains that shot water of all colors high into the air.

"These guards and others like them, keep the peace among the rambunctious crowds who venture here," Beelzebub continued. "Check out our creativity: a yellow and red sky, overhead fireworks, flowers spinning in the air spreading titillating aromas, glowing floating moons for lighting and music." A cacophony of sounds was heard amid heavy drum beats. Soothing jazz played in quieter areas like a soiree.

Perhaps you ladies would like a tour," Beelzebub asked. "The guys will wait here." He glanced at Gabriel and Michael before returning his gaze to the peniels.

Yofiel and Tamor stared into the room, awed by the sights. "I don't think so," Tamor uttered.

"Me either," Yofiel added.

Beelzebub snapped his fingers and the guards jumped to close the doors. Michael looked away while Gabriel continued to gawk at the sights. "Sorry, guys, only my most senior demons are permitted inside." The doors to Café de Erotica closed.

"That, dear watchers, concludes the walking tour of my palace. I hope you liked it. Let's head for my throne room.

"As I already said, Ramkrad is the lower residence of Darkmar. But there's more to it. Ramkrad is a bottomless pit of endless valleys, rock canyons, caves, firepits, tar swamps, lakes of fire and brimstone, lava rivers, mountains, and valleys. There are tunnels in Ramkrad and the upper world of Darkmar that circle the middle world of our planet." He stopped and eyed the four watchers.

"I will not lie to you. Ramkrad is a place as dark as midnight, full of gloom, confusion, eerie sounds, putrid smells, maniacal demons, and monstrous creatures. It pains me to talk about it. The deeper one travels inside our planet, the hotter it gets since the center of the planet is a molten fireball as big as earth. The fireball, or lake of fire as you may have heard about, feeds every volcano on the planet. Creatures of the endless night lurk in Ramkrad including Poquim, the dragon I told you about. There is another dragon above the surface of Ramkrad, called Ichnob. He leads an army of black dragons in the underground world below Demon's Hole.

"Ramkrad demons and the monsters who live there, are the most hideous and meanest creatures in all of Darkmar. Many are fierce, virtually uncontrollable, and will never be released. As I already indicated, it's a land of constant gangs, wars, and despicable acts by creatures who exist only to mutilate and destroy.

"Now, I have described Ramkrad but I will not take you there for the reasons stated. I have shown you parts of my home—the good, the bad and the worse," Beelzebub said in a sarcastic tone. "I do hope you liked it." He stared momentarily at Yofiel. "You ladies are always welcome to visit me at my palace."

Four black beasts approached Beelzebub. The upper parts of the body resembled an ape with fangs like a wolf, horns like a bull, and wings like a falcon. The lower parts of their bodies resembled a snake. Each of the four beasts had four arms. Two held black spears and the other two brandished black swords. Beelzebub consulted with them, then turned and headed toward his palace. The four watchers followed at a distance.

All entered the throne room and Beelzebub left the watchers and traversed the forty steps to his throne. "Beast," he called as he glanced at a nearby guard holding a flaming black sword. "Seize the fair-haired watcher." The command was hardly uttered when Gog seized Michael. He brought him close to the steps.

Beelzebub stared down at him. "Cut his wings off."

"What are you doing?" Yofiel shouted. "Why? He's no threat to you. Let him go. He means you no harm."

A demon stood between the peniels and Michael and held his flaming sword.

"What should I believe you, my little peniel?" Beelzebub jested. "It was the angels who fought us, the angels who subdued us, the angels who beat us, the angels who cut us with their swords, burned us with their spears of fire, disgraced us—their kindred spirits—and threw us away like trash, never to return to Krystar again, never to taste the fruit of the Tree of Life, or walk in the beloved gardens, or reside on the high mountain.

"Oh, to experience that magnanimous peace again. Truly my wretched spirit has known no peace since that day—that terrible day. To taste the fruit again and to experience the beauty and splendor I enjoyed as the most powerful angel in Krystar. And my beauty—my glorious beauty! I was the most beautiful creature in the heavens. They stripped me of my beauty and robbed me of my glory and my power. Did they mean us no harm?" He gestured to Gog. "Cut them!"

A beast grabbed Michael by the hair and dropped him to the floor as another placed a chopping block on the floor.

"No!" Tamor and Yofiel wailed. They charged toward Michael but were subdued by the demons.

Gabriel also charged toward Michael. A demon swooped down from Beelzebub's throne and knocked him to the ground.

Michael reached for a knife in his boot and stabbed one of the demons. The demon fell. Michael leapt to his feet, grabbed a stick attached to his thigh, and struck another. Demons swarmed and threw him to the floor. They placed his right-wing over the chopping block while others restrained him.

Chop.

Michael's right-wing fell to the ground, singed.

"You beast!" Tamor yelled.

"Exactly," Beelzebub roared back.

"You're despicable!" roared Yofiel, lying on the floor.

"Yes, I am," he uttered with a smile.

Michael peered at Yofiel through his tears.

The demons repeated the process for his other wing. He was helpless to prevent it and Gabriel was powerless to help. Afterwards, Michael was dragged to the girls and dropped like discarded waste.

"Bring the other one close," Beelzebub ordered. One of the four beasts flew to Gabriel and marched him to the steps.

"Gabriel, my son, I know you more than you realize. I know what goes on in Krystar. The angels speak well of you. I still have access to your king in Krystar and enjoy visiting with him occasionally, especially when I accuse his family of humans to his face.

"Yes," Gabriel said. "I know."

"My demon scouts tell me you have good leadership qualities and are destined to be a great warrior—they have watched you during your missions to Earth." He paused and turned to Gabriel. "I have plans. Join me my son and I will make you one of my key commanders in charge of many kingdoms in my realm. You will join me and my army when we attack Krystar and claim the universe. You can share in the riches, the power and a glory unknown to angels and humans. Think this through carefully and let me know your decision in a few days. But until then you will be treated as my guest like these peniels. A lightband will replace your chain." He nodded to a nearby demon.

A demon quickly carried out the order.

Beelzebub eyed another demon. "Take the ladies to their quarters on level Casa de Lues. Gabriel will remain here with me. We need to talk." He looked at Yofiel and said, "You will be one level below mine, my darling."

"I'm not your darling, you despicable beast," she countered. She struggled to get to Michael but couldn't because of the demons who held her.

Gabriel looked at Michael as he lay on the floor.

Michael projected the stunned stare of an injured animal.

"Take Michael to Ramkrad," Beelzebub roared. "Throw him in the dungeon."

24

RAMKRAD

Tamor and Yofiel were escorted to their quarters on Casa de Lues—one level below Altus. Yofiel was the last to be escorted to her room. The demon pushed the iron door with his foot.

Screech.

"Whoa," Yofiel mumbled. "That old door hasn't moved in a while." The lonely room greeted its guest as the walls stared in muffled silence.

Small room but the ceilings are high—so it's not too claustrophobic. Ugh, no windows.

The walls, ceiling, and floor were made of a black ironlike material. Her cell, like all the rest on Casa de Lues, was lit by small pits of glowing lava seeping through the walls—a constant reminder of their volcanic residence. Engravings of red and silver dragons embellished the walls and struggled for attention in the dull light.

"That's interesting. An old sword on the wall... probably left by the previous occupant. Okay. I see a table, a chair...." She turned toward the demon waiting in the doorway. "I don't see a bed."

He slowly shut the door with no response.

"She walked to the door and put her ear against it, listening to the fading footsteps. She glanced at the flat rock in the corner of the room. "Hmmm. Must be the bed." *Rock, rock, rock. Everything is rock! At least it's not a dungeon. Poor Michael, I miss him.* She pushed the door open and peered into the lightless hall. "Good. At least the door isn't locked."

"Tamor," she called. No answer. "Gabriel." Only an echo replied. She panicked as she thought about the others.

Where are they?

* * * * *

The demons escorted Michael into the belly of the volcano, allowing him to free-fall along the way to mock the wingless watcher. They traveled through Demon's Hole and entered the open atmosphere of the inner world, finally reaching the surface under which Ramkrad was housed. Ramkrad was like its own world composed of rocky volcanoes with endless caves and tunnels, rivers of lava, and the lake of fire from which there was no escape.

"The Gates of Ramkrad!" one of the escorting demons hollered.

"Move out, watcher," another demon snarled.

How am I ever going to get out of this place? Will I ever see my friends again? Will I ever return to Kanah?

They journeyed up the side of a rocky hill in the direction of the gate. Large spiders with red eyes and stingers began stalking them. Swarms of giant red-eyed wasps with large sharp teeth hovered high in the sky. One swooped down and snatched an escort demon. White gorilla-like beasts began pelting the pack with rocks.

The group finally arrived at the Gates of Ramkrad in the mountain. A sign with the name hung precipitously above the gates. The lead demon retrieved an iron key out of his pouch and struggled to open it. First one, then two, then four demons finally managed to get it to budge. A rush of fiery embers and blowing sand stung their faces as the gate opened to the underworld.

"Go," a demon snarled, pushing through the entrance. Michael fell to the ground and struggled to stand. All passed through and then the lead demon released the huge gate allowing the wind to slam it shut. The resulting vibrations caused a few rocks to fall from the mountain to the passageway ahead.

They traversed a downward sloping path for a few miles before leveling off. It overlooked a valley filled with hills, mountains and streams of lava for as far as they could see. Clouds of molten lava provided scant lighting and black snow fell from the sky, covering their path. The beat of drums, muffled yells, screeches, and sounds of unknown creatures echoed from mountain to mountain. The troupe studied the surroundings before moving on.

"What are those moving lights?" Michael asked the demon entourage.

"Some are our brothers," one of the demons said.

"And the others?"

"Just creatures."

Group of creatures of various sizes and shapes moved sludge and tar from one pit to another. Another group shoveled the same material into wheelbarrows and transported it to other locations for other creatures to move to other places. The activity was unending and appeared disorganized.

"Maddening," said Michael. "Each group undoes the other groups' work. And it's occurring everywhere."

"It's work, isn't it?" a demon snapped.

"Yes, but it's zero-value work. Nothing's getting accomplished."

"Mind your business, watcher," the lead demon growled. He shoved Michael. "Keep moving."

Beasts resembling dinosaurs drove the creatures of the valley with whips—yelling and roaring as they went. Flying monkeylike creatures dove low and bit the unwary. Mosquito-like creatures feasted on the dead and half-dead. Dragons flew overhead. Giant spiders hid in crevices, snatching the unsuspecting. Gangs of ape-like warred against ox-like and then retreated before attacking again. Giant snakes slithered about.

"What are those creatures over there?"

"Those are abacodas," another demon said. "Avoid them or die. They resembled horses but have the faces of men, the hair of women, the teeth of lions, the wings of eagles, and the tails of scorpions. Woe to the creature who stirs their fury. They swarm like wasps and take hours to settle. The whole valley hides when they fly."

"They fly?" Michael asked.

"Yes, they fly," the demon said. "And fast."

"One more question," Michael said.

The demon hissed. "Last one."

"I see some other creatures all over the other mountain in the distance." Michael pointed. "They fill the valley between the two mountains."

"They are called dyquattuors, or dyquats for short—two hundred million of them. They are lion-headed horse-like beasts that breathe fire and smoke like a dragon. Their tails inflict poisonous stings like a scorpion. Their skin glimmers like metal in the sun. They are the meanest and most ferocious beasts in Ramkrad. They await one called Apollyon, a coming prince of Ramkrad. He will be the offspring of Beelzebub, according to the prophecy."

Molten lava exploded from the mountain they on and sprayed into the sky above them. "Run!" the guard demons yelled. Lava rained all over the mountain.

The demons ran into a nearby tunnel to escape the rain of fire.

"Deadend!" the leading demon yelled. "Go back!"

The entourage returned to the mouth of the cave and waited until it was safe to exit. They found another cave further down the path and arrived at a large room at the end of the tunnel. One of the demons opened a metal hatch in the ground.

"Get in!" the lead demon roared at Michael.

"No," Michael retored.

They forced him to the opening and pushed him through, dropping him to the floor. Two of the demons followed, blindfolded him, and then took turns striking him.

"We're your official welcoming party, watcher," they taunted. "Welcome to Ramkrad?"

"You watchers think you're so smart," another said. "If you know so much then tell us who hit you last, brat. Where are your friends now? Even the peniels are stronger than you, little worm. What do they see in you runt? You'll never see them again. We'll visit them for you. I can't wait to get my hands on them." They continued to strike him.

Anything I say will prolong the agony and their enjoyment.

"Your only friends will be rats, bugs, spiders, and snakes," the first demon spouted. "They like to crawl around in the dark and bite. Enjoy. Haha." The two demons flew through the hatch, slammed it shut, and locked it. The sound reverberated through his cell like a cymbal rolling down a flight of stairs.

"Help me!" he cried.

25

VISIONS AND INVITATIONS

Michael lay on the floor, staring at the dark ceiling. The light of the lava in the walls furnished a faint glow. The room contained a chair and a small table both made of thin rock. An unlit candle sat on the table. The floor was full of black soot from charcoal, ash, and old lava rocks. Little critters scurried on the floor and walls. He could barely breathe the hot air due to the putrid smell. Intermittent moans and screeches echoed beyond the ceiling door, including the sound of chains intermittently slid across other metal doors on the floor above him.

I hope demons and any other creatures don't try to come in.

The dungeon room had a small gap around the perimeter where the wall was supposed to meet the floor. He peered through the gap into the adjacent rooms.

"Is anyone there?" he cried. No response. He reached around on the floor but only felt bugs and rocks. He stood and brushed them off. "What have I done to wind up in this place? Why did Beelzebub find me in the cave? Why didn't I leave earth as soon as Gabriel found me? I'll never get out of here! I wish I didn't exist. I'm a pathetic loser. Help me!" Darkness and loneliness engulfed him. The pain of losing his freedom, his home on Kanah, his wings, his reputation, and his friends crushed him. "Let the bugs crawl on me. I don't care."

A light began to glow and his cell lit up as bright as the sun. He squinted to see the image but to no avail. "Who are you?" he shouted.

"I am the messenger," the figure replied.

Michael floated up from the ground as if invisible hands were holding him. He flinched as he neared the ceiling but flew through it as if it were invisible He found himself flying along in the sky above snow-covered mountains. The day was young and the sun, hidden. He flew as in a dream toward an icy cave overlooking a cliff and landed inside next to a small fire.

How can this be? Where is this place? A blast of snow followed him inside, almost squelching the fire. A gale blew in and whistled around the cave leaving patches of ice here and there, kissing his face with rime. He huddled by a boulder, cupped his hands under his legs, and bowed his head away from the wind.

The messenger from the cave reappeared holding a flaming sword in his right hand. His eyes looked like fire and he glowed as he did in the dungeon. "Let him who has ears hear what the spirit says. Capture the sword of darkness."

"How do I do that if I am locked away in the dungeon?"

"All things are possible. You must find a way to capture the sword of darkness," the vision repeated before disappearing.

Michael was temporarily blinded but no longer felt the cold of the cave. "Who was that and what could it mean? Was it the vision that Gabriel spoke about?"

Lightning flashed at the sound of a trumpet blast. He jumped to attention and walked outside. It was dark and the stars flickered. Thunder sounded and lightning sizzled in the distant horizon. The ground shook. Stars began falling from the sky. First one, then another and then all streaked away and disappeared into the corners of the sky leaving an empty canopy of darkness. All of the lights in the heavens abandoned the night except for one. It grew larger and larger and until it resembled the messenger he had seen in the cave. The mountainside glowed in his presence. The messenger roared like a lion and Michael felt his strength leave him.

The figure raised a golden sword of fire. "Hail mighty warrior. Do not fear. You must not cut your hair as a sign of your call. Capture the sword of darkness."

"But I am the least esteemed warrior in my class and I am the weakest and the smallest."

Michael's body went limp, his breath escaped and he floated upward as if dead.

"Where is your faith?" the image asked, just before disappearing in a flash.

"But I'm a prisoner of Beelzebub."

"Where is your faith?"

"But who am I? I am nothing."

"Where is your faith?"

"If the king has called me to do this," Michael replied for the third time, "then show me the way."

Michael shook himself out of the trance, gasped for air, and found himself lying face down on the floor of his dungeon cell. The dull fire returned his blank stare. He peered around the room—he was alone. *Was that a dream? Was the messenger real? 'Pursue and capture the sword of darkness. Do not cut your hair. Where is your faith?'* "Good question. Where is my faith?"

* * * * *

Knock, knock, knock.

"Yes?" Yofiel answered.

"I was sent by Beelzebub to deliver an invitation," a demon said.

The demon waved his hand at the door which made it transparent so she could see him. He wore the red-colored lightband of a trusted senior demon. She opened the door.

"Your invitation." Her name was written in red glowing ink.

She took the envelope with her name glowing in red. She removed the invitation, and read the words written in the same red glowing ink. It read:

To Yofiel:

King Beelzebub Requests The Honor Of Your Presence At A Celebration Gala This Evening In The Stadium Of Flavium.

"I have your dress," the demon barked. He revealed the dress and watched for her reaction. She remained expressionless. He frowned. "My master personally selected it for you," he said, handing it to her.

"I will not wear it," she wailed as she snatched it out of his hands and threw it back.

The demon entered the room and carefully placed the dress across her rock bed. "You will wear it, little peniel, or something unfortunate may happen to one of your friends. Are we clear, dear one?"

She stood silent, staring at the floor. "Clear," she finally muttered, refusing eye contact. The door shut by itself as the demon exited.

She shuffled around her cell until she found herself in front of the dress. She carefully inspected it without touching it. Slowly, as if daring herself, she reached for it and held it in the dim light.

"Beautiful," she said as she gazed upon the fiery-red strapless silk gown. *How did he know this was my favorite style?* The luminescent material glowed, set with exquisite white and reddish-white gems in strategic locations to compliment her curvaceous body. She put it on. Perfect. *I wish Michael could see me. I hope he's okay.*

* * * * *

The demon went to Tamor's quarters, presented the invitation and repeated the message. But he did not give Tamor time to respond before adding, "You must come to the party wearing this dress, or you will never see your friends again." He tossed the dress over her arm and abruptly left.

She stared at the invitation and finally read it.

To Tamor:

King Beelzebub Requests The Honor Of Your Presence At His Table For A Celebration Gala This Evening In The Entertainment Stadium Of Flavium.

Her eyes dropped to the dress hanging from her arm. She tried it on. *I can't believe it. It fits like it was made for me. Purple is my favorite color. I would wear this dress to the gala on Kanah.* The V-neck, sleeved, high-slit, purple silk dress gleamed with gems strategically placed. *I love how the crystals glow like stars.*

26

THE GALA

Knock, knock, knock.

"Yes?" Yofiel asked.

"Your escort to the gala," the demon said.

Yofiel waved her hand in front of the door so she could see through it as the demon had shown her. He was wearing the red lightband over his eyes.

She opened the door. "What's your name?"

"We do not have names, except for the four who guard the throne of Beelzebub."

"Why is that?"

"Names do not matter to our master."

"How unfortunate. Why are you wearing your lightband over your eyes?"

"Beelzebub commanded it to prevent 'undesirable responses' as he put it. He believes your beauty would cause a negative response since we demons do not have self-restraint, whatever that means. Our king said the eyes ignite passion."

"Very well. Can you lead, or shall I?"

"I can see with my lightband. It will guide us."

They flew to level Flavium, one level below the Tunnel of Ekron.

"What's that noise?" she asked in flight.

"The demons in the stadium. They're waiting for you two peniels."

"What stadium?"

"It's our entertainment complex where we have events—fights mostly. It holds a million demons or so."

"What's that bubble?" she asked, pointing in the stadium.

"It's 4DDIG: Four-Dimensional Dynamic-Imaging Globe. It magnifies the images within the bubble and projects holographic images to every seat in the stadium."

"How convenient!"

T-shaped catwalks extended through a circular stage and connected with an outer-circular catwalk surrounding the main stage. The concave walls of the stadium towered into the sky so that the higher seats projected forward to the field below.

The demon dropped Yofiel off in a large, solid-white room beneath the stadium and locked her inside.

A short time later the door opened. "Yofiel!" The two hugged.

"What are you doing here? Tamor asked? "Why are we here? Why are the demons in the stadium?" The stadium began to vibrate as the demon spectators stomped their feet.

""I think they're going to put us on stage. We're to be displayed in that bubble-thing unfortunately. Did you see it?"

"Yes," Tamor replied.

The door opened.

"Gabriel!" Tamor shouted.

"Hi, Gabriel."

"Hello, Tamor and Yofiel. I missed you peniels. How are you?"

They hugged.

"I'm okay," Yofiel answered.

"So am I," said Tamor. "We need to get out of this place."

"Why are we here?" Gabriel asked.

"Beelzebub sent a special invitation to Tamor and me. There's an event in their stadium and we're to be a part of it somehow."

"We want to get out of here," cried Tamor. "Can we get out of here?"

"We'll think of something. But what are you ladies supposed to do?"

"We're the eye candy for these rascals, or so we think," Yofiel replied.

"I get that. The demons haven't seen such beauty since being kicked out of Krystar. You ladies are dressed to party."

"I think we are the party," Tamor said, "Don't ask about the dresses."

"Our friend, Beelzebub, had them made for us," Yofiel added. "Have you heard from Michael?"

"Unfortunately, no," replied Gabriel.

The door opened and in walked Michael.

Yofiel's heart skipped a beat. "Michael!" She ran to him. "Are you okay?" The two embraced. "I was worried about you." She looked back at Gabriel and Tamor. "I was worried about every one of you."

"I'm surviving," Michael replied. "I can barely breathe in my cell." He eyed the girls and inhaled deeply. "Why are you ladies dressed up and where did you get the dresses?"

"We were invited, or forced is the better word, to attend this so-called gala," Yofiel said. "I think we're to entertain Beelzebub and his horde of demons. Can you hear them in the stadium?"

"I do. They're waiting for us?"

"We think so," Tamor replied.

"I'm sorry that I put us in this predicament," Michael said. "This is my fault. If it wasn't for me, none of you would be here."

"If it's anyone's fault, it's mine," Yofiel insisted. "I'm the one who took you to the cave that day."

"But you didn't know Beelzebub would be there," Tamor said. "Who could have known?"

"She's right," Gabriel muttered. "I'm the one who led the peniels to earth. This is my fault."

"Stop it, guys," Michael cried. "It's not your fault. None of us had any idea we would be kidnapped on the return trip to Kanah."

"It's Beelzebub's fault," Tamor wailed.

"Right," Yofiel replied.

"But Uriel and Caleb will hold me responsible," Michael cried.

"Let's change the subject," said Tamor. "Michael, we're sorry about your wings."

"They'll grow back," Gabriel added. "Soon."

Yofiel said, "Those demons will pay for it, somehow."

"In time," said Michael. "What's this gala about? What are they celebrating?"

"Us."

"What do you mean?"

"I think they're celebrating our capture."

"And now we're to be paraded and gawked at," Yofiel said. "Listen to the demons in the stadium. All of them are yelling and stomping."

"Yes, but what about me and Gabriel?" Michael asked.

Gabriel placed his hand on Michael's shoulder. "You and I must be the main event and will fight demons in the bubble. Fighting is their main sport."

"I'm not too sure the demons will think we're the main event," replied Michael. "Unfortunately, they'll enjoy Yofiel and Tamor far more. You peniels are stunning. Your dresses glow and it's making you glow guys glow."

"We love the dresses but I don't want to wear it to any event on this planet," Tamor replied.

"They threatened harm if we didn't wear them," Yofiel added.

Two demons pushed the door open and motioned to the peniels.

I'm scared," Tamor muttered as the platform in the middle of the room.

"Sit there," a demon ordered.

"We'll get through this," Yofiel whispered. "What do you think they're going to do to us?"

"You already said it," Tamor replied. "They going to put us in the bubble on stage. It's showtime."

The demons backed away, leaving the peniels by themselves.

The girls reached for each other's hands in suspenseful anticipation. Their circular platform began to rise as fast as the ceiling opened.

Rancorous sound poured into the room like rushing water from a waterfall.

"Sounds like the ceiling is going to fall!" Tamor shouted. The two covered their ears. The opening of the stadium floor caused a sudden hush among anxiously waiting celebrants momentarily stilled in breathless anticipation.

"Are you ready for this, Tamor?"

"Are you?"

"No."

As the girls rose into view on the platform, the demons of the packed stadium exploded with shrieks of hysteria that pounded the ears. Every demon stood and some charged the stage, as all beheld unimagined beauty mixed with eye-storming colors of the two angelic creatures from another world. The eyes of demons could not process the artistic perfection of the heavenly beings and could scarcely contain the sight..

Beelzebub stood from his seat near the bubble and greeted the peniels with arms raised and mouth wide open exposing his sharp teeth. He approached and cupped their hands, bowing to each.

An escort demon motioned for the ladies to walk the stage. They moved gracefully yet cautiously to the perimeter and continued around the catwalk.

Large security demons dropped conspicuously from the ceiling to enforce crowd control among the chaos. Each guard carried a spear that generated microbursts of lightning bolts. The guards worked to prevent a mutiny by the lustful, covetous spectators who wanted nothing less than to fondle, consume and digest the two visions of ecstasy. Demons acted raunchily with other demons. Beelzebub, ignoring their behavior, left the peniels on stage and returned to his seat.

Yofiel leaned in toward Tamor. "Look," she shouted, pointing. "How convenient that he brought his throne."

"He's creepy," Tamor shouted back, a look of disgust on her face.

The bubble around the stage and catwalk shielded the peniels from the dangerous mob, for even some of the senior demons were untrustworthy. Some tried to get to the girls but were immediately shocked upon contact with the bubble.

Guards zapped demons who refused to behave or were unable to restrain themselves, temporarily incapacitating them. Even a security demon succumbed to the temptation of the peniels and was zapped by two guards at the same time. Yelling, screaming, jumping, fighting, hitting, cursing, slapping and carrying-on continued as the peniels progressed around the catwalk for the next hour. One big demon flew from high in the stadium and licked the bubble closest to Tamor. He was electrocuted through his tongue.

Some demons were zapped more than once. Multiple zaps melted the demon, leaving a black slime of their original self that slithered away to Ramkrad like a panicked snake.

Discordant waves of acrimony filled the stadium when escort demons summoned the peniels to return to center stage. The hiss of angry demons filled the stadium like angry rattlesnakes in a hot, rusty cow trough.

Yofiel flashed a smile.

"Glad it's over!" Tamor said.

"It's not."

27

FIGHTING ON FLAVIUM

"The stage is lowering," Michael said. He and Gabriel moved closer to the center of the room where the platform was descending.

"Here they come." *Looks like they survived.*

"We're next, friend," Michael said, as they moved toward the platform to greet the peniels. "Welcome back, ladies." They hugged them but the peniels remained silent.

"My ears are ringing," Tamor finally said.

"Mine too," Yofiel added. "I can hardly hear."

"Are you two okay?" asked Gabriel.

"Yes, if you don't mind being paraded for millions of deranged creatures," Tamor responded. You two wouldn't understand."

A demon motioned to them.

"And we're next!" Gabriel said, releasing the peniels.

"Beelzebub is near the stage," Tamor muttered.

"Hold your ears," Yofiel offered. "Here comes the noise."

* * * * *

Beelzebub rose from his chair, capturing the attention of all demons in the stadium. One zap from his fingers would send a demon straight to Ramkrad and the demons know it. All drew silent.

"Fellow demons," the king of demons shrieked. "We are family."

The demons responded in a fevered frenzy of yells and cheers mixed with thunderous applause and foot-stomping. The noise continued for several minutes until Beelzebub raised his hand. Silence ensued.

"Not only are we family but we're brothers and sisters who—"

Again the demons erupted in praise of their commander.

Beelzebub jerked his arm up to command silence. "We're family and we're bound with a common purpose to rule the universe together. We will defeat the king of Krystar. We will rule together.

The demons rose from their seats and cheered, hollered and stomped.

"We will rule the universe," he continued over the noise. Planet earth and all humans will belong to us."

The demons roared in approval and could no longer be silenced.

Beelzebub waited for them to settle down. "Dear brothers, I invited our lovely guests as a sign of my promise. When we capture Krystar and the outposts, each of you will get your own peniel watchers. They will serve and please you for eternity."

The exuberant demons stomped their feet like stampeding dinosaurs, causing the walls of the stadium to shake.

The cacophony of deafening sounds continued until Beelzebub signaled the crowd. "Brothers and sisters," he shouted. "We have two additional watchers who are visiting with us and they will join our fighters in the Challenge Circle of Doom. Welcome them."

Hissing and cursing echoed around the stadium as the spectators awaited the arrival of the two junior angels from Kanah. The hissing was replaced by shouting as every demon began chanting "Demons, demons, demons." All observed them as they rose into view on the circular stage.

"Look, Gabriel," Michael said, pointing at demons seated on stage. "Our opponents, I assume." *We're going to be destroyed.*

"No doubt. I count six of them."

Beelzebub approached the two standing alone on center stage and peered at the demons into the stadium. All grew quiet. "Brothers, you have met the peniel watchers." Cheering commenced and quickly faded. "Now, allow me the pleasure of introducing two student watchers from Outpost Kanah." Hissing and groans reverberated around the stadium like a cacophony of howling coyotes. "This is Michael."

"Boo, hiss, cursed watcher, skinny child, runt, turdball," the demons shouted, one after another. Echoes of curses reverberated around the stadium. "And this brave one is Gabriel." More booing ensued. "Should we go easy on them?"

The hiss of a million demons sounded like angry rattlesnakes in a pit. The venom of hate frothed onto the field like a drooping fog.

"The festivities will continue with both watchers fighting two junior demons. Our junior demons are working toward the rank of demon."

A guard motioned toward the six demons, singling out the two junior fighters. The stage is yours," the guard demon shouted over the spectators. "You will fight until there is a clear winner. There are no rules. Begin on my signal."

As the junior demons moved to center stage, a million voices chanted: "Demons, demons, demons..." Louder and louder they chanted.

Another guard presented two watchers with swords. One of the guards pointed at Michael and his opponent. Then he pointed at Gabriel and the other junior demon and closed the palms of his hands together indicating to approach one another.

"Fight like the warrior you are!" Gabriel shouted. He tapped Michael on the back and posited the watcher hand symbol—thumb down with fingers slightly curled to mimic an eagle's claw—the angelic symbol for mighty warrior.

Michael raised his sword to acknowledge him. Both had small, matching silver swords. The junior demons had slightly larger black swords. The little demons were humanoid but with ape-looking faces, sharp teeth, and red eyes. The opponents eyed one another as they positioned for battle. The junior demons glanced at each other and laughed as they pointed at Michael.

He ignored them. *The last time I fought, I lost. I lost badly. But these are junior demons. But I have yet to win a match.* He glanced at Gabriel and tried to compose himself so as not to hyperventilate. *Gabriel looks confident. He should—he's won most of his matches.* He eyed his opponent. *He looks smug but whoa he reeks.*

The two watchers moved closer to their opponents. Michael's opponent shook his finger, taunting him. Michael's legs were shaking. His opponent noticed and winked.

"Come to me, little watcher," the demon shrieked. "I will show you your destiny."

Michael said nothing. He and Gabriel shuffled forward and lunged toward their opponents at the same time. The fighters circled each other many times, jabbing and kicking at each other. Michael was a slightly better fighter than his opponent and blocked most punches and every sword strike while achieving the majority of his strikes.

Gabriel easily dominated his foe and knocked the junior demon off the circular stage several times. As the fight continued, Michael and Gabriel grew more self-assured and successful while the little demons appeared to panic. The demons in the stadium began booing and hissing at the junior demons.

Beelzebub was embarrassed by the lackluster performance of the pair from Darkmar and frowned at the booing. He signaled the guard demon. The guard plucked the junior demons from the fight and threw them off the stage. They were beaten by the spectators as they ran through the crowd. Two other junior demons were dismissed from the stage with no explanation, leaving two senior demons. The guard motioned to them with his sword. The two senior fighters approached center stage.

Beelzebub joined them. "Everyone knows our two respected archdemons, Legion and Endor. So no formal introduction is necessary." The crowd roared and stomped their feet, sending shockwaves through every seat.

The two bowed and waved to the crowd.

"They are huge," Michael shouted.

"They are," Gabriel replied, nodding as he studied them.

"What do we do, Gabriel?"

"We fight."

The two senior demons strutted around the stage with red-eyed, dual-horned, solid-black saber-toothed cats—the animals bit at their leashes. The warriors worked the spectators into a frenzy, then yielded their animals to the guards who led them offstage. The two demons turned toward Michael and Gabriel and lowered their swords.

"Look, Gabriel," Michael said, pointing with his sword. "The peniels." He watched as several demons escorted the girls to their seats next to Beelzebub.

The king of demons stood as the peniels approached and sat after they were seated.

Michael and Gabriel glanced at one another—barely able to hear due to the hollering and foot-stomping. "Fight brave," Gabriel shouted against the deafening noise.

Michael returned the fist-pump. *We're going to be destroyed. I know I will be.*

The guard moved toward center stage with his flaming sword held high, garnering the attention of the crowd. He swung it to and fro in a half-circular motion to signal the start of the fight.

Endor and Legion touched swords and advanced. Legion suddenly vanished and instantly appeared behind Michael. He elbowed Michael in the side of the neck, knocking him to the ground, much to the amusement of everyone except the four watchers.

Endor lunged at Gabriel, who barely deflected the strike.

Michael jumped to his feet and swung at Legion, who disappeared to avoid it.

Legion reappeared behind him and kicked him in the buttocks to the rancorous approval of the demons.

The guard motioned to Legion to cease from disappearing. The demon gave a backhanded motion as if to disregard the directive.

Gabriel and Endor appeared evenly matched, at least at first. Endor finally got through Gabriel's defenses and cut him on the arm. He maneuvered again slice through his jeans, cutting Michael in the thigh.

The crowd roared.

Gabriel charged and plunged his sword toward the demon's midsection. But Endor easily deflected it while dropping to his knees and thrusting his fist into Gabriel's midsection. Gabriel doubled over and fell to the stage while clinging to his sword. Endor spun around and knocked Gabriel's sword into the audience as if striking a ball with a bat. It was a line drive straight into the face of a spectator.

The crowd began chanting, "demons, demons, demons... ."

Meanwhile, Michael pivoted and swung his sword, hoping to catch Legion off guard. But the demon simply held his sword to intercept it.

The crowd hollered so loudly that the stadium vibrated.

Michael sliced downward toward Endor's leg.

Legion swung his sword in a quick circular motion, halting Michael's sword in mid-swing. The demon headbutted him to the groun. The crowd yelled.

Yofiel turned her head to glimpse at Beelzebub as he laughed. She nudged Tamor and pointed at him.

Tamor shook her head and tightened her grip on Yofiel's hand.

One of the guards tossed another sword to Gabriel.

The two demonic warriors drew closer together and then flipped in the air and simultaneously flung their swords across the stage. The swords flew straight into a column, penetrating it deeply.

Michael moved closer to Gabriel. Both were breathing heavily and hurting. Michael gave him a thumbs up though exhausted, mentally and physically.

Endor did a roundhouse kick and elbowed Gabriel in the face, knocking him to the floor of the stage as Legion toyed with Michael. The demons beat them and struck them with increasing force. The demon warriors swapped opponents, inflicting pain with ease before swapping back again.

"Stop it, stop this at once," Yofiel wailed.

The crowds continued to roar and stomp their feet. "Kill them, kill them, kill them," they chanted.

The archdemons looked at Beelzebub who shook his head to deny the request. Endor and Legion flipped in the air and body-slammed Michael and Gabriel. They knocked to the stage repeatedly with single punches.

"Stop the fight, Beelzebub," both peniels cried.

Endor turned to face Legion, who ran straight at him, and together formed a wheel and rolled toward the watchers. Endor released Legion who catapulted into the air and struck both watchers in the face with his fists, knocking both to the ground. The crowd rocked the stadium in celebration of the impending win. The noise was louder than at any previous time of the fight.

The two watchers managed to stand—completely humiliated—and approached the demons while managing to hold their swords. They swung simultaneously at Legion. The warrior demon caught both swords with his hands, jerked them away, and tossed them into the crowd. Discordant shrieks of laughter, cursing, and yelling bombarded their ears as the senior demons dominated the two watchers.

Legion did a roundhouse punch and knocked Michael unconscious. As he lay on the stage, the demon began cutting on the remaining wing.

Gabriel lunged at him but Endor grabbed him by the hair and lifted him off the ground with one hand. The crowd continued yelling and stomping as loudly as they could.

Beelzebub motioned to stop the match and for Endor to release Gabriel. Endor dropped him and Gabriel fell face down to the stage. The guard extended his flaming sword between the fighters to signal the end of the rout.

The demon fighters left the stage. Legion kicked Michael in the head as he passed by.

"You animals!" Yofiel yelled.

Beelzebub pretended not to notice.

The guards threw water on both watchers to rouse them. Both slowly stood.

Beelzebub leaned toward Yofiel and sneered. "Your friend is pathetic. What can you possibly see in him? He is weak. He's no warrior. He is hopeless."

Anger covered her face.

Tamor tried to console her as angered filled her veins.

Beelzebub raised a white towel for one of the guards. The guard took the towel and gave it to Gabriel.

Gabriel wiped his face and passed it to Michael.

"Take them away," Beelzebub ordered. "Meet at the exit gates."

The guys glanced at the peniels through pained eyes.

Yofiel and Tamor attempted to run to them but were restrained. Looker demons surrounded by senior guards arrived to escort them from the stadium.

The guards steered the frazzled watchers offstage and herded them through the jeering crowds, along with the peniels. The defeated warriors bore cuts and scratches from the demon's claws and deep bruises from the punches, kicks, headbutts and body slams. The spectators added to their injuries as they made their way through the stadium. They grabbed at the girls through the wall of senior guards. The guards resorted to shock rods to keep them at bay.

"Did you hear something about an ambush?" one demon asked as they made their way toward the stadium exit.

28

A PLEASANT EVENING

"Sir, I have been informed that there are forty demons outside the stadium waiting to ambush the watchers," a demon reported to Beelzebub. "They plan to kill the watchers and kidnap the peniels."

"Send fifty warriors with flaming swords to meet them at the gates. Tell them to take the watchers through the underground passageway to level Casa De Lues. Destroy all participating in the ambush."

"Very well, Master." The demon turned and flew away.

The warrior demons arrived at the gate and searched for the ambush, while four others escorted the watchers through the secret underground passageway.

Gabriel and the girls were escorted to Casa de Lues. Michael was taken to Ramkrad.

* * * * *

Yofiel found herself back in her room surrounded by the lonely walls. *Oh, Michael. Oh, Gabriel. I hope you guys are okay. This is a living nightmare. Beelzebub is cruel*! The quiet cells were a welcome reprieve from the thunderous noise of the stadium. She drifted off to sleep.

Knock, knock, knock.

Three knocks at the door were not enough to pull her from her sleep.

Knock, knock, knock.

She snapped awake at the sixth knock. *What do they want now?* She stood and waved her hand over the door to see through it. There were two senior demons with lightbands over their eyes.

"Yes," she responded.

"We have another invitation for you, peniel watcher." The door opened automatically.

"Our master requests the pleasure of your company and he also requests that you wear the same dress as before," the second demon added. The other demon read the invitation.

To Yofiel:

King Beelzebub Requests Your Presence at His Table For A Celebration Feast This Evening In The Royal Banquet Hall.

The words were written in glowing red ink as before.

"I refuse to eat with that evil creature!" Yofiel shouted

"You don't have a choice! You will be escorted to the Royal Banquet Hall in eight hours," the first demon insisted. They closed the door and left.

Sure enough, later that day, there was another knock on her door.

Knock, knock, knock.

She waved her hand and saw Tamor with two senior demons. She opened the door.

"Hello, Tamor," Yofiel said, hugging her. "I'm so glad you're here." They shut the door leaving the escort demons in the hall. Yofiel clutched her invitation. "So you received another invite?"

"Yes, but at least it's not another gala."

"True. We need to be leaving soon." They changed into their dresses.

The group made their way to the Palace of Beelzebub on Altus and entered a large room.

"The tables were ornately set," Yofiel observed. "Love the flowers."

"Music too?" Tamor asked. "Nice touch. This place is full of surprises."

"Yeah, mostly bad."

"True."

"I see that Beelzebub invited some of his senior officers," Yofiel muttered, nodding toward a large group entering the room.

"And their demonesses," Tamor replied. "I like their gowns."

"But they're dressed in black."

"They're favorite color, perhaps?" The two laughed.

"I like the burgundy walls with white marble floors," said Yofiel. "And crystal water fountains."

"This I didn't expect," Tamor replied. White, burgundy, and chocolate dahlia and hibiscus flowers were strewn over the table and in vases around the room—all glowed and gave off the smell of lavender and chocolate. Ribbons were draped in the high ceiling.

"Who would have thought?"

The two stood alone in the middle of the circular room. All gazed at them.

"Look, there he is," said Yofiel.

"Ladies, thank you for coming," Beelzebub said as he approached.

"Did we have a choice?" Tamor asked.

"Ladies, please join me at my table." He placed Yofiel to his right and Tamor to his left. The table set for twenty couples was decorated with a silver lace tablecloth, crystal cutlery, a silver candelabra with thirteen black candles, crystal glasses, and flowers. Demons held the chair for their demonesses and seated them on the left-hand side of Beelzebub, while his officers sat to his right. Food was cooked in small mobile firepits near the table.

"What, may we ask, is the purpose of this banquet?" Yofiel asked.

"I wanted to spend time with you peniels in a quiet, intimate setting."

"And the other couples?" Tamor asked.

"They're my most senior demons: commanders, guards, and leaders. I'm honoring them with this special dinner and your presence."

"Their dates—the demonesses—are quite attractive," Yofiel observed.

"Yes, but their beauty doesn't match yours," he whispered. "Theirs won't last forever as yours will—they all turn into old ghoulish witches." He laughed. "It's part of the curse. But your beauty will always be like a flower that blooms for the first time." Beelzebub waited for their response but to no avail.

Attendants interrupted with drinks. Dinner followed.

This is the best food I have ever tasted, Yofiel thought—*but I will not admit it to the demon.* "Where did this food come from?"

"It is roasted pheasant from planet earth," Beelzebub said with a slight but confident smile on his face. "Wait till you taste the desserts and other delicacies—I had them delivered from Paris for this occasion."

Tamor glanced at Yofiel. "Can't wait."

"And where did the flowers come from?" Yofiel asked, venturing her first smile.

"You wouldn't believe me if I told you."

"Earth?" Tamor suggested.

"Of course, yes," he replied. "Hawaii to be exact. Other than Krystar and the seven outposts, no planet in this universe can match the flowers and the beauty of earth. Trust me I know. I've been all over the universe. Earth is a garden, a jewel among planets. But earth, oh wondrous earth shall be mine one day. My demons can have all the other planets for all I care. But the beauty of earth and the flowers in this room—as beautiful as they are—pale in comparison to you two creatures. You are stunning. You take my breath away."

Is the demon blushing! Yofiel wondered.

All in the great room began to eat.

"I hoped you liked your dresses," he said, breaking a long silence. "I designed what I thought each of you would like."

Again, the girls didn't respond. All finished eating and the lights in the room faded as the music turned more lively.

Beelzebub rose from his chair, peered at Yofiel, and asked, "May I have the honor of this dance?"

"No, absolutely not," Yofiel snarled. "You practically killed Michael and Gabriel in your sporting event today and now you expect for us to pretend it didn't happen?"

"Beelzebub, you're heartless," Tamor charged.

The senior demons and demonesses paused at the outbursts.

"Ladies, that simply isn't true—I'm not heartless," he protested. "Yes, I am tough at times. Cruel too. But I enjoy nice things as you do. I can't help it if I was kicked out of Krystar and made into what I am. I could've destroyed Michael and Gabriel yesterday but I didn't. So I gave my demons a break from their endless miseries and let them enjoy themselves. Is that asking too much? I think it's good. So grant me some fun and respite from my misery—I think you call it grace. Yes?"

Yofiel gritted her teeth and refused to look him in the eye.

"Today is the most fun I've had in a long time. I know there are bad things here but Michael and Gabriel are still alive and will remain so. Can't you allow me one pleasant evening?"

Yofiel took his hand as she rose from her seat. The two entered the dance floor and danced alone. She studied his face and he pulled her close. *He is handsome I must admit. I never noticed his green eyes*. She took a deep breath of his cologne—it filled their space as she relaxed her grip in his arms. Her sense of self-preservation and ramparts of stubbornness washed away with each musical note.

He held her close, eyeing her form-fitting gown. The light of a floating moon guided his hand as it drifted downward along her curvaceous body, pausing here and there until her hand met his. His lips brushed her cheeks and touched the corner of her lips.

She started to push away but remained close.

Maybe he has some good in him. How could one so attractive and charismatic be so evil? He's romantic, I confess. I like him this way. But what makes him do bad things?

"I'm working on being better," he whispered.

Can he read my mind? I think not. I hope not... It's good to be held again.

"If you were mine, I would move Krystar and Darkmar to change. I can be good. I can be an angel of light."

"What do you want?" she asked

"You," he whispered as he gazed at her with gentle eyes." They slowed their dancing while other dancers twirled around them. He drew closer. "I would give all of Darkmar for you. You can have half of my kingdom."

She glanced about, finally resting her face on his chest. *I sense his spell on me. I must resist. I don't want to? But I must. I must. I...*

He paused and gently turned her face, moving his lips closer to hers.

Tamor tapped Yofiel on her shoulder, startling her. "May I have this dance?"

"What?" Yofiel asked with a dazed expression. "Oh." Yofiel hesitated. She stepped away—looking at him, wantonly.

Tamor noticed the reddening of her cheeks.

"Of course you may," he replied, belatedly. He eyed Tamor. He took turns dancing with both peniels for the remainder of the party.

"I saw how you were looking at him," Tamor later commented when the two were alone at the table. "That's why I broke in when I did."

Yofiel offered no reply as she stole a glance at Beelzebub standing by the band.

"And your face. You were blushing, Yofiel."

Beelzebub approached the table. "I missed you peniels on the dance floor for the last dance. Join me, both of you. They danced some fast beats as a threesome. Everyone in the room became more animated as the wine flowed.

"The guy can dance," Yofiel said privately to Tamor.

"That he can. I'm surprised." The dancing went on for hours.

But pleasant evenings and dancing do not heal broken hearts nor erase hurtful memories. The two girls talked about Michael and Gabriel between dances. Soon the celebration was over and they were escorted back to their rooms.

Yofiel lay on her bed thinking about the evening. *Do these walls have eyes*? The music lingered in the darkness and whispered in her ear. Visions of the moons stole the darkness in her cell.

I liked him tonight.

29

SHESLA AND GOLGA

Ssscrreeeeecchhh.

Michael was jarred awake as someone or something began turning the wheel to open the door to his cell.

"Who's there?" he shouted, staring at the ceiling.

The groans of the hinges screeched like hard fingernails against a chalkboard as the heavy iron hatch opened and slammed backwards.

"Who's there, I said?" He rose, holding his breath, listening. *What's going on*? Fine time for the fire to be so low. I can barely see.

"Lunch," replied the unseen creature in the ceiling.

Clop.

The sound of feet landing on the floor startled him. *Demons never enter when delivering food. They just toss it to the floor.* Michael drew another breath and held it, trying to anticipate the stranger's next move.

Clop.

What? A second visitor? He glanced around in the darkness, expecting an attack.

"Who is it?" Michael finally whispered, breaking a long silence. "Identify yourself."

Two creatures began to glow.

Michael lifted himself with his hands and legs and receded into the corner of his cell. "Who are you?"

"My name is Shesla," said the taller of the two.

"And my name is Golga," said the second.

"We're the cooks," they said in unison.

"We brought food," added the taller one. "My name is Shesla and this is Golga."

Shesla stood six feet tall with a humanlike face, droopy eyes, a large nose, and floppy ears. He also had a red combed blade and wattle like a rooster except for a diamond image in the shape of an inverted triangle on his forehead.

The second creature was shorter. He also had a humanlike face but resembled a pug with his small ears, flat face, small mouth, and bulging brown eyes that occasionally gazed in different directions.

Michael stared at the intruders. "Things don't go well when I'm around demons. They don't come for social visits and they don't hand-deliver food."

"We're not demons," Shesla answered.

"And our eyes aren't red like those of a demon," Golga said.

"Okay, so you're not demons. But your creatures of the dark who constantly roam around.

"We're not," stated the taller creature.

"Then state your purpose." *If they were going to hurt me, they would've done it by now.*

"I told you we're the cooks and we brought food."

"Then what else do you want?"

"Want is not the issue, need is. We're here to help you—something no creature of Ramkrad would do."

"What I want is to escape and return to Kanah. And what I need is help to do it."

"Yes, but it's not that simple," Shesla said. "Unfortunately, you're going to have to fight your way out of here—we all are. You must learn how to fight like a warrior and we're just the two to teach you."

"How do you know my name?"

"News travels fast here."

"Demons can't keep secrets," Golga said, smiling with his mouth open. "Gossip, gossip, gossip. The stupid critters just won't stop talking."

"Just what I need. Two funny guys who fight with pots and pans? What am I supposed to do? Roast them to death?" Michael started eating. "And by the taste of this food, I should teach you guys how to cook."

"Okay, okay. Golga and I are actually from Krystar and we aren't real cooks."

"Oh, thank goodness. I can handle the dungeon but not your cooking."

"Funny guy you are. Golga and I are elders—two of twenty-four members of the council of Krystar appointed by the king. We're kingdom advisors and protectors.

"Yeah, sure. And I am the king's personal assistant. elders are the greatest warriors and the wisest creatures in all of the kingdom."

"You are correct!" Shesla turned to Golga. "Show him."

Golga's eyes began to project rays of penetrating light, like a laser. He unsheathed his sword, previously hidden, and raised it in the air. It became aflame with fire as he swung it in a circular motion.

Michael threw himself against the wall to dodge the blade.

"As you can see, this is no ordinary sword," Shesla pointed out. "It's the sword of a senior warrior, capable of shooting bolts of lightning and it has situational awareness and becomes one with its owner."

"I see it but I don't believe it," Michael uttered. "That's one interesting cooking utensil."

"Are you serious?" Golga asked.

"He's kidding," replied Shesla.

"If it's the sword of a master fighter, how did he get it?"

"Same as every senior warrior in Krystar—he earned it as I did mine. The king of Krystar awarded them to us."

"Are you guys for real? Both of you are elders, senior warriors?" He pushed away from the wall contemplating the revelation. "So you know how to fight?"

Shesla retrieved a sword from the sheath on his back and tossed it to Michael.

"What's this for?"

"To train with," Shesla replied.

"Are you serious?"

"We have a lot of work to do and the sooner we get started the better."

"It's the sword of a demon!" said Michael. "A junior demon."

Shesla put his arm over Michael's shoulder. "That's all we could get. Golga and I have trained some of the best warriors in Krystar, including your own Sensei Caleb."

"This is too hard to believe. What are you doing in Darkmar? How did you get here? And how can you train me without the demons finding out about it?"

"Golga and I were captured with Beelzebub and his millions of mutinous angels when they attempted to take over planet Krystar and depose the king. We weren't part of the rebellion—we're loyal subjects to the king. But we were corralled with the rebelling angels and thrown out of Krystar. It was an accident. But the king and everyone on Krystar and the seven outposts believes we are traitors. We're not. All of Beelzebub's angels transformed into demons when they were expelled from Krystar. But we didn't as you can plainly see."

"So what does this have to do with me?"

"We believe helping you will build our case for proving our innocence. Besides, we enjoy teaching and serving in the army and we want to help you grow as a warrior. Regarding where to train, the dungeon is by far the best place in all of Darkmar—it's private, hidden, and far away from Beelzebub and his senior demons. And the low-ranking demons and creatures of Ramkrad don't care."

"Look. We still have our blue diamond rings with our names engraved on them," Golga added. "They contain the morning star—the sign of the twenty-four elders around the throne of the king." He took his ring off and showed Michael. "Look closely and you will also see the king's initials."

"I see them."

"All demons of Darkmar, excluding those in Ramkrad, wear the black ring of Beelzebub," said Shesla. "The ring of a demon has the image of a dragon. No demon has a ring like ours. Our rings reflect who we are and we're true citizens of Krystar.

"The color of the dragon is black for a junior demon, red for a regular demon and gold for a senior demon," Golga said. "Our rings prove we never joined forces with Beelzebub."

Michael turned toward a small patch of lava popping through a crack in the wall. "All of that is interesting and I know you want to get out of here as I do, but I'm the worst fighter in my class. You'll be wasting your time. I'm hopeless."

"Where we come from, we believe in a thing called faith. Faith requires one to travel paths that don't exist to claim things that can't be seen."

"Impossible! How does one do that?"

"Everyone has a purpose—even you," Golga interjected. "When you belong to the king, strange things can happen—you're here for a reason. We're here for a reason too. Perhaps for you. All you have to do is take the next step."

"What's the next step?"

"Beelzebub is saving you for something, or you wouldn't be here," Shesla muttered.

"And we need to know why," added Golga. "We also need to know why your friend, Gabriel, is spending so much time in the throne room with the old demon. That's a bit concerning."

Shesla approached the fire in the wall with his back to Golga and Michael. "The next step is to begin your training. Golga and I must go." The two leapt toward the hatch in the ceiling and disappeared.

"Wait!" Michael shouted.

30

TRAINING IN THE DUNGEON

Shesla and Golga. Interesting characters. I wonder when they'll return. Michael impatiently at the hatch in his ceiling.

The next several days seemed to pass slowly. *I wonder how Gabriel and the peniels are doing.*

Knock, knock, knock.

Screech. Bang.

Michael stiffened. "Shesla? Golga?"

"It's us," Shesla replied. The two sprang through the hatch. "Are you ready?"

"To start training? Yes."

"Okay. Golga and I will come every day and work with you for up to ten hours a session. Agree?"

"Agree. It's not like my schedule is full of other activities. I'm all yours."

"Discipline, not just desire, determines destiny," Golga added.

Michael did a double-take. "Good words."

"Many will talk, some will start, few will finish," Shesla added. "We don't stop until you become a skilled warrior."

"Absolutely."

Golga unsheathed his sword and it lit on fire as he swung it about."

"Careful, Shesla, the cell is rather small."

The diamonds in the handle reflected the molten lava clinging to the walls. The blade was saurinite, a material mined on Saurine that was hard and lightweight and maintained original blade sharpness. Golga's presented it to Michael.

"It has your name engraved on the prime end. The messenger had a similar sword."

"What messenger?" Shesla asked.

"I received a vision."

"Okay. When?"

Golga sheathed his sword. "We'll begin your training after we hear this."

Michael told them the details of the visit. "I don't know if it was real or a dream. This place affects my head with the constant screaming, fighting, and the clanging of chains. The smoke, the ash, and the heat don't help either."

Shesla turned and faced the wall. "I suggest you take the messenger seriously."

"And get the sword of Beelzebub," Golga added. "His is the sword of darkness."

"How? I can't get to him. I'm a prisoner, remember? Besides, as you can see, I'm puny. That won't change even if I do learn to fight."

"Golga is right. You must pursue the objective. Watch for the opportunity, come now or later." He eyed him sharply. "I'll give more thought to the visions. Now, let's begin your training."

"Sword control," Golga replied, reaching for the sword.

Michael pointed the blade down and returned it.

Shesla placed a candle on a table in the middle of the room and backed away to the corner of the room, sitting down on the flat rock.

Golga touched the wick with the blade of his flaming sword as Michael shuffled backwards. Golga did a roundhouse and sliced through the wick without disturbing the flame.

"You missed," exclaimed Michael. He turned and grinned at Shesla whose eyes were locked on the wick.

Michael shifted his eyes to the flame and watched as the wick began to leaned over and finally fell to the floor. The three watched as it flamed out.

"Excellent!" Michael shouted. "Will I learn to do that?"

"Yes, with practice, practice and then more practice," Shesla replied. "A warrior of the king must learn to fight with precision."

"Hit me," Golga commanded, glaring at Michael.

Michael squinted. "What?"

"In the face with your fist," Golga added.

"I don't want to hit you."

"Go ahead," Shesla suggested.

Michael gave a confused look and then readied himself. He swung and missed.

"I said hit me."

Michael swung again, with more force and speed, and missed again.

"Come on, watcher. Hit me!"

Michael swung hard and fast but missed a third time. He continued swinging and missing as Golga danced about.

"You see, Michael, there's more to fighting than just striking at your opponent," Shesla uttered. "Fighting involves offense, defense, avoidance, and situational awareness. You must master all four and know when to employ each technique. Your fight objective is to win. Your life objective is freedom. We must fight to win our freedom. We fight for life."

"Exactly," Shesla said. "We begin with basic sword fighting. Keep the demon's sword with you in the cell. Practice with it. You will become a total warrior with many different skillsets using various weapons, including your body. You will learn how to shoot fire and lightning."

"Fire and lightning?" Michael asked. "Really?"

"That's why we're here," Golga replied. "To teach."

Shesla and Golga began the first day of class by showing Michael the sword, explaining the sections and how to hold and swing it. Shesla narrated while Golga demonstrated.

"My hands are tired," Michael said after the first hour.

"Keep going," Shesla barked. Training continued with basic guard positions.

"Okay, that's it for day one," Shesla finally muttered hours later. "We'll return tomorrow." The two left as quickly as they had come.

Michael attempted to slice through the wick as soon as the hatch door was closed. *I can do this.* He held his sword out, steadied it, glanced at the hatch was still closed, and focused on the flame of the candle.

Swoosh.

He sliced through the middle of the candle, knocking the top half to the wall and the other half to the floor. *Crud, how hard can this be*?

* * * * *

"Caleb, it's been forty days since Yofiel, Tamor, and Gabriel left for earth in search of Michael," Uriel said.

"Send a search party. Follow the signal to the lightbands."

"Yes, sir."

* * * * *

A team of four soldiers left within the hour.

"Sir," one of them said to the lead angel shortly after arriving in the cave on Kanah. "We found something on the ground." He held up two pieces of a broken sword.

"Michael's sword," the lead soldier replied. "Now let's go to the cave on earth. The signal for the lightbands is there." The team disappeared from the cave of Kanah and reappeared in the cave on earth. All of the angles glowed automatically in the dark.

"There they are," one of the soldiers said, picking them up.

"They belong to Yofiel, Tamor, Gabriel," the lead angel said. "Michael never received a lightband."

"Sir," another warrior called. "Another broken sword." He held it up.

"Probably Gabriel's sword."

"Sir. Two fire whips," another soldier said.

"Must belong to the peniels," the lead angel replied. "Our mission is finished. Good work. Back to Kanah, team."

* * * * *

Shesla and Golga repeated the skillsets over and over until Michael mastered them. They repeated the process over many, many months in the privacy of his cell. All the while, Michael's wings continued to grow.

One day Michael asked, "Golga, I can put the flame out. But I can't slice the wick without disturbing the flame. What am I doing wrong?"

"Show me." He watched as Michael went through the routine.

Michael swung the sword into the wick, knocking the wick to the other side of the room.

"You lack focus"

"What do you mean?"

"You must focus on the wick, not the flame. And your breathing?"

"What about my breathing? I practice the respiratory pause as you said to do."

"How many breaths?"

"None. I hold it."

"Try one and hold it after the respiratory pause. Don't take in more than you need. Minimize and simplify."

"One?"

"Yes, one." Golga patted him on the shoulders and left with Shesla.

Michael continued after they left. The flame grew as still as a block of ice. He carefully aimed, exhaled, slowly inhaled, held his breath, and swung at the middle of the wick.

"Missed! Darn it. Come on, Michael." He repeated the attempts and failed each time. Exhausted, he fell to his knees and dropped his sword.

Quitters never win, winners never quit? Isn't that what Yofiel told me? Yes, she did.

"Why can't I do this?" he shouted—the echo escaped through the hatch above. "I will not quit, I will not quit, I will not quit!" He picked up the sword again and focused on the flame and then on the wick. He shuffled his feet into position, went through the breathing cycle, and swung in a perfect horizontal motion. The flame flickered, then straightened.

"I missed again!" he shouted. Dropping to his knees again, he stared at the wick. The flame flickered. Then it slightly leaned, then curled and then slowly toppled to the table. He stared as the little fire struggled to survive.

"I did it!"

The smoke of the lifeless candle drifted toward his nostrils. The dim eyes of the dreary dungeon witnessed the birth of a master warrior.

31

THE PROMISE

Ssscrreeeeecchhh.

Michael was practicing some of his fighting moves when he heard the clanging of the chains to his hatch door, followed by the screech of metal on metal as the wheel turned.

Shesla and Golga don't come this early, so who is this? He saw the large silhouette of a guard demon through the hatch as it opened. The creature was too large to enter.

"Bring him to me," the demon barked to an attendant demon. The smaller demon flew into Michael's cell, grabbed him without saying a word, and returned with him in hand.

"You have been summoned by King Beelzebub," Gog said, in a thunderous voice. "Come at once."

"Oh, since when did Beelzebub become a king?" Michael asked. "He was a commander the last time we met."

Gog slapped him to the ground, picked him up with one arm, and pulled him to his face. "I have something to show you, watcher." He clutched Michael and flew further into the mountain and reached a large hole in the ground. He dove down and landed several miles down on the cliff of a mountain and released him. "Tell me, watcher, what do you see?" The creature nodded at him to move close to the edge.

Michael walked forward and looked down. "A sea of fire!"

"Yes, and what do you see in the sea of fire, watcher?"

"Creatures of various sorts, demons, sea serpents. They're in agony."

Gog picked him up and brought him to his face. "I can easily drop you into that lake of fire, watcher. So unless you wish to take up residence down there, then you will watch your words. Comply?"

"I will."

"If he didn't want you alive, you would be dead by now, runt watcher. I could throw you into the lake of fire and you would be forgotten. Or I could return you to your cell and forget to lock it. Who will protect you then? The Ramkrad demons would love nothing more than to eat you alive and defecate you to oblivion. It would make a more handsome you, pretty boy."

Gog snatched him up, flew to his cell where he hurled him to the ground, and hurried away. His two attendant demons picked him up and followed.

Beelzebub spotted them as soon as they entered his throne room. "Hello, Michael. Have you enjoyed your time in Ramkrad? How long has it been? Ten months, I think. Has anything, shall I say, good come out of your time alone?" He laughed.

"It's been a real workout," Michael replied.

Gog slapped Michael to the ground. "Address him as King Beelzebub, scum."

"It has been interesting, King Beelzebub scum," Michael snarled.

Gog punched him in the stomach.

"Gog, is that any way to treat our guest?" Beelzebub asked.

He bowed humbly and stepped aside.

The king of Darkmar stared intently at Michael as if he were staring through him while thinking of something else.

Did the demon bring me here just to stare at me? Michael wondered.

"What do you desire most, Michael?"

"You know what I want," he replied. "The same thing my friends want. Freedom! They want to return to Kanah."

"Interestingly enough, Michael, I have been contemplating how to connect what I want with what you want. The answer finally dawned on me. I like the word "dawn." Too bad we don't have any on this planet. It's always dark underground and dull above ground. Never mind about that. I wanted to hear your response from your own lips."

"Okay, so you have heard it. May I return to my cell now?"

"Is that what you want, Michael? Do you really want to return to your cell in Ramkrad? If you want freedom, as you say, then of course you don't want to return to the dungeon. If you could have your freedom, then certainly you wouldn't remain in Darkmar another day. Don't you wish to return to Kanah? You want to leave right now. Is that right?"

"Of course, Beelz—"

"Then why don't we discuss your path to freedom? You can get what you want by giving me what I want."

"What do I have that you could want? You already have the peniels and—"

"Ah, yes, I do," replied the demon, interrupting again. "Now you're listening. You're correct to say we don't want the things we already have. We demons want the things we don't have and especially those things we can't have. We want more and more because there are always more things to want and it pleases us to get more. Funny thing is we both want something and we both can give each other what we want. I'm the ultimate consumer. If you want your freedom, then you simply need to give me what I want."

"You have my attention. What is it you want?"

The king of the demons stood and stared deeply into his eyes as if he were reading his mind. "I want the fruit on the Tree of Life in the garden of Kanah."

"That's impossible. No one can gain access to the garden and remove fruit without permission. They wouldn't grant that right to me. I'm just a junior watcher, not a senior angel. Besides, the garden is guarded by cherubim. Remember those six-winged creatures? You don't know what you're asking."

"AAARRRGGGHHH," the demon yelled. Lightning bolted out of his fingers and scorched the nearby walls as his anger boiled. He transformed into a ten-foot red-eyed beast with curved horns, long fangs, and oily-looking greenish-brown skin of scales. He picked up a flaming spear and hurled it to the floor near Michael. "Don't tell me what I already know!" His voice thundered through the throne room and echoed into Demon's Hole. He stormed the steps from his throne. The ground glowed like molten lava with each step he made.

The demons made way as he approached Michael.

"I reigned with the king of Krystar himself," he roared within inches of Michael's face. "I know the rules in Krystar and the seven outposts. I know who can go in and out of the gardens. And I also know it's possible to get the fruit. I have done so many times when I lived there." He stench of his breath left a film on Michael's face.

Michael held his breath and remained at attention as the beast spoke.

"Trust me. I know the rules better than you do, little warrior." He transformed back to his regular size and started back to the throne before pausing. "Now do you want your freedom? If you do, then let's talk. If not, then go back to your cell where you'll rot and never see your friends again." The demon hesitated again and eyed him. "Decide now!"

"I choose freedom," Michael said, pausing to consider the risks.

The demon seemed to relax. "Good, good. I knew you were smart." He turned and headed for the throne, before pausing again." I know you care about your friends. You may be surprised to know demons are excellent judges of character. You have character, Michael. That's why I won't try to persuade you to join my host of followers. I know you can never be persuaded. But not so with your friend Gabriel."

"You don't know him as I do."

"Granted," he said, heading up the steps and taking his place on his throne. "But I sense he wants more. He wants it all: the kingdoms of Krystar, the seven outposts, and Earth. No, I will not try to persuade you to join me for I know it is freedom you most desire. You want the freedom of your friends more than anything. I know you would trade your freedom for theirs. That is commendable. So if it's freedom you want, you must give me what I want. I want the fruit from the Tree of Life."

"Why do you want it?"

"Must you ask? I crave the taste and the rush of fresh life from the fruit. It will restore the beauty of my former self. Did you know I was the most beautiful creature in all of Krystar—more awesome and spectacular than all angels? I was as beautiful as the morning star and was called the son of the dawn. I am not certain of the power of the fruit but I must try. In all of Darkmar, there is nothing like the fruit from the Tree of Life and I desire it so—it's all you need to gain your freedom and that of your friends.

"If you want to save your friends, then you must go to Kanah and get the fruit from the Tree of Life. Do so and freedom is yours. Deceive me in any way, or fail in your mission and I will give the peniels to my demons and allow them to have their way with them. And they will spend the rest of their days in Café de Erotica for the sole pleasure of my senior demons. Are we clear?"

"Yes, Beelzebub. You made your point. When do I leave?"

32

BACKPACKED AND READY

"Tonight," Beelzebub said, standing up from his throne. "You will be escorted to the cave in space where I first saw you and your girlfriend—if my demons can find it." He showed three fingers on his hand. "You will have three days to locate the fruit and return here. Take this for the fruit." He tossed a black backpack in his direction and it hovered to him as if self-directed.

"How do I communicate with you when I'm ready to return?" Michael asked.

"You don't. Endor and Legion will meet you at the end of the three days." Beelzebub reached into his robe and retrieved a small, shiny black box. He opened it and retrieved a black opal ring. "You will wear this ring when you arrive at the cave. It has my image. We'll be able to track your movements. You'll get it when you arrive.

"If you're not back after three days, then our agreement is off and you'll never see your friends again." Beelzebub turned to Gog. "Take him back to his cell and prepare to leave within the hour."

Gog escorted Michael to his cell and dropped him through the hatch in the ceiling.

Michael fell to the floor and lay there, contemplating the promise. He knew better than to trust a demon, especially Beelzebub.

What are my options? I can remain in this dungeon forever, or I can return to Kanah where they'll think I'm a runaway or worse, a traitor, I must take the risk.

* * * * *

Gabriel came out from behind the throne. "I told you he would agree to go."

"Am I making a mistake?" Beelzebub asked.

"Michael has never cared for anyone other than himself. He's a young watcher with a self-absorbed personality who puts his interests first."

"Sounds like my demons. But we can't tolerate failure."

"He'll do anything for his freedom. He'll certainly follow through and get the fruit of the tree of life for you."

"He has to. It's our only option."

* * * * *

Ssscrreeeecchhh.

"What the—" The clanking of the chains on the hatch startled Michael.

"It's us," Shesla cried, looking through the hatch.

"Class?"

"Yes, it's time," Golga replied, jumping inside ahead of Shesla. "Why are you lying on the floor?"

"Halt," a senior demon shouted to Shesla from outside. "What are you doing here?"

"I brought food for the prisoner," he replied.

Golga put his finger to his mouth signaling silence to Michael.

"You are not authorized to enter Ramkrad," the demon wailed. He glared at his attendant demon. "Enter the cell and make sure the prisoner is present and alone."

"Michael, quick," Golga whispered. "Open your backpack."

Michael opened the backpack, unsure what Golga was going to do next.

Golga minimized and flew inside. "Quick, throw it in the corner of the room."

The attendant demon jumped through the hatch and landed next to Michael. "Are you alone, watcher?" the demon screeched.

"Yes."

The demon kicked the backpack as he walked searched along the walls. "Clear," he shouted to the senior demon. He jumped through the hatch and locked it.

Golga climbed out of the backpack and returned to his original size. "They got Shesla."

"What happens next?" Michael asked.

"I'll find out. You look rough. Are you okay?"

"Yes, I had an interesting encounter with Beelzebub today—in his throne room. I think he missed me after all those months."

"Beelzebub wouldn't have called for you unless he wanted something. What did he want?"

"He wanted to make a deal for my freedom."

"In exchange for what? The old demon is never up to anything good."

"He wants one piece of fruit from the Tree of Life in Kanah."

"Interesting. Did he tell you why?"

The two spent the next hour discussing the deal and what it could mean.

"I know all the rules for security protocols in Krystar and the seven outposts. Shesla and I know many of the guards and Council Representatives because we trained them. I must go with you to convince the Council to grant your request. Otherwise, they will certainly deny you. You're just an immature watcher to them. They won't entrust you with it. This is also an opportunity to present our case to the Council."

"But how can you go with me? Beelzebub will assign a cook from his kitchen to escort me to Kanah."

"He won't know. As you just saw, I can change my size and hide in your backpack. I can also make myself invisible."

"So, why haven't you and Shesla already escaped if you can do those things?"

"Because we can't get through the gates to get outside the volcano. The doors are locked at all times and they have sensors and other creatures stationed at the exit to detect movement."

"Okay, I get it. So what's the rest of your plan and what case are you talking about?"

"I'll convince the Council to allow us to borrow the fruit. Secondly, I will convince the Council that Shesla and I are not traitors. I'll present our case first before requesting the fruit. Otherwise, they won't listen to me. We have a strong case."

"Okay, Golga. Let's do it."

Clank, clank, clank.

The three heard the chains in the ceiling and the old wheel as it began to turn.

"Quick, Golga, minimize." He zipped it shut as soon as he jumped inside. "Are you sure we can get away with this?"

"I've got your back, literally," whispered Golga.

Bang.

The hatch opened and a scowling demon jumped inside the cell. "Time for you to leave, runt boy. Endor and Legion are waiting for you at the Gate of Darkmar at the end of the Tunnel of Ekron."

"I know where it is," Michael replied.

"Don't get smart with me, watcher," the demon roared. "Get going." The demon grabbed him by the arm and together they flew through the hatch where another demon was waiting.

Whoa! The second demon looks menacing.

They made their way through a tunnel along several passageways overlooking lava pits, fires, and other demons and creatures lurking in Ramkrad. Black snow and ash floated around without ever landing on the ground. The usual smell of ash and sulfur cascaded along the walls and floors followed by unrelenting heat.

A group of frog-looking humanoid creatures with yellow eyes, horns, and sharp teeth lunged at them from behind a crevasse in the walls. The two demon escorts fought intently, tearing the arms and legs from some of the attackers. Two of the frog demons subdued the smaller demon and then the remainder of the pack attacked the larger one.

Michael grabbed the pitchfork from the dead demon and stabbed one of the frog creatures as it clung to the back of the guard. It slithered to the ground. The guard sliced two of the frog demons in half and beheaded another. Three other frog demons ran into an adjacent cave and disappeared into the dark. The guard turned and continued onward without saying a word—he left the other demon lying in the path.

Michael followed closely in the tunnel until they reached the ledge overlooking the valley of Ramkrad. When they finally arrived at the gate, the senior demon unlocked it, grabbed Michael by the arm and leapt into the air towards Demon's Hole which appeared like a big black round spot at the top of the sky. They flew into the hole all the way to the Tunnel of Ekron. There they exited Demon's Hole and flew to the Gates of Darkmar.

Endor and Legion saw their approach and motioned for the tyrannosapiens to open the gates.

"What took so long, guard?" Endor sneered at the demon. "Did you stop for a picnic with your watcher friend?" The two archdemons chuckled.

The senior guard bowed, remaining silent.

Endor motioned for Michael to come forward.

"We were attacked by frog demons," Michael told him.

"Not my problem." The archdemon grabbed him, leapt into the air, and flew to the sky.

33

BACK ON KANAH

"We can only find the door to Kanah if it hasn't moved from its last known location in space," Endor said. "Otherwise, we're going back to Darkmar. That won't make Beelzebub happy."

"Can we fly any faster?" Michael asked.

Legion recoiled at the question. "We're going the speed of light, watcher. That's fast enough."

"It seems slow in the open universe." *If Beelzebub could find the doors to outposts, he could attack us.*

"The cave," Legion shouted. "Lucky for you, watcher."

The three landed on the ledge of the cave. "Here's your ring, runt," Endor sneered. "Stick it on finger now."

Michael placed it on his finger as they watched.

"Remember, you have three days. Fail in your mission and you'll never see your friends again."

"How do I contact you when I'm ready to return?"

"Don't you listen?" Endor asked. "Just report here in three days—with the fruit." The two knocked him to the ground as they took off.

Michael spotted the glowing pearl door, ran through the cave, and entered the forest of Kanah. "Golga, we're here," he said as slid his backpack off his shoulders and unzipped it. "Golga, Golga, are you there? We're here!"

Golga popped his head out. "Viva Kanah." He pumped his fist, jumped out of the backpack, and returned to his normal size. "You could have let me out on the ledge."

"I didn't want the demons to see you," Michael replied.

Golga thought for a minute. "Never mind." He surveyed the area and took in a deep breath. "Oh, the sweet smell of home."

"I thought Krystar was your home."

"It is, but so are the outposts. All have been my home at one time or another. Shesla and I have trained angels on every planet." He started walking down the path. "We have a mission to complete. Let's go."

"I'm with you."

"I'll be invisible in case there are others in the woods. They think I'm a traitor, remember? I'll reappear when we near the east gate."

"And then what?"

"We don't know how you will be received. But we do know about me. They'll immediately usher me to the Council for interrogation. They'll ask how I was able to enter the planet since the door should have prevented my entry.

"You'll eventually be questioned by the Council since you have been missing for eleven months I think. Who knows? They could decide to escort both of us to the Council immediately. By the way, the ring you're wearing, all demons have one. It's how Beelzebub keeps track of them. It doesn't work here."

"That's good to know."

Golga turned invisible. "Let's fly to the edge of the woods.

"Let's do it."

"There it is," Michael uttered, moments later

Golga reappeared and landed. "Are you ready for this, Michael?"

"As ready as ever."

"If we get separated, then let's meet at your suite."

"I have been gone for so long, I may be suiteless."

"Then get another one. I'll find you."

"Okay, Let's go."

The angel guarding the gate eyed them. "Stop," he commanded as the two approached. He unsheathed a flaming sword and held it before them.

"Why are you stopping us?" Michael asked.

"Stand aside watcher," he shouted as twelve warrior angels flooded the entrance.

"You there," a senior angel in charge of the twelve shouted. "We recognize you, demon. You are Golga, former elder, master warrior, and traitor to the king. On the ground! Now!"

Golga was stopped just shy of the gate. Guards rushed to him, confiscated his sword, and dropped him to his knees while other angels chained his arms and placed a lightchain around his ankle.

The east gate guard leaned toward the leader of the twelve. "The Council of Kanah has standing orders to meet with Golga if he ever returned, sir."

"That's why we're here," the lead angel said. "We'll take him, actually both of them." Turning to Golga, he said, "You, traitor, are an unexpected surprise."

"I've notified the Council of their arrival," the east-gate guard interjected.

"Good," the lead angel replied. He kneeled beside Golga. "Why have you returned, demon? And how did you enter the door? It doesn't open to filth."

"I'm no demon, sir. I've come to declare my innocence to the Council."

The lead angel grabbed him by the collar of his shirt and drew close. "I don't believe you, demon."

"Look at my eyes," Golga replied. "You're a lead warrior, are you not?"

"Silence! I'll ask the questions, demon." "He eyed his team. "Be careful with this one. He was one of the best warriors in the kingdom. Too bad we lost him to the dark realm." He glanced at Michael. "Are you also here to declare your innocence? Where are the two peniels and where is Gabriel? Did you leave them on earth?"

Michael remained silent.

The east gate guard returned. "The Council will see them now, sir."

"Very well," the lead angel replied. "Let's go." The team of warriors pulled Golga to his feet and headed through the gates.

The guard of the east gate walked up next to Michael. "They say you ran away to join the army of Beelzebub. Is it true?"

"No, that's false."

"You're lying. I see your demon's ring. You're one of them."

34

GOLGA AND THE COUNCIL OF KANAH

"Traitors," someone yelled as the soldiers escorted Michael and Golga through the streets of Kanah. The shops along the way closed their doors to show disdain. The troupe marched into the castle and floated to the highest floor of the atrium to Council's Circle. They landed on the mezzanine and made their way.

The members of the Council were seated at a semicircular crystal table near the center of a large circular room—each sat in crystal chair ornately decorated like a throne. The Council was composed of seven lead angels appointed by the king of Krystar. They planned and oversaw military missions and battles against demons to protect humans. They also ensured watchers fulfilled their training requirements while on Kanah.

The soldiers stopped at the entrance to the Council Circle as the lead angel continued forward with the two prisoners.

"You may release them," said Council Lead Uriel.

"Yes, sir, Commander." The lead angel bowed and returned to his team.

The Council Circle was adorned with twenty-four crystal columns filled with various patterns of moving fire. The floor around the perimeter of the room looked like clear glass, while the area in the middle of the floor appeared as a heptagon-shaped azure-blue crystal sea. The steeple of the castle rose high above the room and was made of crystal impregnated with a colorful gem—it flashed brilliant colors like a kaleidoscope. The walls sparkled like crystal.

Five guardian angels were stationed around the Council Room. Each had a creature on a leash of fire. There was a tiger with wings, a grizzly bear with glowing eyes, claws, and teeth, a white leopard with glowing green eyes, a white humanoid ox with a flaming spear, a brown humanoid bull with a doubled-bladed sword of light, a white lion with wings and eyes of fire, an eagle with glowing eyes, and a bronze-colored grizzly bear.

"Come forward," Uriel said, motioning to the two. They approached the Council table. "We're glad for your safe return, Michael. Golga, we're puzzled by your return and have no idea what you're doing here, how you got here, or how you entered through the Door of Kanah. So we are very much interested in hearing from y ou."

"Yes sir," both replied.

"We desire to know the truth," Uriel continued. "and hope each of you are found faithful to the king, but doubt it is so with you Golga. Are you both ready to begin?"

"Yes," Golga said.

Michael nodded.

"Are you familiar with the truth-flame, Michael? I know you are, Golga."

"No sir," Michael replied.

"The truth-flame is a revealer of truth; it perfectly assesses all input—facts, thoughts, tone of voice, knowledge, body language, memory, motives, desires, and emotion. It will not harm you. It's as gentle as light but it looks and responds like fire. The colors of the flame remain blue and white for truth but turn red for untruth. Also, the rainbow will glow for truth and fade for untruth. Are you ready to proceed?"

"Yes sir," Michael replied.

"I am," Golga added.

"Please step into the ring."

Michael and Golga stepped inside the twenty-foot ring of gold centrally located in front of the Council and beneath the center of the steeple in the ceiling. The truth-flame immediately engulfed the two.

Michael jerked his foot upwards as if the fire was hot. *Ah, it doesn't burn*. He touched it with his hand. *It's cool to the touch*.

To the amazement of the Council, the flames remained blue and white indicating perfect truth with no impurities or wrongful intent, even they spoke.

Caleb leaned toward Uriel seated next to him. "Interesting."

"Very," Uriel replied.

"Michael, please exit the truth-flame and take a seat. We'll interview Golga first."

"Golga, why did you defect with Beelzebub and why did you return to Kanah?"

"Commander Uriel and Council members, I'm honored to be here. I know you will hear me fully and will consider the facts presented today. Neither I nor Shesla defected. Rather, we were trapped in a sea of millions of mutinous angels when they were corralled by the king's army during the rebellion. Shesla and I were escorted out of Krystar with Beelzebub and his angels. We simply couldn't free ourselves from the pack. We were pressed in on every side in a sea of chaos.

"Uriel and Council members, my first piece of evidence is a ring. I still have my blue diamond ring awarded by the king when I achieved the rank of a master fighter and was crowned as an elder.

Shesla has his ring as well. Please observe." Golga held it up and then presented it to a nearby guard who took it to Uriel for inspection.

"As you know, demons have black rings with the image of a dragon. My ring is not black and it contains the image of our king to whom I am and always have been loyal. If I were a demon, the ring would have sensed it and changed to the black ring of a demon as it did for Beelzebub and his angels." Golga paused for the Council.

"Please continue."

"Shesla and I risked training Michael in combat techniques shortly after he arrived on Darkmar. That is my second piece of evidence. The demons placed Michael in a place called Ramkrad—the hottest, most gruesome area far below the surface of the planet where the worst of demons are imprisoned."

"How were you able to visit Michael while he was imprisoned?" another Council member asked.

"We were never specifically authorized to enter Ramkrad but as trusted servants of Beelzebub, we had no travel restrictions within his kingdom. We have full access to Darkmar, just not to Ramkrad. Few creatures elect to visit there—it's a locked-up, forgotten place. So it's rather easy to enter."

"Interesting," the Council member said. "And why did you train him."

"We wanted to prepare him for a day when we could join forces and escape together—we knew it would be a team effort."

"Was Gabriel trained?"

"We wanted to but Beelzebub was trying to recruit him to join his dark realm and kept him close. He was closely watched by Beelzebub and his spies."

"And Yofiel and Tamor—the peniel watchers?"

"Their quarters are located close to Beelzebub's quarters near the top of the volcano which stands over his kingdom. The area was closely guarded as they were."

"Why didn't Shesla return with you today?"

"A guard demon apprehended him while attempting to enter Michael's cell. I was already in the cell at the time and escaped detection."

"Understood. Tell me about Michael's training."

"We provided training in various forms of combat over ten months. We also instructed him in the ways of the king which including principles of leadership expected of a warrior. He's aware that all warriors must defend Krystar, the seven outposts, and humans with a blue or white aurora."

"My third piece of evidence is the Door of Kanah—it allowed my entrance to the planet today. If there were evil in me, then Sir Calidoor would have certainly prevented my entrance. My brown eyes are my fourth piece of evidence. They are not red as they are for demons.

"Finally, the fifth piece of evidence is the truth-flame. It has validated my truth to this Council. So, in summary, Commander Uriel and honored Council members, Shesla and I are innocent of treason based upon the following: my ring, the training we provided for Michael in Ramkrad, the Door of Kanah, my brown eyes and finally, the truth-flame.

"Thank you, Golga," Uriel said. "You may exit the truth-flame. Please give this Council one hour to review your testimoy and we'll inform you of our decision."

"Thank you, Council," he said, stepping out of the truth-flame. The guard returned and escorted him to his seat next to Michael. After one hour, the Council was ready to render their conclusion.

"Golga, please approach the table," Uriel asked. "The factors are complex in the multiplicity of events surrounding your case.

"The truth-flame did not reveal any untruth as you pointed out. Your blue diamond ring did not transform into a demon's ring, as you also pointed out. Beelzebub always confiscates the rings of angels captured in battle. Why he did not obtain your ring is unknown to us. But your eyes have not turned red as they do for true demons. Finally, as you also said, you were not prevented access to Kanah by the door.

"However, we are quite surprised and find it difficult to believe that you were accidentally ushered out of Krystar with Beelzebub and his demons during their mutinous self-aggrandizement. If that is true, while we trust the objective evidence presented to this Council, we must review our procedures and determine root cause and corrective action to prevent a recurrence. We don't anticipate ever having another revolt in our kingdom. The twenty-two other elders are still on Krystar. That we know. Do you know of other angels removed from Krystar as you and Shesla were?"

"None known, sir. Shesla and I have checked all senior demons in Darkmar."

"On behalf of the king of Krystar, this Council apologizes for the egregious oversight. We no longer consider you or Shesla to be traitors to the king. You are loyal warriors and servants. A proclamation of this Council assessment and confirmation shall be issued and proclaimed throughout Krystar and the seven outposts, effective immediately. Nevertheless, we will request a meeting with Shesla upon his return to Kanah, if he can escape Darkmar. We will also study whether it is possible to send a special team to rescue Shesla if we can locate Darkmar. But we doubt this is possible. It's a dark planet, hidden from light." He glanced at a nearby guard. "Remove his lightchain, soldier."

"Thank you, Uriel and Council Representatives, for your time, consideration of the facts, and your decision."

"Welcome home, Golga," Uriel said. The entire Council rose and applauded. "We will hold a welcome celebration for you and Shesla together when he returns."

Golga smiled. "Thank you. Uriel, if it is acceptable to you, I would also like to present a request for Michael."

"No, Golga. Allow him to make his case. We are mindful that you support him."

35

MICHAEL'S TURN

"Welcome again, Michael, to the Council of Kanah," Council Lead Uriel said. "Our Council will listen to your story, and we may ask questions to help us to understand or to clarify facts. Please come forward."

Michael entered the ring. Blue and white flames rose and engulfed him as the rainbow arced over the fire.

"Sometimes facts are forgotten or are misrepresented unintentionally," Caleb added. "The truth-flame helps to ensure accuracy and completeness. Just relax and be yourself. We are family."

Michael nodded. *I'm glad Sensei Caleb is a Council Representatives.*

"We were concerned about you and the three others: Gabriel, Tamor, and Yofiel," Uriel continued. "We sent a search party to the cave and to earth. They found the lightbands of the others in the cave. They also found two broken swords, which we identified as belonging to you and Gabriel. Please tell us the whole story from beginning to end so we understand where you and your friends have been and everything that has happened."

"Council Lead and members of the Council," Michael began, "the story I have to tell is quite incredible and will take some time to present if the Council will permit."

"Yes, please continue," replied Uriel.

Michael relayed the story beginning with his and Yofiel's visit to the door in the forest, their subsequent confrontation with Beelzebub in the cave, their time with Leah and Vince on earth, the kidnapping by Beelzebub and his demons and finally, the kidnapping and imprisonment on Darkmar including his loss of wings, his training with Shesla and Golga and the gala event.

"I came to know Shesla and Golga who, at great risk to themselves, visited me in my dungeon in Ramkrad—as Golga reported—and trained me over many months in martial arts and various forms of combat. I am honored to call them friends. Here is a ring that Beelzebub gave me to so he could monitor my actions while here. But Golga said it doesn't work on Kanah."

"He's right," Uriel said. "And Beelzebub knows that. Strange that he asked you to wear it."

"Perhaps Beelzebub just wanted Michael to be seen wearing it," Caleb said.

"I agree," Hadessah added. "You should take it off, Michael."

"Will do," he replied. Michael removed the ring and put it in the pocket of his jeans.

"Do you have anything else to add, Michael?" Uriel asked.

"Yes sir. I returned to Kanah to present a request, sir."

"Let's hear it," Uriel replied.

"Beelzebub has agreed to free Yofiel, Tamor, Gabriel and myself in exchange for one piece of fruit from the Tree of Life. He gave me three days to return, or the deal is off and we'll never see them again."

"Absolutely not!" Uriel charged. "You don't know what you're asking. Beelzebub can wait until Darkmar freezes over to get fruit from the Tree of Life. The Tree of Life is intended only for residents of Krystar. It may strengthen the demon as well as his army."

"I agree with you, Uriel," Caleb said. "The fruit will certainly enhance his power. If he gets his hands on it, he and his army may become indestructible."

"What reason did he state for wanting it?" Hadessah asked.

"He said it will restore the beauty he enjoyed while living on Krystar."

The red color of the rainbow fire began to consume the blue and white colors and grew larger.

"Michael, the red fire reveals impure thoughts," Uriel observed. "You know stealing is wrong and is against protocol. Once evil enters into the mind of a watcher, or an angel and is acted upon, that one becomes a demon and without remedy. You would be forever banished."

"I understand, sir. If I may ask, with all respect to the Council, is it right to allow our friends to remain imprisoned on Darkmar?"

"No, Michael, it's not. Perhaps there is another way to achieve the objective. Our army is too small to attack Darkmar. We're a small outpost with a relatively small contingent of warriors. The army of Krystar will not assist since historically take defensive steps as opposed to offensive maneuvers. They defend the kingdom—Krystar, earth, and the seven outposts—when Beelzebub attacks. And I don't believe the other outposts will join us to save three watchers. We would sacrifice more angels than we would rescue and they may take additional angels captive. But the Council will review the matter and consider possible options."

Uriel around the Council table. "Does anyone have any other thoughts or questions?"

"I have an idea," Caleb said. "We could create a replica and allow Michael to take it in place of the real fruit."

"Beelzebub would detect a counterfeit," Uriel replied.

“Only if he touches it,” Caleb answered. “If we produce a quality copy, he may never suspect it based on visual observation.”

“But if he handles the fake, it would not give him an electrical shock as the real fruit would,” Hadessah said. “He will be tempted to touch the fruit, fake or not.”

“Perhaps,” said Uriel. “Let’s discuss it privately.” Turning to Michael, he said, “Please give the Council a few minutes to consult together. You may exit the truth-flame.”

“Yes, sir.”

The Council members huddled together to discuss the option. After a short meeting, the members took their seats. “Here are our thoughts, Michael,” Uriel said. “We believe Beelzebub will renege on his agreement and will refuse to honor the agreement once he has the fruit.

“He has a poor track record of resisting temptation which means he’ll likely touch it for one reason or another. He’ll know it’s a fake at that point. Even if the counterfeit caused a shock, he’ll still find out it’s a fake once he tastes it. So we believe the plan will fail. We cannot knowingly send you to Darkmar without assurance of success.

“If we were to give you the real fruit, we feel he would attempt to grow more fruit from the seeds. The risk is unacceptable.

"So the only option that presents no risk to the kingdom is Caleb’s proposal. If Beelzebub handles the fruit, it would be after you and the others have left Darkmar. But again there is a significant risk.

“You, Michael, must decide if you’re willing to take the risk. If you are imprisoned, we will not attempt a rescue as said—I doubt we could find Darkmar since it constantly moves around in space and is cloaked in darkness. The Council recommends against your return but we will allow you to make the decision.”

"Thank you, Uriel and Council. I do not need to think on it any further. I must go and do all I can to save them. They're in this predicament because of me. I accept the risks."

Hadessah waved her hand at Michael. "What will you do if he touches the fruit in your presence and discovers that it's fake?"

"I will say that it was a test to see if he would honor the agreement. I will then tell him I will return to get the real fruit as long as the peniels are released. Only Gabriel would remain."

"And if he reneges and puts you in jail upon your return?" Hadessah asked.

"Then at least the peniels would be free. Gabriel and I would have to figure out how to escape."

"The plan sounds plausible," Hadessah said. "But it's fraught with risk."

"Fellow Council members, are we all in agreement?" Uriel asked. All nodded.

"Michael, this Council has one more test for you before you leave Kanah. Caleb will provide the counterfeit fruit for you after you complete it."

"What's the test, sir?"

"Caleb's class, your former class before all of this happened, meets soon. We propose that you prove your fighting skills to this Council. The Council is aware that you've never won a sparring match and we want you to demonstrate the skills learned under Shesla and Golga."

"Very well, sir. I will do as you and this Council request."

"One more thing. Do not discuss your mission with anyone outside of this Council room. Understood?"

"Yes sir. Thank you, Commander Uriel and Council Representatives, for your time, consideration, and your decision. I will submit to the test and then leave as soon as I get the counterfeit fruit from Sensei Caleb." Michael turned to leave. *The Council's plan is the better plan*. He caught Golga's eye. "Do you want to come to my class?"

"I wouldn't miss it for anything." The two flew to the first floor of the castle and headed out the door ahead of Caleb.

"What do you think of the Council's plan with the counterfeit?" Michael asked.

"It won't work."

36

BACK IN CLASS

"What do you mean?" Michael asked.

"You're doomed if you show up in Darkmar with counterfeit fruit," replied Golga. "Beelzebub will most certainly touch it. And when he's not electrocuted, he'll know it's fake. It will be a dealbreaker. At best, you will be thrown back into your cell. At worst, you'll be tortured for eternity and live on the edge of death."

"But I will say it's a test."

"It won't matter. If he were willing to let the Peniels go, then he would have released them to come on this trip. Look, you need to get to your class. I will meet you in your suite."

"Okay. We'll talk later." He started jogging through the streets. *I can't wait to see my classmates again. Oh, city that I love. Your light reflects the heavens above. Little Kanah—home of my friends. May our feet walk your streets again.*

What if Golga's right? I can't bear the thought of Yofiel and Tamor being with those dirty demons. He slowed his pace. *Focus. I'm here for them, am I not?* He viewed the arena in the distance and resumed jogging to relieve the stress. *They will be surprised to see me. Wonder how they'll react? Come on, Michael, you can do this.*

"Well, lookie here," Oren said. "Who is this that honors us with his presence? It's the quitter, the one who ran back to Krystar because he couldn't take it."

"Where have you been?" a student asked.

"Rumor is you went to earth and fought a demon," said another.

"We heard you found a secret door in the woods?" a fourth asked. "Is it true?"

"I heard you deserted Gabriel and two peniels on Darkmar," another sneered.

"Someone said you saw Beelzebub himself," Oren said. "The rumors are lies. We know the truth—you were on Krystar this whole time. Why did you return? You're not wanted here."

"Is it true you have a girlfriend on earth?" someone asked in the back of the pack.

"Class, class," Sensei Caleb shouted. "Let's get started. We have a full agenda. We'll begin with sparring and then I'll introduce a new technique. Michael, come forward. Oren, you too."

"With pleasure," Oren said, smirking as he glared at Michael.

"Someone loan Michael their sword since he doesn't have his with him," said Sensei Caleb.

"Beat him good," a student whispered to Oren.

"Michael doesn't stand a chance," another said. "Never has. Never will."

"You deserve what's coming," spouted another student as Michael walked onto the sparring mat.

"Déjà vu," muttered someone. "Prepare to lose, loser."

The two stood ready to begin while the rest of the class encircled the mat as they always did. All of the students anticipated a fight, though it was supposed to be a friendly sparring match.

"Begin," Caleb shouted, barely visible behind the students. The two fighters approached one another, words drawn.

Michael settled into a middle guard position to defend from attack and gripped the hilt tightly.

Oren looks eager to attack. Be patient, Michael. Familiar feelings of inadequacy crawled over him like a cold chill.

He thought about the countless sparring sessions with Shesla and Golga and the techniques drilled into him over and over. Gone was the shy, weak student of the past. Feelings of confidence engulfed him like the darkness of Ramkrad as he recalled the hours of training in the dungeon. *I can do this. I'm an expert fighter.*

As he and Oren began circling the center of the ring, Michael glanced into the bleachers and saw Golga. He looked at Oren. He looks confident. He glanced in the bleachers and saw that Golga was no longer there. *Am I seeing things? Focus. Be ready.*

Oren attacked with his sword pointed at Michael's midsection. He easily deflected his charge. Oren appeared confused by his foiled attack. His attacks had never missed before. He lunged at Michael again, without respite, from a closer position. Again, Michael deflected him.

Caleb moved closer to the edge of the mat—a look of intent on his face.

Oren continued to attack and each time was thwarted by Michael's defensive maneuvers.

Oren is getting angrier with each attempt. Good. It's *to my advantage. Always fluster your opponent, as Golga would say. Keep them guessing.*

Oren charged again.

Again, Michael deflected Oren's sword but this time he spun low to the floor with leg extended and kicked the legs out from under Oren, sending him to the mat.

"Ooh," the class sounded.

Shesla was hard on me but I'm glad he was. It's paying off.

Michael felt relaxed for the first time in a sparring match with Oren, or with anyone.

I'm in control. I can do this. Memories of his lack of confidence faded like dying embers on the walls of his cell.

Furious by now—confusion convulsed to a craze—Oren jumped up and charged. Michael deflected the attack, flipped him in the air and pinned him to the mat with his sword at his neck.

Oren knocked Michael backward. He looked around at his classmates to see if they were still on his side.

They looked as confused as he is.

"Go get him, Oren," one of them yelled. Oren appeared less confident, but continued the struggle in search of his former success.

"This is the same Michael who was in our class. Right?" a classmate asked another beside him.

"I think so," the other said. "Can you believe it?"

"No."

Oren overheard the comments and snorted, then dropped his sword to the mat.

Michael reciprocated.

Oren charged and hit him below the belt, breaking a class rule.

Michael fell to one knee.

Oren wasted no time and swung straight at Michael's face.

Michael deflected the incoming strike and struck his much-larger opponent in the chest with his fist, forcing him backwards. He stood as Oren lunged again. Michael deflected the next attack and kicked Oren's legs out from under him. While Oren was horizontal in the air, Michael struck him in the stomach, sending him to the ground. Michael jumped on top of him, placed his hand around his neck, and pinned him.

"Stop," Oren managed to yell after a moment of not breathing. "You're the victor."

Everyone in the class except for two or three of Oren's most loyal friends, shouted in excitement, encircled Michael, and congratulated him for his victory.

"Congratulations, Michael," one shouted.

"Great footwork!" said another.

"He's changed," another muttered.

"What happened?" Oren asked as he lay on the mat.

"You lost," a friend replied.

"Did that really just happen?" he asked, breathing deeply, gazing at the high ceiling without blinking. "I can't believe it."

"Neither can we," replied another.

Michael helped Oren to his feet.

"What changed, Michael?" he asked. "You're different. How did you get so good?"

"Practice."

"I would give my life to fight like that," a classmate said.

"I have," Michael replied. "For the last eleven or so months."

All laughed.

Combat Master Caleb approached the two fighters. "I believe you," Caleb exclaimed, shaking Michael's hand. "I believe every word you told the Council today even before your rematch with Oren. You could not have done what you did today without the help of master trainers, besides me that is. I saw moves today that I've seen only Golga and Shesla do. Good job. I'm excusing you and Oren for the rest of today. You both earned a break."

"I need it," Oren muttered.

"Thank you," Michael replied. "I think I'll go to my suite."

"Fine," he said. "Oh, I had someone deliver the item we discussed to your suite. But come to my place in an hour or so and let's talk."

"Okay," Michael replied. He knew the item was the counterfeit fruit but Sensei Caleb didn't say it in front of Oren and the others. He turned to leave as Sensei Caleb embraced Oren.

"Michael," Oren called. "Wait." He hobbled forward.

Oh no. Is he going to attack me or what?

"Good job. You won fairly. You did great. Please forgive my rudeness in the past. I was wrong. I acted big in front of my friends like today but I see how dumb I was. Forgive me. Here. Take my sword since you don't have one. You may need it."

"No thanks."

"I insist. Please. You need one."

"Thanks, Oren."

"See you around."

Michael stared in disbelief. "Wait, Oren. I have a wild idea and would like your thoughts. Do you have a few minutes."

"Of course. What do you have in mind?"

"You must promise not to repeat what we're about to discuss."

"Michael, I know I have not been your friend up to this point. I regret that. But I give you my word."

Michael explained his agreement with Beelzebub and the plan to escape from Darkmar with the peniels and Gabriel. "Remember. This is a contingency plan in case the demon holds me on Darkmar. If I'm not successful, or if Beelzebub doesn't release me, then I will have to break out somehow. If I give you the current coordinates of Darkmar, would you be willing to come with some of the class to help us if I don't return in seven days? You wouldn't need to enter the volcano, but wait outside the gates in the entrance of the mountain."

"That's asking a lot and I'm not sure if it's possible."

"None of us are sure, Oren. And you will have to leave here without notifying our leadership, or they may prohibit you from leaving."

"I know. Give me the coordinates. I'll talk it over with the guys."

"You must make them pledge secrecy."

"If we come, then we'll hide near the Gates of Darkmar, as you call them."

"When we escape through the gates, I'll look for you. But all of Darkmar will be on our tails, Oren."

"For sure."

"Sounds like a plan. I hope Darkmar doesn't drift too far from the projected coordinates."

"If they do, we won't find you."

* * * * *

Caleb put his index finger in front of his mouth. "Uriel, this is Caleb. I just wanted to let you know that Michael's match is over. Yes, he performed in a stellar manner. What...? Yes, I do believe him.... He couldn't have done what he did if he wasn't trained by a master warrior, a really good master fight. Possibly, yes, it could have been someone other than Shesla and Golga but I doubt it. I.... I.... Did I hear you correctly? Some of the Council members think Beelzebub trained him?"

37

SUITE MEETING

"Golga, are you here?" Michael shouted. *I hope he found this place*. "Golga?"

I hear water in my spa. *Who's in my tub*? *No, he can't be*. Michael slowly opened the door. "Golga. What are you doing?"

"Getting rid of the grunge of Darkmar that's baked on my skin," he replied, holding a stiff bristle brush. "There are no spas in Darkmar."

"Point taken," Michael said. "Caleb said the fruit was delivered. Where is it?" asked Michael.

"In the box on the den table."

How did I miss it? He found the box and opened it. "It looks real! It even smells real. Let's hope it works for Beelzebub." Michael returned to the spa with the counterfeit fruit. "Check it out."

"Towel please."

Michael flung a towel his way. "What do you think?"

Golga caught it before it struck him in the neck. *Pop*. He snapped the towel toward Michael. "It looks good."

"Caleb wants me to stop by for a visit before we leave. When I return, we'll head to Darkmar."

"Sounds good." Golga drew quiet and stared at the floor while drying off.

"Why so serious?" Michael asked.

"I can't stop thinking that Beelzebub will discover the replica. Bad things will happen if he does. Have you thought this through? I can't believe the Council is allowing you to return with fake fruit."

"They're not."

"What do you mean? We heard what they said."

"I mean they prefer I do not return to Darkmar but they're not preventing me as long as I understand the risks. You know this."

"Yes, I do. But the thought of fooling the old demon is gnawing at me."

"Me too. But I have to do this." He paused before leaving. "You know I have to do this."

Golga nodded. "I'll put the fruit in your backpack. See you when you return."

Michael jogged away. *Sensei Caleb's a chocolate freak. I'll stop and get some chocolates to show my gratitude for his support.* He exited the castle and flew to the only candy store in the city.

"Are you Michael, who they say fought a demon and was imprisoned on Darkmar?" the shopkeeper asked.

"Yes, that's me."

"Sorry, we don't serve traitors. Please leave."

38

COUNTERFEIT FRUIT

I'm no traitor. The angel of the chocolate shop meant no harm, but believes I'm a traitor.

Michael flew to Caleb's suite high in the castle. They spent the rest of the day talking about his time on earth and Darkmar.

"I need to leave soon," Michael finally said. He rose from the couch.

Caleb remained seated on the sofa chair. "Of course; but there's one more matter to discuss."

"What?"

"Some of the Council members doubted your testimony."

"What?" Michael sat back down.

"It's true. Some think you could have been trained by Beelzebub, or by one of his senior demons instead of Shesla and Golga." Caleb shuffled in his chair. "Hey, I believe you. So do Uriel and Hadessah. It doesn't matter who doesn't. I know how you have changed. You are more confident now. They don't know you as I do. But wearing the ring hurt your credibility. It was noticed."

"It doesn't work, it means nothing to me. Beelzebub made me wear it for the trip when I testified."

"Perception matters. You understand the ring is not congruent with who you are?"

"What should I do?"

"The only way to prove your story and clear your name is to go to Darkmar as you plan to do and return with everyone. Do that and you win."

"My plan is to save my friend, not my reputation."

"Save your friends and you won't have to concern yourself with redeeming your reputation. But some doubt you'll return. Understand that we've never had a case of demons kidnapping watchers. Angels? Yes. But not one has ever been rescued from Darkmar—even those captured in battle. Uriel admitted that we don't know where Darkmar is located. It's hidden in a cloak of dark matter far out in space and we believe it's constantly moving like earth, the planets, and the stars. Some think Darkmar could be a disappearing dark star or even a black hole.

"Beelzebub wants to build a new kingdom of demons in the omniverse, the universe beyond the human space-time continuum. He calls it Genesis. But he is unable to enter since he can't fly faster than the speed of light to escape this universe. That's why he wants one of our caves. He believes it will provide a portal to Genesis. We think it's his escape plan if he is not able to defeat the king when they decide to attack Krystar."

Alarms began to sound all over the outpost. Caleb abruptly stood. "You must leave Kanah now. Do not allow any of the guards to stop you. They do not know that you have been sanctioned to leave. They will confiscate the counterfeit fruit thinking you have stolen it. Speak to no one. Leave now."

Knock, knock, knock.

"Come in!" Caleb shouted.

A guard entered as Michael stepped away unnoticed and quietly listened by the door.

"Sir, there was a breachan unauthorized entry into the Garden of Kanah," a guard reported. "The Tree of Life has been compromised."

"What? Impossible. How did they get past the cherub who guards the east entrance to the garden? How did they get past the flaming sword in front of the tree? Did we catch the intruder?"

"No, sir. We're searching now."

"Was anything taken?"

"Yes, sir, one fruit."

"Notify Uriel and the Council. I will meet with them immediately."

"They are being notified now, sir."

Michael slipped out of the door, raced away, and burst into his suite. "Golga?" He ran frantically from room to room. "Golga, where are you?"

"I'm here," replied Golga, stepping out from another room.

"Let's go. Where's the fruit?"

"In your backpack by the front door. Get it."

Michael raced to the backpack.

Golga grabbed another pouch and met Michael by the door. "Let's separate so as not to draw attention. I'll meet you on the path by the woods and we'll fly to the door."

"Can you open a portal here?"

"No, I tried."

"Okay. See you there."

They dashed out of the suite, leaving the door wide open. Michael sprinted through the streets toward the east gate. "Golga, are you still with me?" There was no response and so he took to the air.

"Halt there," shouted the angel guarding the east gate.

Michael attempted to escape but the guard shot a bolt of lightning that exploded around him, stopping his forward momentum and causing him to fall to the ground.

"You were ordered to stop, watcher," he barked. "Your clearance must be verified. There's a reason the alarms are sounding all over the city." The guard scanned him with laser rays from his eyes. "Interesting. You have been granted special clearance by the Council and are ordered to leave the city. Go now."

The Council must have cleared me to leave after all. He flew through the gate and over the path in the direction of the woods.

"Golga? Golga, where are you?" Silence pervaded the forest—only the wind acknowledged his call. *He's not here yet. Where did he go*? After waiting for an hour, Michael took to the sky. *Perhaps he's waiting at the door.* He landed by the door, turned the blue diamond doorknob and entered the cave.

"Golga, are you here?" He searched the cave and the ledge. He sat down and held his ring up toward the stars.

Nothing. Did Golga and the demons leave without me? Surely not. Beelzebub is desperate for the package—this I know. A noise jolted the silence.

"Michael, Michael!" Golga called from the pearl door.

Michael twisted and looked toward the mouth of the cave. "Golga, I'm here. On the ledge." He ran to the entrance and spotted the silhouette of a figure standing in the doorway at the opposite end. "Come on, Golga. Let's go."

"No, you need to come here."

"But Endor and Legion will be here any moment." He shrugged and then jogged through the cave.

"What are you doing?" Michael asked, exiting through the pearl door. He was startled by a shadowy figure behind Golga. "Who's that? Oh, Sensei Caleb. What are you doing here, sir? What's going on?"

"I was caught with the real fruit," Golga said.

"What do you mean?"

"I stole it."

"What?"

"You two have been summoned to the Council," Caleb interjected. "I came to bring you two back with me."

"But Beelzebub is waiting."

"The Council is expecting us," replied Caleb. "The demon can wait."

39

CAUGHT

"Golga, please come forward," Council Lead Uriel said as soon as they arrive with the escort team.

Caleb took his place at the table with the other six Council members.

"There was a breach in the Garden of Kanah today and fruit was removed from the Tree of Life without authorization," Uriel said. "A review of the scanners reveals it was you, Golga."

Michael glanced at Golga.

"You entered the garden undetected, defeated the flaming sword, and took the fruit from the Tree of Life," Uriel continued.

"You know the protocol of this Council. The members will ask questions about the breach. Please enter the truth-flame."

Blue and white flames rose and surrounded Golga as the rainbow arched overhead. A small red flame appeared and grew until it filled the ring. The rainbow faded.

"Golga, as you see, the flame has turned red because you entered the garden and removed fruit without authorization. You purposely disobeyed our decision. I would like to ask the first question which is one the whole Council wants to know. Why did you do it?"

"To save our friends in Darkmar."

"Was Michael aware of your plan?"

"No. We both believed the Council would grant his request to take real fruit to Darkmar. I decided to steal it after the Council denied his request. You said that Michael would be walking into a trap with counterfeit fruit. Yet, the decision of this Council would allow him to do so. Everyone on the Council believes Beelzebub will touch the fruit and discover that it is fake. Beelzebub would torture Michael and the others for eternity. I don't think he would kill them. He knows their spirit would return to Krystar where they would be recreated and freed from him, but he will make them plead for death. My reason for stealing fruit from the Tree of Life was to save Michael and his friends. Please forgive me, Uriel and Council members, for going against the decision of this Council. For that I am guilty."

"Your decision to steal the fruit, when you were aware of our decision to use the counterfeit, constitutes disobedience of a Council directive," Uriel said. "While your reasoning is commendable, you could have given Beelzebub and his demons a possible military advantage, as the fruit would strengthen them and make them more formidable in battle. Did you consider this before you stole the fruit?"

"Yes. I planned to have Michael submit the real one to Beelzebub and then replace it with the counterfeit after he is convinced that Michael has fulfilled his mission."

"Golga, you are an elder, a legendary fighter of Krystar, a highly respected member of the infamous Thirty—the honored league of the king's mighty warriors. How could you plan to deliver fruit from the Tree of Life, knowing it could compromise our ability to protect humans from demons—the prime directive of the armies of Krystar and the seven outposts?"

"All I can say is I would have done it to save just one. I am willing to give my life to secure their release, even to be cast out of the kingdom. We still have the opportunity to save them, or try."

"How did you get past the cherub who guards the entrance to the garden and the same question regarding the flaming sword in front of the Tree of Life?"

"If I may first say, sir, and members of the Council, I apologize for my error in judgment and request mercy to spare me from what I deserve. I realize the seriousness of what I've done.

"Knowing the guard has four faces and can see invisible creatures, I decided to teleport directly to the flaming sword in the middle of the garden instead of minimizing and making myself invisible. I also knew I could not transport beyond the boundary imposed by the guardian sword.

I moved the flaming sword out of its protective domain and substituted my sword in its place. I fought the flaming sword, moved it aside causing it to flame out and fall to the ground and placed my sword in the eternal flame. I was then able to get past the flame as my sword permitted my passage. So I approached the tree and took the fruit. The alarm sounded. I grabbed my sword and teleported out before time stopped and froze me in place. It did partially affect me but I was able to keep moving."

"Fewer than five warriors in our entire kingdom could defeat the flaming sword and do what you did," Uriel said.

"You are truly a mighty warrior," Caleb added.

"Here, here," Hadessah murmured.

"The eternal flame accepted your sword because it's identical to the sword of the eternal flame—a master sword," Uriel replied, glancing at the other Council members. "We must change the static eternal flame to a dynamic flame so that the guardian sword can never be separated from the eternal flame as was done." The entire Council nodded.

"Golga, we agree that you were never disloyal to the king, and you are commended for attempting to save your friends," Uriel said. "But you stole the fruit. For such an act an angel would be found guilty and removed from the Kingdom. Once disbanded from the kingdom, you would transform into a true demon. But this was a test."

Michael noted a look of confusion across Gabriel's face.

"A test? Sir, I do not understand."

"Gabriel. This Council was not completely convinced of your immunity to evil since you have been in Darkmar for many years now. We wanted to see if you would allow your friends to be tortured, given the high probability that Beelzebub would touch the fruit and punish them for upon learning that it was fake. You made the better choice by chosing life over protocol. You will not be charged for disobeying a Council directive. Your case is dismissed."

"Thank you, Uriel and Council members."

"We agree with the plan to switch the fruit in Darkmar, though there it still presents significant risk," Hadessah added.

"Is this Council saying that Michael and I may take the real fruit to Darkmar?"

"We are," replied Uriel. "You are free to go."

"Uriel and Council members, I plan to return to Darkmar with Michael. We will do all we can to save Yofiel, Tamor, Shesla, and Gabriel. But I have a request."

"Before you do, we have one more item to discuss. Where's the real fruit?"

"It's in Michael's backpack, sir," Golga replied. "I placed it there when he was visiting with you."

Uriel glanced at Michael. "Come forward, Michael."

Michael approached the table.

"Do you have the real fruit and where is the counterfeit?"

"I have the counterfeit, sir, in my backpack," Michael replied. He retrieved the counterfeit.

"And the real fruit?"

"Here, sir," Golga replied. "In my pouch."

"Good. Exchange them so that Michael presents the real fruit to Beelzebub. Once you show the real fruit to Beelzebub, Michael, you or Golga must swap it for the fake when it's safe to do so—after he gets shocked by the real fruit, of course. It pains me to say this, for it would mean we would never see you again but if you two are unable to return, then the fruit from the Tree of Life must be hidden so that no demon will ever find it. You know the real fruit cannot be destroyed because it's a source of eternal life and can never be extinguished."

"We understand, sir," both said.

"Okay, Golga, what else did you wish to discuss?"

"Thank you. We humbly request that the Council direct the Army of Kanah to Darkmar."

"Why, Golga?" Uriel demanded. "Did we not just agree on a plan?

"My request is predicated on Beelzebub reneging on the agreement. He will not honor his word, Sir. I respectfully offer three reasons why I believe it is in the best interest of the Council to send the army."

"First, Beelzebub plans to marry Yofiel and produce a prince. A prince is coming, sir—a prince of the bottomless pit, as the prophecy says. We can delay the fulfillment of the prophecy. Second, if Beelzebub can grow more fruit from the seeds, then he will be able to provide fruit for his entire army. Instead of dying on the battlefield from their injuries—causing their spirits to slither away to Ramkrad—they could continue fighting. There will be no stopping them. Lastly, we will lose three watchers and an elder to Darkmar."

The members of the Council conferred together. Turning to Golga, Uriel said, "We agree with everything you said. But we cannot go to Darkmar. We'll lose more warriors than we could possibly save and that assumes we can locate Darkmar and the prisoners, a highly doubtful endeavor. Second, the fruit from the Tree of Life is an instrument for life. To Beelzebub, however, the fruit is an instrument for death. We will not go to Darkmar and fight for what is essentially a weapon. We do not fight for weapons. We fight for life. Also, the prophecy you speak of is a predestined truth that will be fulfilled regardless of events. We can't stop what the king has ordained. It will be fulfilled as the prophecy says."

"Yes, sir, I understand," Golga replied. "Thank you and Council members for your consideration."

"Stick to the original plan, Golga," Uriel charged.

"Yes sir."

"May we discuss Gabriel?" Michael asked.

"Please," Uriel replied.

"I fear Gabriel may have defected to the army of Beelzebub. It's a mystery as to why he has chosen to join the dark realm."

"Have faith," Uriel said. "His purpose will soon be revealed—good or bad. You two must return soon, so you are free to go."

Michael and Golga left the Council room, exited the castle, and headed for the door.

"Are you ready for this?" Golga asked.

40

BACK TO DARKMAR

Michael and Golga ran through the east gate and flew as fast as they could.

"There's the area," Michael shouted after a short flight.

"Okay."

They landed by the door, entered the cave, and hurried to the ledge.

"They're not here!" Michael said.

"Who?"

"Endor and Legion."

"Relax. Your ring should work now. Lift your hand."

Michael aimed the demon's ring toward the stars.

"I see something," muttered Golga moments later. "Over there."

"Quick, mini—"

Golga minimized and jumped into Michael's backpack before Michael finished his sentence.

Endor and Legion arrived in a flame of fire and landed with swords drawn in case of an ambush.

"Do you have the fruit from the Tree of Life?" Endor demanded, storming toward Michael. He snatched his sword and tossed it aside and then he jerked his backpack from him. "If you don't, then you die today, watcher boy."

"I got it," Michael grumbled. "Like I said I would."

Endor picked him up by the neck and dangled him above space. "Don't get smart with me, little runt, or I may take your head off and kick it to the stars." He threw him to the ground and started to open the backpack.

"No." Legion protested. "We're prohibited."

"&#%X#%," Endor cursed.*

"We must be in Beelzebub's presence to gaze upon it, Endor," Legiòn added. "Remember?" He eyed the backpack and glowered at him.

"x%#@&,"* Endor cursed again and threw the backpack at Michael's face.

"Are the peniels okay?" Michael asked.

"You will find out soon enough," Legion gruffly replied. "Let's go, now." The two demons yanked Michael at the same time, causing him to almost drop the backpack.

Michael gasped.

"You ignorant, careless watcher," Endor snarled. "You could have lost the fruit in the cursed darkness. Your deal would have been dead."

Michael pulled tightly on the pack straps.

They leapt off the ledge and flew through space toward Darkmar. Hours later they landed in front of the gates of the volcano. "We must hurry," Legion insisted. "The Master waits." They flew through the Gate of Darkmar into the Tunnel of Ekron and on to the palace of Beelzebub.

They ushered Michael into the throne room. The king of demons loomed aflame on his throne. Two archdemons, Gog and Magog, stood with swords aflame.

Beelzebub saw the group approach, flamed out as he transformed into an angel of light, and began to shine brightly. He stood and floated from his throne to the floor at the bottom of the steps as Gog and Magog flanked him. "Do you have the fruit from the Tree of Life?" he demanded, excitedly rubbing his hands together, looking back and forth at Michael and the backpack.

Michael glared back, struggling to speak, mesmerized by his luminance. "Yes, I have it."

"Speak up, watcher," the king of demons demanded impatiently.

"Yes, I have it." He swung his pack to the front, kneeled, and unzipped it. "The mission was a success."

Beelzebub stopped him by grabbing Michael's shoulder to get his attention and then nodding at Endor.

Endor took the backpack from Michael and retrieved a white box. He smiled as he presented it to Beelzebub

"Bring the crystal vase," Beelzebub barked, turning around and slowly walking toward his throne, staring at the box.

Endor tossed the backpack aside and followed along with Legion.

An attendant demon brought a sparkling round crystal vase on a black tray. Beelzebub passed the box to Endor, removed the lid from the vase, and set it on the tray. He then lifted the vase and tilted it towards Endor.

Endor eyed Beelzebub and then removed the lid from the white box and slowly leaned it forward. Demons in the area gasped as the exquisite fruit rolled into the waiting vase.

Beelzebub's face lit with glee as the shiny red crystalline colors danced inside like a verboten temptress.

"Spectacular! Take the vase," Beelzebub ordered, eyeing Endor.

"But Beelzebub, you know—"

"Endor, I know. Do it."

Endor carefully took the vase and held it out.

Beelzebub gingerly reached inside. *ZZZZtt*. An electrical shock shot through his hand.

"X%#@&,"* he cursed. "Put the *X%#@&** lid back on. I shall take it in my quarters." Beelzebub held out his throbbing hand and

watched as it healed. He looked at Michael and then transformed into his monster version and then headed for his throne.

"I have done as you asked," Michael said loudly. "I brought the fruit from the Tree of Life. Now release us as you agreed."

Beelzebub stopped on the steps and turned sharply to Michael without uttering a word.

Michael waited and waiting for his reply. *His face looks like it's going to explode*!

Beelzebub's face turned red and he burst out laughing.

41

THE LIE

The four archdemons joined Beelzebub in his hysterics. They laughed and laughed until their king left his throne.

Beelzebub danced down the stairs and drew near to Michael—his gaze piercing him through. Endor and Legion followed closely behind. "Don't you know what has been written about me since time began?" he uttered. "I am the father of lies!" He laughed some more.

His breath stinks! Michael thought. Whew.

"You and your friends will never leave Darkmar now that I have my prized possession—the fruit of the Tree of Life. After endless years of waiting, I finally have all I need to put my master plan into action. You see, Michael, the fruit will be my wedding gift to your peniel friend." He whipped around, slapping Michael with his hair and headed back toward his throne. "We're to be married in a week."

"Scumbag," Michael uttered through clenched jaws. "She'll never agree to it."

Endor backhanded him, followed by Legion lifting his long leg and shoving it into Michael's chest. Michael fell to the floor.

Beelzebub didn't flinch but continued up the steps then stopped and turned. "I assure you she will. She was practically mine already when I had her dancing in my arms recently. We'll share the fruit during private moments in my quarters and together we'll grow stronger. The beauty that I knew on Krystar will return to me—Yofiel and I will live together in love for eternity.

"Together we'll produce a son, a prince to rule Ramkrad—the underworld of the kingdom of darkness. His name will be called Apollyon." He continued up the steps. "By doing so we will fulfill the prophecy that a prince of the bottomless pit is coming. Then I will take the seeds and grow a planet full of fruit for my demons who, along with me, will grow in strength. Thank you for helping my plan become reality. Dreams really do come true, my child."

"You will not get away with it."

"And who will stop me? We'll take over Krystar, the outposts, and earth. The humans will be our slaves on earth and the angels will be our slaves on Krystar. I may even rebuild this place. But some of you will be thrown into the lake of fire. We will rule the universe for all eternity from the mountain of Krystar—my original home."

"Liar."

Endor punched Michael in the stomach.

"Does not the prophecy say that the sun will turn black, the moon blood-red, and the stars will fall from the sky? I will elevate my throne above all others and will be worshiped by every creature. I will be more glorious and powerful than your king. Oh, that great day is now in sight!

"All of this is thanks to you, Michael. I even owe you for introducing me to my future bride." He gestured to Endor. "Take him out of my sight and let him rot in the dungeons of Ramkrad."

Endor grabbed Michael to leave just as Gabriel entered the room.

"Aaahhh, Gabriel, my son," Beelzebub crowed as he sat on his throne.

Endor paused for a moment—unsure who he was addressing.

"You see, Michael," Beelzebub continued. "One of your own has joined us. Unlike you, he sees the future and has made the wise choice to join us. He will personally command a legion of my best fighters against your king. He will be rewarded while you lie forgotten in your cell. He will share in all the pleasures of eternal carnality, infinite power, and indulgent realities.

"Millions of voluptuous peniel angels are there for the taking—and I mean millions—all of immaculate, unchanging beauty. They are and will always be young and beautiful—unlike my demonesses who are cursed. They will age and turn into creatures of the dark as my demons did when they left Krystar.

"Just think about it—the universe, the planets, moons, and stars—all will be ours, as will all nations and the glorious cities of the earth. All creatures and things in the universe will be ours: diamonds, gems, planets, fortunes, and wonders. We're talking about dreams, parties, and fantasies beyond the realm of imagination. If you were to join us, then you, like Gabriel, will be extremely rich with many mansions—why settle for one mansion which is all your king promises? Why not partake of the glory and the ecstasy that will be ours? Otherwise, you will rot in the fiery pits of Ramkrad with the king and his angels, where the only song they will sing is a dirge."

"I belong to the king of Krystar and I am his," Michael retorted. He eyed Gabriel. "You can't be serious. What are you thinking? You know we win in the end according to the prophecy. Beelzebub knows his time is short. Don't do this."

Beelzebub flew from his throne to the floor, strode briskly to Michael, and backhanded him. Michael flew into the air and fell to the floor.

"Don't quote that dung prophecy in my presence, watcher. It's a lie written by imperfect humans who were consumed with perpetuating myths."

"It may be a myth, demon but it's a true myth. You of everyone should know that."

"I do know it, watcher. But I'm not talking about me. I'm saying most humans believe it's a myth—a fantasy." He waved a hand at Endor and said, "Take this x%#@&* trash out of here now."

Endor dragged Michael out of the throne room by the hair.

"Gabriel, don't do it. Gabriel. Gabriel!"

"Someone shut that varmint up," the demon yelled.

Legion hit Michael with such force that he knocked him unconscious. The two demons dragged him to the edge of Demon's Hole and raced to Ramkrad.

Golga slipped out the backpack during the flight and flew away unnoticed.

Legion opened the hatch and dropped Michael to the floor of his cell.

I'm doomed. He was alone again—barely conscious after coming to—in the darkness of his eternal home, deceived by Beelzebub, separated from Yofiel and distraught at his betrayal by Gabriel.

Will Gabriel join Beelzebub and his demons? Certainly, Yofiel will refuse to marry the demon. This can't be happening. I'm with no hope of escape. He leaned against the wall and closed his eyes. *What am I going to do? This fate is unacceptable.* He stood up and stared into the lone fire in his cell, his breath slowing while his thoughts settled as much as they could. His body drew still like death as the light of the fire volleyed in his eyes.

"It can't end this way!"

42

A WARRIOR IS BORN

Michael was startled awake at the sound of the wheel on his dungeon door. *Who can this be? How long was I asleep?*

"Michael, are you okay?" Golga asked, looking down through the hatch. "It's me and Shesla."

Friends!

"I'm all right," Michael replied. "What happened to you, Shesla? You were taken captive the day Golga and I left for Darkmar."

"It's like this," Shesla replied, jumping down into the cell and throwing a sword into the wall. "I heard you needed another sword."

"Don't tell me," Michael replied. "News travels fast. Yes, they took it in the cave."

"Let me tell you how I got out. There are benefits to being Beelzebub's chef. He will allow nothing to get in the way of his delicacies and pastries which I prepare for him daily. His rules are meant for demons, not him. He hates any inconvenience and me being in prison was an inconvenience. But I'm glad that the arresting demon failed to mention that he found me here. No telling what may have happened if Beelzebub knew."

"Anything else?" Michael asked.

"Beelzebub plans to marry Yofiel,"

"I know. Beelzebub just told me. She'll never agree to it."

Shesla put his hand on Michael's shoulder. "He told the peniels you accepted a deal and left Darkmar. Both believe you have abandoned them. Golga and I have been unable to tell them otherwise since escorts have been assigned to them full time. That's his way of watching them."

"I would never abandon them!"

"We know, Michael," replied Shesla. "The old demon told Yofiel he will love and protect her always. She's probably convinced that he is her only option for survival. This is not good."

"She must hate me and think I'll a traitor."

"Hate you?" Golga asked in jest. "No. Traitor? Yes."

"You're not helping, Golga. What happens when he no longer wants her?"

"His evil will consume her," Shesla replied. "And she, being pure, will shrivel to nothing and die, or will wish to."

"Oh, wretched watcher that I am. There's no escaping this dreadful place. Everyone believes I'm a traitor. Beelzebub will be strengthened by the fruit and will eventually attack Krystar and the outposts. Wait. Did you exchange the real fruit for the counterfeit as Uriel said?"

Shesla shook his head. "I couldn't. Guards are posted in his private quarters. I can't get near it."

"All of us are powerless to do anything," Michael said, kicking a rock against the wall. This is because I delivered the fruit right into his hands." Michael fell to the floor in agony.

"Michael," Shesla called.

"Leave me alone!"

Shesla and Golga slid to the floor against the wall and drew silent. They watched him and waited.

After a few hours, Michael shuffled his feet and stood up. "Shesla and Golga, it cannot end this way." He walked across the cell and pulled the sword from the wall. "We can't stay in Darkmar. We must escape." The dancing fire in the corner of his cell caught his look of desperation. He rubbed his hands against his jeans and then rubbed his face.

Shesla and Golga continued to silently watch. "What are your thoughts, Michael?" Shesla asked.

"I see fire in your eyes," Golga added. "Maybe it's a reflection."

Michael nodded with a resolute expression on his face. "Redemption."

"What?" Golga asked.

"Our home." Michael turned toward them. "We need a plan."

"I like the sound of it," Shesla said.

"So do I," Golga added. "But what?"

"We must tell the girls the truth," Michael continued. "Figure out a way to get to them. We're not letting it end this way."

"We're with you," Shesla said.

"Tell Yofiel that I haven't left and that I'm not leaving without her. I'm no traitor. We'll escape before the wedding, together."

"We'll find a way to get to the peniels," Shesla said.

Shesla glanced at Golga. "We must go. Michael, we'll be back as soon as we get to the peniels."

"Be thinking about the plan. We'll talk when you two return."

"Right." Shesla leapt up through the hatch.

Golga started to leave and turned to Michael. "Did something change in you today?"

"I realized something. We're family and this isn't home."

"Redemption!"

"Something like that."

43

PENIELS IN THE PALACE

Shesla and Golga flew to Beelzebub's palace on level Altus. "I thought the girls were on Casa de Lues, one level down," Golga said.

"If we don't find them here, we'll go to Casa de Lues."

Beelzebub's palace contained fire-illuminated images and gargantuan life-like statues of dragons and demonic creatures. The halls and walls were illuminated by hot lava pits, torches, and strings of lights. The floors looked like the sea with specks of glowing crystals that appeared like the reflection of stars on a calm sea at night. There were flowers made of diamonds and rubies and flowing streams of liquid fire.

"Check this room out, Golga," Shesla said as the sneaked through the halls on their way to Beelzebub's quarters.

"The sign says '*WAR ROOM*,' Shesla. Let's go inside, just for a minute."

"Fine. Whoa. It's a model of the universe, complete with floating stars and rotating planets."

"I see earth," Golga said, pointing.

"No doubt this is where he and his commanders plan their battles with angels. Look, another room. Check it out. This is his private banquet hall. The floor looks like the night sky with moons and stars."

They tiptoed past Beelzebub's palace, dodging patrol demons, finally reaching his private quarters.

Shesla pointed inside. "No sign of the guards." He opened the door a little wider. "Here, my friend, is the only bed on the planet—a double-king-sized playground made from the bones of dragons."

"Can I have the head of dragon stuffed above my bed like that one, Shesla?"

"Who wants it? It probably drools."

"Never mind."

Shesla pointed around the room. "More trophies."

"Those are some wicked looking beasts. He has a reputation as a hunter who prowls around like a roaring lion with his demon-hunting parties."

"I see no human heads."

"Good. Let's help to keep it that way."

A rainbow of colored fire danced on the walls, circling the room like a dancing snake. Sparks emanated from the fire and formed floating bubbles of light.

The two entered the room, leaving the door partially ajar. "Yofiel, Tamor, where are you?" Shesla muttered in as loud a whisper as he could muster without shouting. He cocked his head.

"Where are you guys?" Golga blurted.

Shesla jumped. "Quiet! Do you want the demons to find us? You know Beelzebub wouldn't hesitate to throw us to the dragons."

"True." They crept along the floor. "Wait."

Shesla jumped again. "What is it?"

"The peniels don't know us. We know who they are but they have no idea who we are."

"We still must find them."

"We're under the bed," Yofiel mumbled.

Shesla and Golga glanced at one another in shock. "It's safe to come out," Shesla said. "We're friends of Michael and Gabriel.

"Michael's a traitor," Tamor said, still under the bed.

"No, he isn't," Shesla. "We'll tell you about it later. Just trust us. We must get out of here before we're discovered."

The peniels crawled out from under the bed.

Shesla and Golga lost their breath at the sight of them.

"Are you okay?" Yofiel asked.

"Flowers must blush in your presence," Golga stuttered.

"Whoa," replied Yofiel. "Thank you for your kind words. Are you okay?"

"Michael did not tell us that you were peniels."

"We are."

Tamor nodded in agreement as she rose from the floor.

"You are lovely too," Golga said.

"He always tells the truth—bluntly," Shesla said.

"Thank you," Tamor said. "We were looking around in Beelzebub's room and heard you two coming. So we hid under the bed."

"We thought you were demons or some other creatures that Beelzebub keeps for pets," Yofiel added.

"We're not demons," Golga replied.

"So you're friends of Michael and Gabriel?" Yofiel asked.

"Yes, we are. I'm Shesla. This is Golga. We're elders from Krystar. But as far as Beelzebub knows, we're his private cooks. We'll explain later. We have a message from Michael. He's no traitor. Beelzebub's the traitor." They told the girls about the events of the last few months and Michael's recent trip to and from Kanah. "He wants you two to know he hasn't left you here."

"The person you described doesn't sound like Michael," Yofiel said. "The Michael I know lacks confidence and is immature. But don't tell him I said that."

"That may have been true last year when you arrived, Yofiel," Shesla said. "But something about fighting demons, spending time on earth, being kidnapped, fighting with Beelzebub, and being thrown into a dungeon for these months has changed him. He went from being a sheltered watcher who had never seen a demon, to fighting demons and spending hours alone in a miserable cell, thinking about what matters—friends, family, you, Tamor, Gabriel, us. It's called maturity."

"How can you be sure?" Yofiel asked.

"Golga and I spent many hours over the past few months teaching him how to fight and about the conduct and leadership skills required of an angel warrior. He shared his thoughts and his struggles through the process. We saw him grow from a watcher who lacked confidence and skill to a confident warrior with solid warrior and life skills. He demonstrates leadership skills and is now a master fighter."

"Are we talking about the same Michael?" Yofiel asked.

"We are," Golga replied. "Blue eyes, blonde hair, had his wings cut off, traveled to earth, was kidnapped."

"Okay, Okay, I believe you," replied Yofiel.

"Why didn't he come himself?" Tamor asked.

"We haven't seen him in months," Yofiel said. "I miss him."

"He's a prisoner in Ramkrad and has the lightchain on his ankle—he can't leave his cell," replied Golga.

"I wish I could go to him," Yofiel replied. "The last time I saw Michael and Gabriel was at the gala of Darkmar."

"I'm happy to hear he did not desert us like Gabriel," said Tamor. "At least Michael was trying to save us."

"How sickening that Gabriel, his best friend, our friend, joined the demons," Yofiel said. "Unbelievable. He's a traitor."

"Have faith, peniels," Golga said. "Maybe something good will come of it."

"How could it?" Tamor asked.

"Faith is brightest when night is darkest," Golga told her.

"Good words," Shesla said. "And true."

"Beelzebub is a liar and he lied to us about Michael," Tamor said. "There's nothing good about that."

"But there is a part of him that wants to be good," Yofiel said. "He means well sometimes."

"Be careful, Yofiel," Shesla said. "He's deceptive." He turned and scanned the demon's room, crept to the door, and then peered into the dimly lit hall. "Let's go."

Yofiel gave a surprised expression. "Where?"

"To Ramkrad to see Michael."

"We can't leave," she replied. "We're prisoners. Our lightbands limit us to Altus and Casa de Lues."

"Not quite," Shesla replied. "Remember, we live here. We know the rules. Creatures called lookers roam the halls of Darkmar like silent glowing alarms—looking, watching, staring. You can tag them."

"What does tag mean?" Tamor asked.

"You touch them with your lightband and a light beam forms between you and the looker," Golga replied. "They look like white glowing towels with two black eyes and a halo like the flame of a candle."

"We saw them when we first arrived on Darkmar," said Tamor.

"Just tap your band and then tap the looker to connect your lightchain," said Golga. "As long as you're connected to them, you're free to roam but they remain with you. They're weightless. But you must return within four hours, or the looker will melt and what's left of them will drag you to Ramkrad, where you will be bound for as long as he is there."

"Quick, there are two of them now," Golga said. "Run and tap them. They'll follow. Trust me."

44

A DUNGEON VISIT

Yofiel and Tamor ran into the hallway and tapped the two lookers. They held their wrists out to show Shesla and Golga the flexible beams of light between them.

"Amazing," Yofiel said. "I see it but don't feel it."

"I do," Tamor said. "It feels like air blowing across my arm."

Shesla and Golga joined them and together the troupe made their way through the palace to Demon's Hole.

"We have the same lightbands that the demons have, so we can fly," Shesla reminded the peniels.

"So we're able to fly," Golga said as he jumped from the ledge.

"You can't fly," said Shesla. "Neither can the lookers. They float."

"So what are you saying?" Tamor asked.

"You can float!" Golga shouted as he flew around behind the peniels and nudged them forward, knocking Yofiel over the edge.

Tamor caught her balance and backed away.

"Oh!" Yofiel shouted as started falling before she began to float. *This is easy.* "Come on, Tamor,"

Tamor held her light beam and pushed her looker over the ledge. As the rope-light tightened between them, it gently pulled her over the edge into the air toward Yofiel.

Shesla flapped his wings once and floated under the peniels. "Remember, the light will tighten like a rope if you get too far away from your looker escorts. You can pull them along—just hold the light beam like a leash. Hold your hands out in the direction you want to go."

"Follow us," Golga said.

All floated down in the direction of Ramkrad and then they began to fly. After a few hours, they arrived at the Gates of Ramkrad. Shesla opened it with his key and the group leaned into a blowing wind of black snow. He tried to prevent the gate from slamming shut as the wind blew against so it wouldn't loosen any rocks on the mountains along the passageway.

"Shesla, the girls are gone," cried Golga. "I see the lookers."

"The peniels turned invisible when we passed through the gates. It happens automatically for prisoners escorted by lookers in Ramkrad. Invisibility keeps prisoners safe from the underworld demons and creatures."

"Peniels, can you hear us?" Golga asked.

"We're here," Tamor replied.

"The abaddonite is a mineral that weakens you, and it's here on Ramkrad," Shesla said. "Best we avoid it if we can. Let's walk."

The four journeyed along the path overlooking the valleys and distant mountains.

"Dragon," Golga shouted, breaking a long silence.

"Over there Shesla shouted, pointing toward a large boulder. The four ran and hid as the dragon flew overhead. It made several passes, blowing fire with each pass, before flying away into the horizon.

"You two peniels don't need to hide since you're invisible," Shesla said.

"We wanted to hide anyway," Yofiel replied. "It looked too scary to just stand there even if it couldn't see us."

"Agree," Tamor added.

"Look," Golga said, pointing further down the path. "Ramkrad demons."

"Stay down," Shesla said. A herd of wild demons came screaming by like a pack of rabid coyotes. The demons saw the two lookers but ignored them.

"They looked like wasp creatures of some sort," Yofiel said.

"There are creatures here that we've never seen before," said Shesla. "Let's keep moving."

They walked around tar pits, through tunnels and along ledges overlooking hot molten rivers of lava. Black snow continually fell beyond the mountain tunnels. Huge fire dragons and beasts of all sorts were seen in distant valleys. Shesla and Golga constantly darted behind large rocks and in and out of caves to escape detection. Screams, hyena laughter, roars of various creatures, and moans echoed from below. They finally exited the ledge and entered a particular cave in the mountain.

"This is the tunnel that leads to Michael," Golga said. They exited the tunnel and entered a large open pit. He knelt at one of the many iron hatch doors on the floor and began to turn the wheel.

"Let me help," Shesla said as the two lifted the hatch. on one of them.

Michael, who was practicing some of his fight moves in his cell, heard the noise and glanced at the ceiling. "Who's there?" He steadied himself against an unwanted visitor.

"Michael, it's us, Shesla and Golga," Shesla replied. "Yofiel and Tamor are with us but they're invisible due to being connected to the lookers."

Yofiel entered first.

"I see you, Yofiel, or part of you," said Michael. "It's as if you're outlined in light. I see your form."

Yofiel laughed. “Michael!” The two hugged as the others entered the cell. She slapped him.

“What was that for?” Michael asked.

Yofiel shoved away. “We thought you left us.” She frowned.

“But—”

“We knew you wouldn’t do such a thing. Beelzebub is such a liar.”

“But I—”

“You can say that again,” replied Tamor.

“Hear, hear,” Golga said, standing in the dim corner of the cell.

“Thank you, Michael, for doing what you did, for risking your life and your future for us,” Yofiel said. “It was brave.”

“That’s what friends do,” he replied. His smile began to fade as he focused on a small flickering fire on lava oozing through the wall.

“What’s wrong? Yofiel asked.

“We must leave this place.”

45

THE PLAN

"We can't leave, Michael," Yofiel confessed. "We are constantly watched by demons and even because of the wedding. We're prisoners in this awful place and they'll never let us go."

"What are you saying? We must leave. Staying here is not an option. You can't marry that demon."

"I don't want to marry him. But it's not about what I want. You know I have no choice. Tamor can't leave either."

"She's right," Shesla added. "The girls are Beelzebub's most prized possession. The old demon will hardly let them out of his sight."

"Can one of these lookers get them to the Gates of Darkmar?" Michael asked.

"No," Shesla said. "All lookers and all demons must be granted permission to enter the Tunnel of Ekron. Even if we're able to get them there, how would we open the gates? Remember the giants and the tyrannosapiens? And come to think of it, you're also stuck here in your cell."

"Which is exactly why we need a plan, guys," Michael said. "Come on. Help me out here. We're going to get out of here together. So, think everybody."

"First, we have to figure out how to get rid of your lightchain so can get out of here."

Yofiel blinked a look of surprise. "Whoa."

"What is it?" Michael asked.

"I just remembered that Tamor and I recently found a secret door in Beelzebub's quarters. They contain weapons. But we saw something peculiar."

"There was a knife floating in light between two points of a half-moon crystal vase, or that's what it looked like."

"Sounds like the knife of Beelzebub," Shesla said. "It's a knife made of light. The edge of the blade shines as bright as a welder's flash—as bright as the sun. The rumor is it will cut through anything. If anything will remove your lightchain, it will."

"Excellent," Michael exclaimed. "So the first action is to go to Beelzebub's palace and get the knife."

Tamor glanced at Michael. "And bring it to you."

"Shesla and I will do it.," Golga said. "What's next?"

"Don't forget to find the fruit—the real fruit," Michael said. "I assume it also in his suite. Uriel and the Council want it returned to Kanah."

Shesla pointed at Michael. "Absolutely. That's the second action item. We'll find it."

"The wedding has been moved to two days from now," Yofiel said.

Michael sneered. "Then we only have two days to plan and execute."

"Shesla and I will help with any necessary preparations," said Golga. "We've been tasked to prepare a feast for six hundred and sixty-six wedding guests—all senior demons. We'll add some ingredients slow them down a bit. It won't stop them from coming after us when the explosions begin but it will daze them. But thousands more will not attend the wedding and so most of the demons in Darkmar will attack."

"We will add some ingredients to some bombs," Shesla said.

"Where do we get the bombs?" Michael asked.

"I wish Tamor and I could help," Yofiel said. "This plan has to work."

"You peniels will have your hands full at the wedding," said Shesla.

"Let's finish the plan," Tamor said

"Demon work parties make bombs in the pits of Ramkrad for warring against angels," Michael said. "They stockpile them in pits and caves. So the third action is to get them."

"And place them where?" Golga asked.

"The gates of Ramkrad and everywhere else including Demon's Hole, around the wedding venue on Flavium, Beelzebub's palace, and from the Tunnel of Ekron to the Gates of Darkmar. That's the fourth action item."

"We should also place some on level Flavium where the wedding is to take place," Shesla added.

"Exactly," Michael replied.

"We can use your backpack and I'll get more so Shesla and I can help gather all the bombs we need," Golga said.

"So far, so good," Tamor said. "What next?"

"The fifth action is for the three of us to fly from Ramkrad to Flavium one hour before the wedding and find you peniels," Michael said. "We'll remove your lightbands with the knife. Then we'll rush to the Gates of Darkmar as fast as we can. We should be able to fly."

"It depends on the abaddonite," Shesla said.

"Yes and we must be prepared to improvise," Yofiel said. "Expect surprises. The plan sounds too simple to work."

"Simple is good," observed Shesla. "Plan the work and then work the plan."

"Yofiel makes a valid point," Michael admitted. "We don't know what we don't know, so we must be situationally aware and respond accordingly. If we get separated, then meet at the gates."

"And this gets us to action six," Shesla pointed out. "We ignite all of the bombs when we arrive at the gates."

"The high-pressure valves on the outside of the mountain are designed to spew hot lava," said Golga. "So we'll place a few of the bombs on the valves to set them off. The demons will think the volcano is exploding."

"Add it to action item four too," Michael replied. "The plan is coming together, team."

"I suggest we place a bomb at the central valve in the Tunnel of Ekron," Golga added. "The giants at the gates will hear the explosion, see the smoke in the tunnel and quickly open the gates."

"Good idea, Golga," replied Shesla. "Include it with action item four."

"That would be awesome," shouted Shesla. "Imagine millions of Ramkrad demons set free. Imagine lava exploding all over the underworld of Darkmar."

"More importantly, we'll be able to fly away as soon as the giants open the gate," Michael said. "Hopefully, Oren and the others will be waiting outside to help fend off the demons who will come after us."

"Don't count on it," Shesla replied. "The odds are that he didn't find this planet."

"While I was on Kanah, I gave Oren the last known space coordinates and the projected orbital trajectory. He will calculate the expected location of this planet and hopefully join us with the rest of our classmates."

"We won't be safe until we reach space and then outfly the demons if they chase us," Golga said.

"Escaping through the gates and flying away is action seven!" muttered Yofiel. "The plan is getting complex!"

"Think freedom!" replied Shesla.

Tamor nodded. "We do."

"The demons will be surprised when they find out we used their bombs against them," Golga observed.

"Team, we have a plan," said Michael. "Simple? Not so much. Risky? Much."

"It will work," Shesla replied.

"It must," Michael replied. "Shesla, could you bring some bombs to the gates?"

"Make that action eight," Golga said.

Yofiel cocked her head. "If Oren comes, what will they do?"

"They'll set off explosions on the volcano and surrounding areas to confuse the demons and get them off our trail. I'm to meet him and his team outside, above the gates somewhere."

"But Oren doesn't know we'll be breaking out earlier, Michael, because of the wedding," Yofiel said. "Will he come too late?"

"He said they would come early to review the landscape and set up," Michael replied.

"Remember, the atmosphere is thick and visibility is nonexistent," Shesla said. "Everyone stay close when we fly away, but don't stop in case you're being pursued. Golga and I will find you once we're in space. Just keep flying."

"Don't forget we have to evade detection by Fierian, the dragon," said Tamor.

"True," Michael nodded. "Any other questions?"

"Will abaddonite prevent our flying?" Yofiel asked.

"We will be weakened but it's not as strong above the surface as it is underground," Shesla replied.

"Any other questions?" Michael asked.

"We have the plan," Shesla said. "We execute in two days."

"Three hours before the wedding," Michael added.

46

GABRIEL AND THE ARACHTOIDS

"Okay, let's go," Shesla said. Everyone hugged and then departed, leaving Michael alone. The group traveled the dark paths and rocky caves on their way to the ledge outside of the mountain.

"Shesla," Golga whispered, "we're being followed."

"I noticed."

A group of eight green-eyed, humanoid hornet-looking creatures was stalking them. A spear barely missed Tamor though she was invisible. The four rushed frantically through intermittent caves and narrow passageways overlooking molten lava pits and creatures from the lower world. The demons gained on them as they swarmed through the tunnels. Closer and closer they came. Shesla began fighting the first one to catch them.

Another creature flew over a ledge inside a tunnel and attempted to sting Golga. Tamor gripped a rock and smashed it in the head. The demon was barely fazed but it bought enough time for her to unsheathe her sword and thrust it into its belly—neon-green goo came streaming out as the creature fell to the ground. It melted into a green gooey pile and slithered away.

Yofiel unsheathed her sword, ran up behind the creature that Shesla was fighting and sliced through its neck.

"Thanks, Yofiel," Shesla said. "Let's go."

The four ran through the cave, stopping here and there to fight the remaining six. Shesla, Golga, Yofiel, and Tamor exited the tunnel onto the passageway overlooking the valley of Ramkrad.

"Look, Ishnob the dragon," Golga shouted after spotting the beast in the sky. The dragon let out an ear-piercing screech as it flew overhead and circled.

"The green creatures are coming!" Tamor shouted. The group darted into a small crevice in the rocks as the winged beast approached. Ishnob released a hundred-foot flame, charring the demons and glazing Golga in the seat of the pants. The six green demons were annihilated in the blaze.

Shesla and Golga peered out as the dragon flew across the valley and disappeared.

"Let's fly!" Shesla roared. Shesla and Golga picked up the penicls and flew in the direction of the Gates of Ramkrad. They landed and quickly opened the gates and took to the air again toward Demon's Hole.

"My lightchain is heating up, Shesla," Yofiel said.

"We're almost there," he replied.

The four landed on Altus. The girls tapped their lightchains and detached themselves from the lookers.

"Why didn't the lookers sound the alarm when we were under attack in Ramkrad?" Tamor asked.

"They only sound the alarm when a prisoner escapes, or when a big fight breaks out," Golga replied. "They don't sound off for small skirmishes."

"Was that what we had?" Yofiel asked. "We were attacked."

A cluster of twelve bony creatures, called arachtoids, descended on silken ropes and surrounded them.

The four drew their swords. "What are these creatures?" Yofiel shouted.

"Never seen them before," Shesla replied.

They were humanoid skeletons except they had faces like spiders with eight white spider legs.

"They sure are ugly," Tamor muttered. "Big red eyes and two horns covered with hairy bristles."

The spider creatures exposed their fangs and claws and began spitting webs over them.

"Stop," Gabriel ordered as he came into view. "Back." The creatures stopped spitting and backed away. "What are you two doing with the peniels? Identify yourselves."

"I'm Golga and this is Shesla, sir. We're cooks for Beelzebub."

"We saw these two creatures being attacked and came to assist," Shesla added. "Nothing more, sir."

"Why are they of any concern to you?" Gabriel asked.

"They aren't, sir," Shesla replied.

One of the spider creatures punched at Shesla, hitting him in the stomach.

"Stand-down!" Gabriel ordered the creature. "Stand aside now."

Shesla doubled over.

Gabriel looked at the peniels. "What are you two up to? Or, rather, where have you been?"

"We went to visit Michael in Ramkrad," Yofiel said. "You've forgotten that you have a friend there."

"Traitor!" Tamor shouted. "You're despicable."

"Are you in command of these creatures?" Yofiel asked.

They're arachtoids," he replied. "They listen to me. Why did you visit Michael?"

"To check on him. That's what friends do."

"Leave us," he shouted to the arachtoids. The creatures quickly ascended on their silk ropes and disappeared into the darkness.

"Do you realize the risk you took going to Ramkrad? Lookers can't protect. Don't you realize that Ramkrad demons and creatures are uncontrollable? They could have torn you to pieces."

"We met a few," Yofiel replied.

"What do you care if we are torn to shreds?" Tamor chided.

Gabriel paused and met her eyes. His face softened. "Now tell me, what is really going on?"

"We told you already," Tamor replied.

"You don't understand. I'm not a traitor. I'm still your friend. I'm loyal to the king."

"King Beelzebub?" Tamor sneered.

"No, to the king of Krystar. I only pretended to join Beelzebub so I could be in a position to help. I'm just not sure how to help right now. I'm concerned Beelzebub will get suspicious of me."

"You should have thought about that before joining him," Tamor said. "Where is he now?"

"On earth. He spends most of his time there, manipulating humans."

"How do we know we can trust you?" Yofiel asked.

"Test me."

"How?"

"You decide."

"Gabriel, this is Shesla and Golga," Yofiel said. "They're elders from Krystar who are here for reasons I won't get into. They escorted us from Ramkrad."

"I've heard of you," Gabriel said. "What are two master warriors doing in Darkmar?"

"Don't tell him anything," Tamor said. "He may report it to Beelzebub."

Gabriel turned to Tamor. "Tamor, forgive me. Please forgive me. I'm no traitor. I know I hurt you. But I didn't mean to. I care for all of you deeply."

"You proved otherwise when you accosted us with your bony spider friends," Tamor said.

"I'm being watched and so I must play the part."

"Now that you know who Shesla and Golga are, if something happens to them, we'll know that you informed Beelzebub," Yofiel said.

"I suggest we accept the risk," Shesla said. "We need all the help we can to execute our plan."

"What escape plan?" Gabriel asked.

Shesla, Golga, and Yofiel spent the next hour informing Gabriel of the escape plan.

"I like it," said Gabriel. "Count me in. I'm with you, not Beelzebub. You guys have to believe me."

Shesla put his hand on Gabriel's shoulder. "Go see Michael. Convince him. Then we'll talk."

"He won't believe me if you two don't come with me. Will you come?"

47

GABRIEL IN RAMKRAD

Gabriel, Golga, and Shesla left the girls in the palace and flew to Michael's cell in Ramkrad.

Knock, knock, knock.

"Michael, it's us—we're back," Shesla said after he opened the iron hatch following the three knocks they occasionally used to signal their arrival. "We have a visitor."

"Who?"

"A friend," said Golga.

The three jumped through the hatch with Gabriel the last to enter.

"Well, what do you know?" Michael said. "The traitor."

"Michael, I'm not a traitor. I'm your friend."

"You fooled me and everyone else."

"Think about it. This is the first time I've been alone with you without Beelzebub or his demons."

"So what are you saying?"

"I'm saying that I pretended to join Beelzebub to gain an advantage. I mean it. I'm still your friend—your best friend and fighting companion as Shesla and Golga are to each other. And I'm still loyal to the king. Nothing has changed."

"You hurt us, you know."

"Forgive me,my brother. I did it for us. Now that they think I'm with them, I'm not sure how to put it to good use."

Michael stood there and stared at Gabriel before breaking silence. "All right, I believe you."

"Forgive me."

"There's nothing to forgive."

"Actually, there is."

"What do you mean?"

"I struggled with the decision. I almost joined them. He made it so appealing."

"That's what you call temptation, friend," Shesla said.

"But you didn't join them," added Golga. "That's what counts."

"I have an idea, Gabriel," Michael said.

"Say it."

"We planning to escape."

"So I hear. Shesla and Golga told me."

"Are you in?"

"Absolutely. So what can I do?"

"Let's talk about it." The four sat down in the middle of the cell and spent the next hour reviewing the details and discussing contingency actions.

"I agree we must escape before the wedding," Gabriel said. "Beelzebub moved the wedding up again"

"Yes, two days from now," Michael said, turning to a burning piece of molten lava oozing out of the wall.

"No, tomorrow."

"No!" Michael said, turning to the three. "He can't. We're not ready. When did it change?"

"He informed his senior demons before leaving for earth with several legions."

"Legions?" Golga muttered.

"Something about blitzing the nations."

"What do you mean?" Michael asked.

"He's after more recruits. He has the fruit now."

"Unfortunately true," Michael responded. "That's my fault. Who's he recruiting?"

"Humans. He's after the undecided—those with no aurora."

"Why legions?" Golga asked again.

"To achieve his quotas," Gabriel replied. "Those who don't achieve their daily quota are crucified and hung on the walls until their body rots. Then their spirit turns to mush and flies away to Ramkrad."

"Beelzebub is loyal to no one," Golga replied.

"Aren't they permitted to earn enough rank and eventually leave Ramkrad?" Michael aske.

"Only the sane ones," replied Golga. "Insane demons, the spirits of humans, and other creatures are imprisoned there forever with no chance of parole."

"So how do humans get the black aurora?" Michael asked.

"We don't know exactly," Shesla replied. "Demons influence humans who'll listen."

"Do they talk to them?" Michael asked.

Shesla unsheathed his sword and swung it around. "No. They shoot invisible pulses of dark energy, some positive, some negative. Positive pulses tempt humans to do bad things to get good things; negative pulses tempt humans to do good things to get bad things. Beelzebub's best demons can get some of them to have false beliefs."

"Which is exactly why we battle demons," Shesla replied. "It's a cosmic war where humans must choose sides."

"Humans are more valuable than they know," Gabriel added.

"And more wars are coming," Golga added.

"Okay, enough talk," Michael said. "We execute the plan tomorrow." He stood and tossed the backpack to Gabriel. "Put it somewhere out of sight."

"What's in it?"

"Nothing yet. We need to fill it with bombs and place them around Darkmar."

"It will be a job to gather the quantity we need," Shesla said. "We're running out of time."

"I can help," Gabriel said.

"Go on," replied Michael.

"I'll gather a group of junior demons and have them collect bombs from the storage pits and place them in strategic locations."

"Perfect," Shesla replied. "Except for one thing."

"What?"

"Junior demons will report it. They'll not keep quiet."

"I'll tell them this is a secret war game. And I'll say they were individually selected by Beelzebub to participate because he believes they have potential. Demons fight for status and rank to earn privileges such as visits to Café de Erotica."

"I like it," Michael said. "The plan will work. One more thing. Do you want to come to my cell three hours before the wedding, or do you want to meet on Flavium?"

"I suggest we meet on Flavium close to Demon's Hole one hour before the wedding," Gabriel replied.

"Beelzebub may task Golga and me with more requests for the kitchen, so don't wait on us," said Shesla. "We'll be there as soon as we can."

Michael caught sight of molten lava pushing through a hole in his cell. "This plan sounds too simple to work."

"I need to go," said Gabriel. "I have work to do."

"We'll head out with you," replied Shesla.

"Tomorrow then," Michael said. "Gabriel, are you sure about your part?"

"I'm good. I'll gather the demons now."

48

EXECUTE THE PLAN

"Golga, we're done in the kitchen," Shesla said. "Let's go. It's two and a half hours till 'I-do' or 'see-you-later.' Our assistants will do the rest."

"Time for action item number one," Golga chimed. "Get Beelzebub's knife."

"And number two," Shesla added. "Find the fruit."

The two flew from Flavium to Beelzebub's palace on level Altus. They made their way to the hall adjacent to his quarters remaining undetected by senior demons and lookers.

"There it is," Golga said. He slowly opened the door to the demon's bedroom and the two slipped inside.

"Wait, Shesla," Golga whispered.

"What?"

He pointed. "They weren't here before."

"They're his wedding gift to Yofiel," Shesla whispered. "They're called dembots--living statues."

Seven?"

"That's what I count."

"They'll see us."

"No, they can't. They can't get out either."

"What do you mean 'living statues'?"

"They're animated and lifelike."

Golga stared. "It's dark in their cages. I'm going to get a closer look."

"Not now, Golga."

"I'll be quick." He approached the cage and called out each one to Shesla as he pointed at them. "A twelve-foot red and black dragon."

Shesla waited patiently.

"A scarlet humanoid muskox-looking animal with horns like a rhinoceros and teeth like a lion. A muscular, baboon demon with two horns and teeth like a tiger. A snake with three heads and teeth like a shark. And a skeletal humanoid creature with blood flowing in the veins on the surface in dendritic patterns. It has two horns, sharp teeth, and a scorpion's tail. Who created these things?"

"We need to stick to the plan, Golga."

"Almost done. An ape with snakeskin. One more in the middle of the room is a humanlike creature with the head of a ram. It looks like Beelzebub with two circular horns pointed downward and hooves like a goat. It has a sword in one hand and a hatchet in the other. All of them have red eyes except for the snake. It has yellow eyes."

"Okay, come on now," Shesla whispered. He crept back to the door and peered into the hallway. "A looker is coming. Hide." They slid under Beelzebub's bed and watched the light of the looker as it roamed the room before exiting.

Shesla took a long breath. "It's gone. Let's go."

"Where's the secret closet?" Golga asked. "Turn the light on."

"No, we'll attract attention. I'll search this way and you go that way. Feel around the wall." The two searched the entire room for several minutes.

"Found it," Golga whispered, prying it open with the tip of his sword. "Whoa, look."

Shesla stepped behind him. "Three crowns. One of gold, another of purple musgravite crystal and another made of faceted black spinel—fascinating."

"Look," Golga whispered. "It's Beelzebub's sword." He went inside ahead of Shesla. "It's double-edged and made of a special black superalloy outlined in gold. I like the inlaid lightning bolts. Superb."

Shesla studied it. "I like the gold handle with the black spinel gems."

"Over there," Golga said, pointing. "A light in the back of the closet."

"We're taking too long, Golga."

"We're here aren't we? This stuff is awesome. It's the knife."

"This is better than I thought, Golga. It has a diamond handle and the blade is pure light."

"Where did he get it?"

"Who knows?"

Golga reached for the knife—it was floating between two points in a semicircular diamond vase. "Did you see that?"

"Yes."

"It tried to cut me." He attempted to grab the knife again but it kept turning."

"It's in defense mode," observed Shesla.

"I know what to do."

"What?"

"Stop time. Remember? Just press the tips of four fingers against the tip your thumb and then open your hand palm out."

"It won't work.'

Golga flicked his hand and the knife stopped rotating as time slowed.

"It worked! Good work, Golga."

Golga reached forwards and grasped the knife. The edge of the blade began to shine brightly. "The legendary knife of Beelzebub. It was thought to be a false legend."

"Take the black metal box on the table, Golga. I think it's for the knife."

Loud ear-piercing alarms sounded in the palace.

"What the—?"

"Let's get out of here," Shesla shouted.

"But the fruit?"

"We'll have to come back. Quick, disappear. I forgot. We can't go invisible now. Beelzebub put something in place to prevent it and it is especially strong near his quarters. He's panophobic and doesn't want anything to go wrong on his wedding day. Let's go."

The two closed the closet door and headed for the door. Six senior demons rushed in with spears of fire—all looked human with the heads of a ram.

Shesla and Golga unsheathed their swords and began to glow.

"Angels?" the lead demon hissed. "What are angels doing in our house? Kill them slowly. I want their swords."

"I want their heads," another cried. The demons moved in and started swinging and jabbing.

Shesla and Golga fought and sliced them until each demon melted into black putty and slithered away like snakes fleeing a fire.

"Hurry, more are coming!" Shesla shouted. The two ran out of the palace and dove into Demon's Hole to Ramkrad.

* * * * *

Knock, knock, knock.

"I was wondering where you guys were," Michael said as the hatch slammed open.

Golga retrieved Beelzebub's knife, squatted, and slowly cut through Michael's lightchain. "Time to fly."

"It worked!" Michael exclaimed. "I like the knife."

"Told you," Golga said. He tossed the lightchain into the corner of the cell and returned the knife to the box. "Here, take it. You'll need it for the peniels."

"Thanks. What about the fruit from the Tree of Life?"

"Here's a sword for you," Shesla said.

"Thanks. And the fruit?"

"We didn't get it," Shesla replied.

"What? Why not?"

Shesla shook his head. "An alarm sounded when we took the knife and we had to fight our way out. We'll go back when it quietens down."

"Keep the knife," Michael said as he handed the box back to Golga. "You may need it to get the fruit."

"He's right, Golga. We need to go."

"Remember to replace the real fruit with the counterfeit, Shesla," Michael said. "Do you have it?"

"I do," Golga replied. He held out his pouch.

"Good. There will be no turning back, friends." He knew he was talking to himself more than he was telling them. "We must escape or Beelzebub will torture us for causing catastrophic damage to his kingdom. He's going to lose many demons today."

"There will be chaos followed by a mutiny of the demons," Golga added.

"Agree," Michael replied. "Some of his demons will taste freedom for the first time when they escape through the gates of the volcano. They will be difficult to corral. We're going to create a mess. Did Gabriel get the bombs placed?"

"He should be finished soon," Shesla replied. "As soon as we exchange the fruit, we'll meet you in Flavium."

"Right," Michael replied. "We need to stay on schedule. I guarantee you Beelzebub will—he has a wedding to attend in two hours and he won't be late."

"Neither will we," Golga replied.

"Get your lightchain in case they come looking for you before we get away," Shesla said. "We don't want to leave any evidence of your escape other than you not being here. Throw it into a fire pit along the way." The three left through the hatch.

"Wait. I left a backpack full of bombs near the hatch," Golga said. "I need to find it." He searched the area. "Found it. These are for the Gates of Darkmar."

"We'll make good use of them for sure," replied Michael.

The three made their way through the tunnels and rocky paths overlooking valleys of smoke and fire and remained undetected by lurking creatures until they arrived on the path leading to the Gates of Ramkrad. They hid by several ravenous groups of creatures along the way. They exited through the gates and made their way to Demon's Hole.

"That's one ugly hole in the sky," Golga said as they drew closer. "Looks like a—"

"We know," Shesla said.

"Is that why it smells like—"

"Who knows?" Shesla said. "It's the only way from the underworld to the palace."

"A scary thought," Golga said.

"See you soon," Michael shouted as exited Demon's Hole at level Flavium.

Shesla glanced at Golga. "We have an hour and a half to get to the palace, find the fruit and return here to meet Gabriel and Michael."

"Is it safe to return to Beelzebub's suite yet?" Golga asked.

"Let's just go find the fruit and leave."

The two hid from several demons and lookers along the way. They reached Beelzebub's private quarters and Shesla cracked the door open.

"Hold it," Golga said, "Look. The statues."

"They're the same. Ignore them. We have work to do."

"I know, Shesla but this time the lights are on in their cage. I can clearly see them."

"No worries. Come on." The two slipped inside.

"Why would Beelzebub present dembots to Yofiel as a wedding present?" Golga asked.

"I can only imagine," Shesla replied. "I think they are for himself—probably to be used as guards for the palace."

"Perhaps he trusts them more than his demons."

"Probably," Shesla said. "Demons are not known for their loyalty—no one knows that better than he does. Let's find the fruit."

The two looked all around the room. "It's not in any drawers," Golga reported. "And it's not under the bed."

"I looked in the hidden closet," Shesla said.

"Oh no."

"What is it?"

"I found it."

"That's good," replied Shesla.

"Inside one of the cages."

"Which one?"

"The one that looks like the monster version of Beelzebub. Look at his right hand."

"We have to figure out how to open the shield."

"But the dembot will get out."

"It's a statue, Golga."

"You said they're lifelike."

"It's a display piece, nothing more."

"Are you sure?"

"Where's the knife?

"I'm not too sure about this, Shesla."

"We'll cut a hole just big enough to get the fruit. Here."

Golga retrieved the knife and pressed the blade against the shield near the fruit. "Did you see that? It cut like I was cutting through air. I'm keeping it." He returned the knife to its box.

"Get it," Shesla said.

"Sorry, I can't."

"You mean you won't. Step aside." Shesla slowly reached through the hole and grasped the fruit, then flashed a quick smile.

The statue grabbed Shesla's arm, yanked it forward, and slammed him face-first into the shield. The dembot slid his other arm through the hole, reached for Shesla's neck and began choking him.

Golga took the fruit from Shesla and tried to free him from the creature's grip.

The creature backhanded Golga and then returned his hand to Shesla's neck.

Golga tried to stop time, but couldn't. The black metal box spilled to the floor revealing Beelzebub's knife. Golga snatched it and instinctively sliced through the arm of the beastly statue.

The dembot let out an ear-piercing yell as his arm fell to the floor.

Shesla gasped for air and pointed toward the door.

"Quick," Golga muttered. The two ran as the creature blew a dart through the hole and contacted a button on the wall. All seven shields opened and a strange fog was released into the room.

"The cages are open!" Golga yelled as he tossed the counterfeit on the bed. They ran out of the room and headed towards Demon's Hole.

"Fly!" Shesla yelled as he approached Demon's Hole and jumped into the air with Golga close behind. The two were unable to flap their wings and began free-falling.

"Hang on!" Shesla shouted.

49

FUMBLING ON FLAVIUM

"My wings!" Golga shouted as the two approached level Flavium while still free-falling.

"It was the fog released by the dembots," Shesla shouted. "Keep trying!"

"It's working!" Golga shouted after several more attempts to flap his wings. "I'm okay now."

Shesla began to fly and was able to slow his descent. "It's good we got out of there when we did, or that fog stuff could have totally incapacitated us.

They two made their way to the ledge on level Flavium and then retracted their wings to avoid unwanted attention. "Any sign of Michael or Gabriel?" Shesla asked.

Golga surveyed the area. "No, I don't see them." He looked up. "I don't see any sign of the dembots either?"

"As far as I know, we lost them. Keep your eyes open."

Golga walked ahead of Shesla. "What time is it?"

"One hour until the wedding. We're on schedule."

"I'm here," Gabriel said, running toward them. "Who has the knife?"

"I do, and also the fruit," Golga said.

"Quick, cut my lightband," he asked, extending his arm.

Shesla threw his hand up. "Not yet. You have the demon's lightband which means it will protect you from the abaddonite so you can fly. Clearly, you have Beelzebub's trust to have it. Don't cut it until you reach the gates."

"You're right."

"I'm here guys," Michael said as slowly approached with a pensive look. "You ready for this?"

"Absolutely," Gabriel replied. "Why so serious?"

"Who has the fruit?" Michael asked.

"I do," Golga replied. "We left the fake one in his suite. They'll believe it's the real one, at least for a while."

Michael nodded in agreement. "By the time Beelzebub figures it out, we'll be gone."

"We may have a problem," Shesla offered. "Let's get out of sight and I'll explain."

"What?" Michael asked as the four walked toward the wall that surrounded Demon's Hole.

"We encountered dembots in Beelzebub's quarters," Golga explained. "The fruit was in one of their cages."

"To make a long story short, they escaped and may come after us," Shesla said.

"I'm sure it's been reported to Beelzebub by now," Michael said.

"But I doubt the dembots recognized us, Michael," said Shesla.

"True, but his guards will be watching and looking for activity," he replied. "We have to stay out of sight. Let's go find the girls."

Golga held out the knife. "Here. Keep it in the box until you need it."

Shesla held out his hands. "Lightbands for you and the peniels," Shesla said. "I found them in Beelzebub's suite."

"Good thinking," Michael said. "We forgot to plan for that detail."

Seven dembots landed on the ledge. "There they are!" one of them shouted, charging the four.

"Michael, go find the peniels!" Shesla shouted as he and Golga drew their swords. "We'll fight them off. Execute the plan."

Michael hesitated, unsure what to do.

"Now, Michael!" Shesla shouted.

Michael turned and ran. *How will I find the peniels by myself?*

One of the living statues threw a firenet at him, causing him to trip and fall. It shriveled into a small block. He picked it up and disappeared into an adjacent hallway.

"Stand down," Gabriel commanded the dembots.

"Shut up, traitor," one of them hissed. "Today you lose your head, watcher!"

"My cover is blown," Gabriel grumbled.

"Get behind us," Golga shouted.

"I'll fight."

"Not these guys," said Golga. "They're programmed to kill. Get behind us."

Gabriel drew his sword and stood behind the two.

"There's too many of them!" Shesla said. "Get Gabriel out of here before guards come."

"I'm not leaving you, brother."

"Go, I said! Do it for Gabriel. The peniels and Michael will need you. Go!"

"I'll come back for you!" Golga turned and rushed to Demon's Hole with Gabriel.

"Take the spiral stairs," Golga yelled.

"Let's fly!"

"We'll be seen. We'll fly when we're out of sight."

* * * * *

Twenty senior demons landed on the ledge and surrounded Shesla and the seven dembots. "Halt!" one of them commanded.

The dembots ignored them.

"They're as stubborn as Ramkrad demons and that's where they belong," another guard shrieked.

"Throw the firenets," the lead guard ordered. The guards threw firenets over the dembots. The creatures tore them off and ran off. The guards chased them. One of the dembots, the dragon, turned and blew fire, stopping burning several.

Meanwhile, the remaining guards took Shesla captive.

"Take him to Beelzebub," the senior guard commanded. They entered a room where the king of demons was being manicured, styled, and perfumed by attendant demonesses.

"Master," the lead demon called.

"Yes," Beelzebub said.

"The dembots escaped from your quarters and we found them fighting this demon on the ledge.

"What?" Beelzebub said. "All seven dembots escaped—they were secured in their cages in my private quarters? How did this happen?"

"We do not know yet, sir. Someone cut a small hole in the shield of one of the statues."

"Which one?"

"The one that looks like you, sir. We found the fruit in your suite but your knife is missing."

"Please tell me this is not happening on my wedding day!" he hollared as he rose and threw a towel from his shoulders. "You imbeciles." He pointed at one of the senior demons in the pack and fired a bolt of lightning from his finger. The sound of thunder echoed in the surrounding area as the demon was fried in place. Beelzebub breathed fire on three others. They melted into thin black snakes and slithered away in the direction of Ramkrad. The rest of the pack fell to their knees, trembling with fear.

"We almost lost the fruit, you incompetent buffoons. Do you know how important the fruit is to our plans of universe domination?

"We do, sir," one of the guards responded.

"You must not," Beelzebub retorted. "The fruit is my wedding gift to Yofiel. Search all of Darkmar with every demon if you must. *&#%X*#%*. Secure the fruit. Find the knife. Find the seven dembots!"

He transformed into a ten-foot humanoid with the head of a ram, red-glowing eyes, scaled-skin, and leather straps around his chest, legs, and wrists.

"What have you to do with this?" Beelzebub demanded as he spun on Shesla.

"Sir, I saw the dembots arrive on Flavium and I attempted to corral them."

"Why?"

"To prevent them from disturbing you on your wedding day, sir."

"What do you know about the thieves who trespassed into my suite, stole my knife, and attempted to steal my fruit?"

"I know nothing of it, Master," Shesla said. "I've been in the kitchen for days preparing the food for your wedding feast."

"Let's see, shall we? I hope your words prove true for your sake." He extended his right hand with the palm up. Smoke formed and began twirling in his hand. A three-dimensional hologram formed as the smoke dissipated revealing a video of Golga and Shesla in his quarters followed by the ensuing melee. "Why do you lie to your master, cook?

"Look at this. Another cook—your assistant, Golga. You two are thieves. Do you realize I could destroy you where you stand?"

"I do, sir," Shesla replied, hanging his head.

"Take his sword," Beelzebub ordered the guards. "Find Golga! Get the fruit!" The guards assimilated a horde of demons and flew in search of Golga.

"My protégé, Gabriel, is a disappointment," Beelzebub said. "I know you know him. My demons reported that he was fighting beside you before your capture. I had such plans for him." Beelzebub screamed with fury. "You, my friend, are guilty. My dembots are loyal creatures. I can trust them. They followed you to reclaim my knife. Tell me where Gabriel went."

"I didn't see him, sir," Shesla replied.

Beelzebub slapped him to the floor. The guards in the room pointed their spears at him. "Liar. He was with you, which means he's against me." Beelzebub snatched him up by the neck. "I should destroy you now, but I have a wedding to attend. I'll tend to you afterwards—you'll pay for your disloyalty." His eyes widened as he drew back and punched Shesla in the stomach. "Throw him in a cell until we find the other traitors!"

50

A WEDDING CEREMONY - NOT

Where could Yofiel and Tamor be? Michael searched many rooms on Flavium. *I hear noises behind that door.*

Could it be them? He cracked the door open and peered inside. *What is this place? A cathedral*? *Sure looks like one.*

There was an altar at the head of the room lined with statues of wolf creatures. The great cathedral had rows of chairs on both sides of a wide center aisle.

No doubt this is the place for the wedding. Yofiel must be close. He watched as attendant demons escorted senior demons and demonesses to their seats in preparation for the ceremony. Everyone was wearing black. The room was surrounded by red and black lifelike statues, each breathing a thin stream of fire to add to the demonic ambiance. Strings of red and white lights and black ribbons hung from the ceilings. A choir of demons played fiddles mixed with drums near the altar.

Nice setup but I feel the negative energy of the demons. He carefully pulled the door shut and continued searching.

Demonesses coming up the hall! One of them held a deep-black, strapless silk gown.

It has to be Yofiel's dress. It glittered with diamonds and droplets of gems framed in glowing yellowish-orange material.

That can't be real lava. They're getting close. He hid in another room along the long hallway and watched them pass by.

Those aren't demonesses. They're witches. He followed them along the curved hallway kissed in burnt yellow from the many torches along the way. He darted in and out of doors countersunk into the walls. The witches stopped and reached for the doorknob—it turned by itself, and the door slowly opened. The coterie of creatures disappeared as the door silently shut behind them.

Michael ran to the nearest room, touched the doorknob, and pressed himself against the wall to peek inside as the door opened. *I see nothing, hear nothing. No one's here.* He entered and placed his ear on the adjoining wall where the witches were. *Yofiel! Her voice. I found you.* He heard his heartbeat. *As soon as the demonesses leave, I'll come to you.*

He jerked his head toward the door. *What's that noise?* He dashed back to the door and peered into the hallway. The notes hung in the air like waves splashing on a beach. Tiny creatures twirled round and round further down the hallways.

Papeons! No, They're fairies. He watched as they sang and danced in the air until they were upon him. They paused to gaze at him through the door.

"I can't close the door," he muttered. *I'm frozen*! The creatures were very beautiful to look upon, like miniature angels. Their beauty and the sound of their voices were intoxicating, their iridescent wings wafting the scent of vanilla and lavender. He stared in complete stillness, mouth open, feet frozen in place.

The little fairies began to fly back from where they came, slowly at first. He took a reflexive step after them—one, then two and the next steps came easier as he began hurrying after them as if they were pulling him along. He resisted less and less, caring less and less who might see him. They lured him on, increasing their speed. The little creatures left a trail of glittering light as bright as the iridescent gems—the colors changed from white to the colors of a rainbow as they fell to the floor creating silent explosions of light.

Stop, Michael. Go to Yofiel. But the pull of desire was great upon him.

Am I so easily overcome by temptation like a human? Fight this, Michael. Don't go. Stop!

The creatures outpaced him as they flew faster and faster. They entered a room through a half-opened door with red light spilling into the hallway.

He caught up to where they were and peered inside. "Yofiel!" *Am I dreaming?*

A female wearing a form-fitting purple silk gown with colorful gems was reclined on a white velvet chaise longue. She was encapsulated in an aurora of purple light. There was no sign of the singing fairies. The smell of lavender incense filled the room. Michael hurried inside as she rose to meet him.

"Yofiel!" he exclaimed and the two hugged. "I just heard your voice in another room down the hall. How did you get to this room so fast?"

"Demonesses."

Michael hesitated. "I thought they were witches. They sure looked like witches."

"You saw them?"

"Yes, in the other room." He paused. "We need to go." He pulled her forward but she didn't budge. "What's wrong?"

"I'm to remain here. Stay with me."

"We must go now! You know the plan."

"But I'm frightened." She lay on the couch. "Hold me."

He started to lay next to her but was startled by a noise at the door.

"No!" a creature shouted, bursting into the room.

The creature wore a white robe and looked just like...

"Yofiel!" Michael yelled. He sat up and turned to the lady on the couch. "Then who are you?"

The woman rolled on the couch and transformed into an old hag with hollow eyes full of black light. Her dress changed into a damp, smelly, rotten purple rag. She reached for him. "I am Yofiel. Come to me." Her voice sounded as if several people spoke at the same time.

"No, witch!" he shouted. "Stay away from me."

The witch transformed into a female wolf-like beast with sharp teeth and red eyes and lunged at him.

He jumped from the couch but fell to the floor. "Yofiel," he yelled. "The witch has tied me to the couch."

"You'll never leave me, my little prince. You're mine now." She smiled, exposing her rotten teeth.

"I don't think so," said Yofiel. She clutched a knife on her thigh and cut him loose.

The witch jumped to her feet. "Over my dead body."

"Your already dead, witch!" Yofiel exclaimed. She retrieved the purple bottle of mercy water from Leah, removed the top, and jerked her arm toward the witch.

"What have you done, watcher?" the witch screamed, as the liquid splashed in her face and chest and began to burn. The witch pointed a crooked figure at Michael and sent a lightning bolt at him knocking him to the floor. Smoke emanated from her clothes as she began to melt. "You have ruined me, you little tramp." Little demons made of smoke appeared and began to fly around her.

"You have failed to keep him from her," hissed one of the demons of smoke.

"To Ramkrad with you!" another smoke demon screeched.

"Off with her, off with her, off with her," they chanted over and over as they flew faster and faster.

"No, no! Send me anywhere but Ramkrad! No, no!" She melted into a green pile of slimy mucus as yellowish-grey smoke rose from the muck and exploded. She and the smoke demons disappeared.

Yofiel turned to Michael who was still lying on the floor. "Michael!" She shook him but he didn't respond. She had a few drops left in her bottle and emptied it on his forehead.

"How did you know I was here?" Michael asked, coming to, and then sitting up. "We have to go."

"The witches left me and I looked out of my door to make sure they left and saw you go here. I must return before they're back." The two ran to her room.

"Nice dress. I saw the witches bring it to you. That's how I found you."

"I refuse to wear it. But I like it. They made it. So they're threatening to put it on me."

Michael retrieved it and handed it to her as her robe slid away exposing her form-fitting black pants and matching shirt. "Let's take it with us."

"I like your hair pinned up."

"I'm keeping the diamond-encrusted headband."

"Okay, so let's leave."

"I can't."

"Why? What are we waiting for?"

"If they don't find me, they'll send a thousand demons to stop us before we reach Demon's Hole. I have to put the dress on and make them think I'm going through with it."

"Yofiel, you know the plan. I'm here for you and Tamor. Give me your arm. We have to remove your lightband. I have Beelzebub's knife." He cut it off. "Here, put this on. It's a demon's lightband so you can fly. The guys will be waiting for us at the gates. We're getting out of here."

"But Beelzebub will hunt for me if I do not go to him soon. You know that, right? How can we possibly get out of here?"

"We stick to the plan. Where's Tamor?"

"In another room. They won't let me see her until the ceremony starts."

"Yofiel, listen to me. We're leaving—together. We've set bombs all over Darkmar, as we said we would. Remember our plan?"

She smiled and then retrieved a scarf out of her pocket.

"Is that the pink one I gave you?"

"Yes. Beelzebub yanked it off when I ran out of the cave. I reclaimed it from his bedroom of all places. I'm wearing it to commemorate our escape."

"That's what I want to hear."

Knock, knock, knock.

"I'm surprised they knocked. Hide. They're here to get me ready."

"Or escort you to the Cathedral. Tell them you'll agree to put the dress on but only if Tamor comes here to check you over. Tell them you want her to make sure everything is perfect for Beelzebub."

Yofiel ran to the door and spoke with the witches, then rushed back. "I can't believe it. They're going to get her. What do we do when she comes?"

"Maintain distance from the witches and stay as close to me as you can. Pull Tamor close to you. Watch for my signal."

"Okay."

Knock, knock, knock.

"That was fast. Michael, I'm scared."

"Me too." They embraced. "We'll get through this together."

The door opened. "Yofiel!" Tamor squealed with subdued joy as six witches followed her into the room. The two peniels hugged.

"I thought you said you would have the dress on when we returned." one of the witches shouted. "Get dressed now, tramp. The master waits."

"What does our master see in this skinny thing that we don't have?" one of the witches asked another. They let out a hideous, high-pitched laugh. The witches had darkened red eyes, rotten yellowish teeth, green-smoke exhaling from their mouths when they spoke and drooping skin infested with sores. Puffs of black smoke—like dark energy—emanated from their bodies as they shuffled about.

"Puny peniel watcher," another witch jeered. "Get dressed now or we'll drag you to the chapel by your long, pretty hair." They cackled and snorted.

"I should wear the dress and marry the master myself," the first witch said. "I don't think he would notice the difference." They cackled.

"You would make a prettier bride, indeed, my beauty," another replied to her.

"I would just like to have someone with teeth," another said. They laughed loudly.

"I would kiss him all night," said a witch with a long, crooked nose and a third eye on her forehead. Green tears fell from her eyes. The group cackled so hard their skin peeled and some of their hair fell out.

The peniels moved closer to a nearby couch where Tamor retrieved Yofiel's wedding dress. "Exquisite. This is a keeper."

"I love your dress. Let me look at you. Oh, a strapped, single pleated emerald-colored gown with a belt of white roses set. You are to die for, peniel. Too bad Gabriel isn't here to see you. And the diamonds pasted to your arms is a nice touch."

"I'm keeping the necklace and bracelets of painite crystals."

"Yofiel, it's almost time for your wedding. What are you going to do?

"Hurry, you little twig," one of the witches screeched. "Get dressed, or we'll do it for you. You have two minutes."

Yofiel tossed the dress on and then Tamor placed blue sapphire gem bracelets on her arms. Just as Yofiel finished dressing, Michael charged out of a closet.

"Guards, guards!" yelled one of the witches.

"I'll kill him myself," another witch hissed. She transformed into a batlike creature with horns, bristly black skin, and red glowing pupils. It threw fire at him.

He dodged it and retrieved the firenet from his pocket and flung it at them. The molten rock shot open like fireworks and wrapped around the witches. Their faces mashed together, gagging their mouths. They moaned from the heat of the lava as it melted their skin.

He removed Tamor's lightband and threw it to the floor. "Follow me," he shouted. The three ran out of the room and into the hallway toward Demon's Hole.

Beelzebub and Endor met them in the hall and blocked their escape. "Thought you would escape, did you, children?" Beelzebub snorted as his senior demon sneered. "You are quite the deceiver, Michael. Did you think I would not find out about your plot? Surely I knew you would come back for your little sweetie, delightful as she is." He glanced at Tamor. "Same can be said of you, my lovely dumpling. How does one create such works of art? Perhaps I should marry both of you."

"They are more than art," Michael said. "They peniels."

"Exactly," replied Beelzebub. "Too bad there aren't more of them in my palace. But Yofiel and I have an appointment to join our spirits together in unholy matrimony."

Yofiel frowned. "I shall never marry you," Yofiel shouted.

"So disappointing to hear you speak that way, my love," Beelzebub said. "But marry me, you shall—right now.

Speaking of disappointment, your friend Gabriel is a loser, a liar, and a traitor—a total waste of space. He shall pay dearly for his betrayal. I shalt not kill him. No. Instead, he will be kept alive and tormented in my pits of destruction for eternity."

"You evil devil!" Tamor snarled.

He ignored her comment. "And you, Michael, will join him. To be barely alive in Ramkrad is worse than death, believe me. Or perhaps I will give you to the witches."

The witches giggled as they ran out of the room.

Beelzebub glanced at Endor. "Get my bride."

"Never," Michael yelled as he stepped in-between them

Endor slapped him to the ground and then shuffled Yofiel forward.

"Send him to Ramkrad and cut him open—but let him live," Beelzebub ordered. "Keep his cell unlocked so demons may visit and have their way with him. Do the same with Gabriel when you find him. Let the roaches, maggots, and worms make their home with them."

Michael nodded at Yofiel. He got back to his feet while reaching into his pocket, then threw a bomb toward the demon posse as Yofiel broke free. Michael, Tamor, and Yofiel dove behind a statue of a serpent as the bomb exploded and filled the area with smoke. The three grabbed one another by the hands, raced past several demons discombobulated in the melee, and disappeared in the smoke.

"Get them!" Beelzebub shrieked. "Get them now!"

51

THE ESCAPE

"Stay close," Michael said to the peniels as the three ran away. "Here is an extra lightband, Tamor. Put it on. It will enable you to fly." They ran to Demon's Hole, flared their wings and leapt into the air. They flew to Tunnel of Ekron and headed towards the Gates of Darkmar.

* * * * *

"Here they come," Golga said. "But I don't see Shesla."

"I see Michael and the girls," Gabriel said, waving at them.

Magnon, one of the tyrannosapiens, spotted Michael and the peniels in the air. He roared and began throwing boulders the size of their heads at them. The watchers landed in the tunnel and ran to Gabriel and Golga, who were standing by a cave in the wall of the tunnel. Magnon charged, blew fire, and began grabbing at them as they ran inside the cave.

"Get back everyone," Golga cried. All darted behind boulders to avoid the reach of the beast.

"Where's Shesla?" Golga asked.

"I was hoping he would be here," Michael replied. "The last I saw, he was with you and Gabriel, fighting the dembots."

"Then he must have been captured," said Golga. "He told me to get away with Gabriel before the demons could arrest us."

Tamor glanced at Gabriel. "What's the traitor doing here?"

"He's with us," replied Michael.

"Always was," Gabriel said.

"He only pretended to join Beelzebub," Michael added.

"How can we be certain?" she asked.

"He's good. We can trust him."

"I want to believe it."

Gabriel smiled. "Then believe it. What I want is standing in front of me."

She smiled.

He kissed her on the cheek and the two hugged.

Magnon latched on to Yofiel's dress and started dragging her out of the cave.

She screamed and began removing her wedding dress.

Michael tossed his sword.

She caught it and dug it into the hand of the creature. The beast released her but managed to knock him against the wall.

Michael ran to him. "Are you okay, friend?"

"I'm okay."

"Thanks, Gabriel," Yofiel said. "That was close."

"Has anyone seen Shesla?" she asked.

"Not yet," Golga replied."

"We can't wait much longer," Michael.

"He's not coming," said Gabriel. "He would have been here by now."

Golga jerked away, facing the mouth of the cave, listening to Magnon still slashing about in the tunnel. "Gabriel's right. He's not coming. And we cannot go back for him either."

"We don't know where he is," Michael said.

"You're both right," Golga said. "We stick to the plan. Which reminds me, everyone remove your lightbands.

"Right," Yofiel replied.

The giants and other creatures began beating on the entrance of the cave causing a rockslide.

"The passageway is covered," Michael shouted.

"We're stuck," Tamor yelled.

"Stand back everyone!" Golga pointed his sword sending a bolt of lightning into the pile of rocks forming a small opening into the Tunnel of Ekron.

"That's another reason I want a warrior's sword," Michael whispered to Gabriel.

"Time for fireworks," Gabriel said.

"Let's do this," Michael said.

"Make it happen," Yofiel added, as she and Tamor tossed their dresses aside. They still had their black stretch pants and pull-over shirts.

"Let's get out of here," Tamor chimed.

Michael pressed the button to detonate the bombs.

Magnon and other creatures spun around as the bombs began exploding. A plume of smoke flooded Demon's Hole and rushed into all levels of the volcano. Rocks tumbled as the mountain shook. Lava spewed in random places. Crocdor and Magnon hurried to open the gates—anticipating the mass exodus of legions of demons and creatures from the underworld. In a matter of minutes, a sound like the rushing of many rivers was heard as innumerable demons and creatures poured into the Tunnel of Ekron in the direction of the gates.

"Go, go, go!" Michael hollered. "Let's get out of here before the demons get here."

"Meet on the mountain across the valley," Gabriel shouted as they ran through the dust. The five separated in a dust storm that spread beyond the gates. Explosions reverberated high on the mountain as molten lava began shooting into the sky.

A demon tackled Tamor from behind as she ran outside in the sandy wind. Yofiel jumped on his back, reached for the knife in his belt, and stabbed him until he fell.

Tamor removed his sword from his scabbard, chopped his head off, and stuck it in the sand.

Two other demons landed nearby on the ledge and spotted the peniels. The demons smiled at one another, confident the female watchers were easy prey.

Both peniels charged the demons. Tamor did a backwards flip and released the sword in midair, hitting the demon between the eyes. Yofiel ran toward the other one at the same time, spun around on his head, and sliced his neck. Both demons fell at their feet.

Michael ran through the gates to the ledge overlooking the valley. He glimpsed at Golga who was stood facing the tunnel.

"I will return for you, my brother," Golga shouted into the wind. He turned and started running toward the edge of the cliff. Crocdor saw him and sprang forward, hitting him with his tail.

Michael ran to assist but was knocked to the sandy ground by the beast. Crocdor grabbed Golga, rushed to Michael, and snatched him with his other hand. The beast held Michael high against the gate while choking Golga with the other hand.

Michael reached for his knife. *It's gone!*

The peniels spotted Michael and Golga through the dust storm and hurried to them. Yofiel struck the beast in the leg while Tamor flew toward its face and jabbed her sword into its neck. Magnon dropped Michael, released Golga, and roared so loud that the ground shook. The beast slapped Tamor against the gate and then knocked Yofiel to the ground causing her to slide across the ledge.

She lifted her head and spotted Gabriel lying face down in the sand near her. "Gabriel!"

Michael managed to lift off in the wind and fly to the steeple above the gates. He pushed on a boulder, but it wouldn't budge. Oren and his classmates landed nearby.

"You made it!" Michael shouted as the two fist-bumped.

"Barely. We almost didn't find this planet."

Michael looked at the rest of his classmates. "Thanks for coming. We need every one of you."

"We stick together," Oren replied. "Looks like you could use a little help with this rock."

"What, this little thing?"

Meanwhile, Golga hobbled in the direction of Tamor. Magnon lumbered toward yelling loudly as he neared them.

High above the gates, Michael and the others loosened the boulder from the grip of the mountain. They rocked it back and forth until finally dislodging it. It hit Magnon in the head causing the beast to stumble and fall in front of the gates.

Crocdor saw Magnon fall and charged Golga and Tamor.

Yofiel yelled as it ran by her. She saw Gabriel move. "Gabriel, Gabriel, are you okay?" She helped him to his feet. Five demons attacked the two of them. Gabriel threw a knife at one and his sword at another. The two demons disintegrated. They began fighting with the other three.

Yofiel retrieved knives from both thighs as she fought with two of them. One managed to grab her jump on her back. The second demon aimed his spear at her stomach. She quickly twisted. The spear entered the demon clutched to her back. It fell to the ground.

Tamor speared the second demon in the back and then helped Gabriel to subdue the third demon. All three demons melted into black slush.

Fierian, the dragon, flew overhead and torched Crocdor. The tyrannosapien somersaulted, landing on his feet, seemingly unaffected by the flume of fire. He threw a large stone at Fierian but missed. He hurled another rock at the trio. It glanced Yofiel's shoulder, knocking her face down on the sandy ledge.

Several apelike demons came alongside Crocdor and hurled spears at the three of them. One caught Tamor in the midsection. Golga rubbed his eyes. "Tamor!"

Eyes wide, she fell into his arms.

"Tamor," Yofiel yelled, running up to them. "No!" Yofiel and Golga held her and then gently lay her down. They watched as Tamor's body turned into sparkling glitter. The outline of her body reached for Yofiel and the two joined hands until she was carried away in the sandy wind.

* * * * *

"I'm going to find the others on the ledge," Michael said to Oren. "Meet us on the mountain across the valley. We need you and the others to fend off the demons coming out of the tunnel."

"Will do," Oren said as he and the others took off.

Michael flew to the ledge and could barely see in the dust storm. The sand ripped at his eyes. He saw Gabriel, Yofiel, and Golga fighting demons and joined them. Together they fought their way closer and closer to the edge. But a whirlwind separated the four of them.

Beelzebub stormed out of the gates with several of his senior demons and spotted Michael. He flew to him, knocking him to the ground. Michael stood and wiped the sand from his eyes in the howling wind. Fierian screeched above as its shadow penetrated the dust and swept across the ledge. Fire from the dragon's mouth destroyed a troupe of demons with each pass.

"I've had enough of you, child warrior," the king of demons roared. "You've wreaked havoc in my home. Today I shall slice you to pieces and spit your into the bottomless pit." Beelzebub pulled his sword and leveled it at Michael's midsection as it lit on fire.

Michael started to unsheathed his sword but the old demon knocked his sword toward the cliff before Michael could get it.

Michael rolled on the ground and grabbed a stick.

"Am I a dog that you come at me with a stick, you little soldier of your cursed king? You stole my bride, destroyed demons, and freed Ramkrad creatures. You have created a mess of my empire.

"I will put it back in order—I guarantee it—and you'll suffer for each rock I put back in place. You'll live in eternal agony for this. I'll soon bring all my demon army against each outpost and take them over, one by one—I will find a way. I will have Yofiel for my wife. Mark my words, watcher. Now come to me and I'll feed your body to Fierian and let him excrete you out at the opposite end."

"You come at me with your mighty sword of fire, but I fight in the name of the king of Krystar," Michael roared.

"I shall do to you as I did last time but much worse, you little dung."

I must hit him early—he doesn't know that Shesla and Golga taught me how to fight. I must surprise him.

Beelzebub approached. Michael struck at his side but he deflected it, barely.

"Oh, so you learned a new move did you?" the king of demons hissed. "My turn."

Beelzebub lunged forward. Michael dodged and struck him in the shin while the demon elbowed him in the head. Michael stumbled.

A huge molten boulder fell from the mountain, startling Beelzebub. The rush of a million demons finally reached the gates and began spilling out onto the ledge. Giant spiders hidden in the dust storm picked some off as they ran about.

Michael lunged at Beelzebub, who managed to thwart the incoming strike. But the impact caused Beelzebub to drop his sword.

Michael threw a small pocket bomb toward Beelzebub.

The king of demons rolled away in the direction of his sword and retrieved it.

Michael spotted a bow and arrow in the sand, scooped them up, and shot it.

The demon caught it with his hand and then threw a ball and chain back at him. It wrapped around his leg, causing him to fall.

As Michael stood, the demon charged and struck him in the face with his fist.

Michael fell on his back but quickly rose.

Beelzebub swung with his sword but Michael dodged and struck the demon in the head with the stick. The demon fell back, dropping his sword in the sand.

Beelzebub hefted a spear and started to ram it into Michael.

Yofiel fired an arrow that pierced the demon's hand.

Beelzebub pulled the arrow out, tossed it aside, and shot a lightning bolt at his would-be bride. It knocked Yofiel to the ground.

Michael charged the demon but several demons landed between them. Michael snatched Beelzebub's sword and ran toward Yofiel. A tornado of sand and fire tumbled across the ledge and separated Yofiel and Michael from the demons, some of who were flung into the valley by the wind. Michael and Yofiel ran toward the ledge.

"After him," Beelzebub yelled. Twelve demons gave chase.

A demon threw a spear in Michael's direction but missed. Another shot an arrow just as the two unfolded their wings and leapt into the air.

The arrow skimmed Michael's side. He knocked an arrow into his bow and let it fly. It pierced the demon in the throat and it fell into a stream of lava. Michael flew caught up with Yofiel. A demon standing on the ledge aimed an arrow but was consumed by Fierian who passed overhead. Michael and Yofiel were soon separated in the smoky, sandy sky.

Oren and the others shot arrows of fire at the pursuing demons. Many demons were struck and disintegrated in flight. The wings of Michael and Yofiel caught on fire and they tumbled to the mountain across the valley.

Thousands of other demons continued fleeing through the gates. Some were consumed by spewing lava, some by the rocks falling from the skies and others by Fierian and the spider creatures. Some of the demons fought other demons out of the mass chaos brought about by the sand storm.

Golga landed on the mountain across the valley where Oren and the others were. "You guys made a big difference. Thanks for coming."

"Absolutely," Oren replied. "I can't tell whether the demons are pursing you guys or fleeing the volcano or both. It's a chaotic mess of lava, sand tornados, and demons."

"True," Golga replied. "I can barely see anything. Have you seen the others yet?"

"I saw Michael but he left to fight on the ledge and we flew to this position to get ahead of you guys." Oren and the others continued to spray the sky-bound demons with flaming arrows.

"Glad to see you two," Gabriel said to Michael as he and Yofiel landed. "We lost you in the sand storm."

"I had a date with Beelzebub," Michael said. "We fought. He got away but I got his sword."

"Excellent," Gabriel said. "Do you know what that means?"

"No. what?"

"You just accomplished the command from the vision. You have the sword of darkness."

"You're right. I'll show it to Uriel and Caleb when we arrive."

Gabriel looked around. "Where's Tamor?"

Yofiel teared up.

"What's wrong?" Gabriel asked.

"We lost her. We lost her. We're so sorry, Gabriel. We lost Tamor."

Gabriel hugged her.

Michael put his arm around his shoulders. "I'm sorry, brother." He turned and watched as Yofiel walked away and stared over the valley. He looked toward the gates of Darkmar and saw Beelzebub staring back.

Several demons charged the watchers from the sky. Michael, Gabriel, Golga, Oren and the who team shot arrows and fought them off. One of the demons caught Michael from behind. Yofiel ran up and stuck a knife in its back. The demon disintegrated.

"Thanks, Yofiel."

Some of the dragons made several passes and blew fire. The team took cover behind the boulders on the mountain.

"We must leave now," Michael said. "We can't hold off the few we've seen and more will come. They'll flood the sky like ants on the ground."

"You guys go," Oren shouted. "We'll cover you and catch up."

"Agree," Golga said. He was the first to leave.

"Yofiel," Michael shouted, jolting her out of a trance. "We must go."

52

THE REUNION

Michael, Gabriel, and Yofiel jumped from the cliff and flew into the sky behind Golga. A band of demons flying in air spotted them and began shooting flaming arrows and hurling firenets at the fleeing troupe.

Golga looked back and saw what was happening. He extended his right arm with his palm facing the pursuing demons and launched a shockwave. The demons were knocked unconscious and some fell into the valley. He shot lightning bolts that exploded, annihilating others.

A horde of more demons chased the group as the fled in the sky. Fierian was joined by Poquim in attacking the continuous stream of demons as they rushed through the gates and leapt off the ledge into the air. Thousands more were fried in the air. Some of Michael's classmates were destroyed as they flew from the mountain.

Michael and the others stopped at the sound of a trumpet blast. "Look, the demons are returning to the volcano."

"Great," Yofiel said. "That means they're no longer chasing us."

"They look like a swarm of wasps returning to their nest," Gabriel added.

Michael waved. "Here comes Oren and the others."

Oren and the surviving team pulled up next to them in the air. "What's with the trumpet blast?"

"Beelzebub is calling his army back to Darkmar," answered Michael.

"He knows it pointless to pursue us," Gabriel said.

"And he knows the real battle will be when he and his army decides to attack Krystar," added Golga. "Let's get out of this place."

"Agree," Yofiel muttered. The group sped away through Darkmar's atmosphere, through the dark matter hiding the planet and entered the starry space where they flew faster than the speed of light. They headed toward an area where the cave was last seen.

"There's the blue spiraling fire," Golga said, pointing.

"And the cave," Gabriel added.

They landed on the ledge and walked inside toward the glowing pearl. Michael opened it and they entered Kanah.

Golga kneeled and kissed the ground.

"Why did you do that?" Michael asked.

"It's good to be back."

All of them took to the air and flew to the city of Kanah.

Uriel and Caleb met them at the east gate with Tamor standing beside them.

"Tamor!" Yofiel said, rushing to her. "I'm so sorry you were hurt."

"My spirit returned to Krystar and I was recreated."

"We're glad you're back," Gabriel added, joining the two. "I'm sorry I failed to protect you."

"All of us did the best we could," replied Tamor. "Things happen in battle."

"Welcome to Kanah, everyone," Uriel said. "Great job. Your mission was a success. The Council is aware of your arrival and is assembling to meet with all of you. We will meet you there."

Caleb gave a thumbs up to Michael and Gabriel. "Welcome home, warriors."

The streets were lined with watchers and angels who waved and cheered as they passed by. Streets and buildings were strewn with banners of congratulations and signs of welcome. Some signs read "The Fantastic Four" for Yofiel, Tamor, Michael and Gabriel; other signs read "The Super Six" to include Shesla and Golga. Another sign read, "Welcome Home Little Warriors," referring to Caleb's entire class of student warriors.

Uriel and the other Council representatives stood and applauded as the entourage entered the Council room. Uriel remained standing when everyone took their place. "We are glad to have each of you back, and for Michael and Golga completing the mission. The fruit of the Tree of Life has been returned, and Gabriel, Yofiel, and Tamor are home. We welcome you back to Kanah." The Council rose again as everyone in the room clapped.

"I would like to recognize some of you individually. Welcome home, mighty master warrior Golga. You are hereby promoted from master warrior to senior master warrior." Thunderous clapping and shouting erupted when Uriel made the announcement.

"Where is Shesla?"

"He was captured during the escape. Gabriel and I were fighting by his side, inside Darkmar, during the escape when he told us to flee so we could help the others to escape. My brother sacrificed his freedom for us."

"He did a brave thing," Uriel said. "That's exactly what I would have expected him to do. You would have done the same."

"I would."

"Do you have the fruit from the Tree of Life and the counterfeit, or does Michael have it?"

"I have the real fruit, sir. We left the counterfeit in Darkmar."

"Well done, soldier," Uriel said. "Did Beelzebub handle the real fruit himself?"

"He did, sir. And he regretted doing so as you can imagine." Golga opened the backpack, retrieved a pouch, and uncovered the fruit. Everyone clapped.

Uriel smiled and nodded to the rest of the Council. "Excellent. Place it into the truth-flame."

Golga hesitated.

"We must validate its authenticity, Michael."

Golga placed it on a stand inside the ring of the truth-flame, and it floated upward and hovered just above the stand. It glowed brighter and brighter until it lit the whole room.

"The real fruit floats and glows in the truth fire, as you see," Uriel said. "Now hold it and tell me if you feel anything."

"I feel something beating within." He handed it to him.

"Yes, like a heartbeat." Uriel handed it to a guard. "It's the heartbeat of life." He held it out toward a nearby soldier. "Return this to the garden."

"Yes sir," the guard replied.

"Thank you, Golga," Uriel said. He eyed Michael. "Welcome home and come forward, Michael, mighty watcher. You are hereby awarded the angel warrior's sword of fire." All rose and cheered. Sensei Caleb came forward and presented the sword.

As Michael gripped the handle, the blade lit on fire and his name glowed in the ricasso like molten gold.

"Sir, during our escape, I battled Beelzebub and managed to acquire his sword. May I unsheathe it, sir?"

"Congratulations, Michael," Uriel replied. "No warrior of the king has ever captured Beelzebub's sword. You have done well, young watcher."

“If I may also inform the Council, I received a vision instructing me to get the sword of darkness. This is the sword.” He unsheathed it and held it out. “Did the vision command me to get it?”

“Some watchers have been known to receive visions as part of their training experience at the academies, though not all do. You will never receive a false vision. So be sure to follow the directive but do not broadcast their message since they are meant for you.”

“Yes sir,” replied Michael.

Uriel looked at the other watchers. “Welcome, mighty watchers Gabriel, Yofiel, and Tamor. Please come forward.”

"This Council believes a senior angel should have been notified of your plans to leave Kanah in search of Michael on earth. You jeopardized your safety and the safety of the peniels. Nevertheless, you—all three of you—are commended for your desire to help your friend. You have demonstrated maturity beyond your years. But your actions resulted in serious risks to yourselves, as evidenced by your ensuing capture and imprisonment on Darkmar. It also presented risk to our outpost if the demons were able to gain a military advantage with the fruit from the Tree of Life.

“However, this is a day of celebration. No consequence will be levied upon you, young watchers, in light of the bravery you displayed. Welcome home.” All in the room rose and applauded.

“Come forward, Oren, please. You, Oren, as well as your classmates and all watchers before this Council who participated in the battle of Darkmar will be awarded the angel lightband. It will include a single red stripe to acknowledge bravery during wartime conditions on Darkmar. We have never seen such a display of commitment to one another within a single class in the history of this academy.” Everyone in the Council room stood and applauded.

Michael ran to Yofiel and hugged her. “Can you believe it? I have the warrior’s sword.”

She beamed a smile. “Let’s celebrate.”

"Gabriel, I want you to have my warrior sword."

"No. It's yours. Thank you, brother. I cannot accept it. But I appreciate the thought."

"You don't understand. I wouldn't be here today without you. I know what you did. We stay together, we fight together and we have each other's back no matter what. We are friends and brothers forever. Take my sword and hold it until both of us are promoted to the rank of angel. We will take possession of our warrior swords together. Please."

"For you, I will," he said.

53

THE DANCE COMPETITION

After three days of celebration with the citizens of Kanah, Michael, Yofiel, Gabriel, and Tamor joined Hadessah and two other couples at the theater to practice dance routines for the Krystar Dance Competition.

"Oh, dears, we missed you so," Hadessah said as they approached. "I am so glad you are safe. Welcome home. Congratulations, Michael, on getting the angel's sword of fire and to all of you for being awarded an angel's lightband. I can only imagine the horror all of you experienced all these months. If you do not wish to participate in the dance competition, I understand."

"What?" Tamor asked. "We need to attend the Gala of Kanah after being on Darkmar—if we still have the opportunity.

"We need to work the stress off," Gabriel said.

"I'm not sure we will ever get over what we went through," said Michael.

"Some things you never get over but you'll get through it," Hadessah said with a big smile. "And yes, you still have the opportunity, though the rest of the team is well ahead of you. They can practice on their own now. So I can dedicate myself to you four. Rehearsal continues first thing in the morning. Do you want to be competitive, or do you just want to enjoy the experience of participating?"

"Hadessah, we dance to win," Michael replied. "With all due respect, we need to work as hard as you're willing to work us since the gala is in six days."

"Dancing is to the soul what medicine is to the body," Hadessah replied. "If we do this my way, then there are no breaks at all until three hours before the Gala and we start now."

"Let's do it," Tamor insisted. The others nodded.

"Do you think we can be competition-ready in such a short time?" Yofiel whispered to Hadessah.

"Oh, girl, yes," Hadessah said.

* * * * *

Teams began arriving at the Coliseum of Kanah from the other six outposts the day before the Gala. The stadium was a semicircular arc structure made of moonstone that glowed like a full moon on a cloudless night. It towered above the dancefloor made of blue Benitoite gems that looked like a sea of glass that glowing with fire—a flame would appear upon contact with a dancer's foot. The blue sky of Kanah canopied above the coliseum as combinations of aqua, purple, green, yellow, and red auroras danced in the air.

Flowers we here, flowers were there, were everywhere. Even the trees grew flowers in their branches. Rainbows were aflame and dropped colored fire that dissi-pated in the air. Waterfalls adorned the walls of the coliseum. Inside, floating spinning stars bubbled over with molten lava that transformed into butterflies of light. Dance teams from all seven outposts took turns practicing but left out the some parts of their routines to keep them secret for the gala.

The day arrived for the three-day event to begin. All guests and dancers entered the coliseum and took their place. The sky over Kanah appeared dark blue. The Gala of Kanah opened with "The Sky of Kanah" presentation. Flares shot into the air from all directions and exploded into many colors and shapes generating a choreographed symphony of sound with two- and three-dimensional images. Laser lights complemented fireworks with musical notes.

After the presentation, the seven dance teams were introduced and then took to the floor for their opening dance. The female dancers wore colorful gowns that glittered with diamonds and precious gems of many colors—the gowns and the gems glowed in unison with their team music. The visiting male teams wore formal black or midnight blue dance attire.

The coliseum had Four-Dimensional Shared Virtual Space (4DSVS) technology that allowed each spectator to magnify or pull images close in for viewing. The judges were composed of seven angels—one from each outpost.

The competition continued with each team taking the floor one at a time. Team Kanah, as the host team, performed last each day. Rumors of their dance circulated in the coliseum—everyone was curious to see it. Each team performed various dance routines over the three days. On the last day, all teams entered the dance floor and danced in one synchronous ensemble.

"I am beside myself with excitement," Hadessah said to Caleb.

"Oh, that explains my double vision," Caleb joked. "I see two of you."

"Oh, stop it," she said. She saw Golga smiling at her from across the dance floor and waved.

The time finally arrived for Team Kanah to perform their dance. The dance was introduced as "The Dance of the Papeons" and represented a composite, small-group, single-couple-led dance performance.

The dance began similarly to the flight pattern of the papeons as seen by Yofiel and Tamor in the fields of Kanah. The male Kanah dancers wore coats of many colors that shined like stars;

the ladies wore rainbow-colored gowns with sparkling gems and glowing strings of light all over their bodies and wings. Each couple leapt effortlessly into the air in a single file and flew in a slow-motion, helical pattern, revealing curved motions of grace in perfect rhythm to the music. The papeon mirrored them as they danced.

Routines in the air were followed by floor routines to mimic the smooth, circulating, sweeping movements of the papeons. They repeated the dance patterns with increasing speed and tighter turns as they flew around like a rollercoaster leaving a trailing of glowing glitter in the air. Accompanying pipe music and rhythmic drumbeats intensified as the dance progressed.

Spectators began swaying and dancing back and forth to their movements. Even Hadessah began shaking her hips. Caleb and Uriel laughed as they saw Golga mimicking Hadessah's moves. The dancers flew closer and closer to one another. The routine ended with the partners floating to the floor with foreheads on one another's shoulder as the papeons disappeared into the horizon behind the stage. Everyone gave Team Kanah a standing ovation, much louder and longer than they had for the other teams.

The team dances were followed by freestyle dancing of all twenty-four teams on the floor at the same time. The judges observed all dancers though it was not a judged dance. As the end of the competitions drew near, the judges invited all spectators to join the dancers on the floor. Dancing continued for hours.

At last, the dancing stopped in anticipation of the judges' announcement of the winning team. The seven judges walked to the center of the dance floor.

"The winning team for the Gala is Team Kanah," one of the judges announced. Team Kanah hugged one another and was immediately swarmed by the other teams. Hadessah made her way to the floor. Team Kanah lifted her into the air and flew over the other teams on the dance floor.

"Congratulations, Hadessah," each member of Team Kanah said as they landed on the floor. "We did it."

"You watchers and peniels did it," she exclaimed. "Teamwork prevailed

"Did you expect anything less?" Golga asked. The two embraced.

Everyone laughed.

* * * * *

"I have a surprise for you," Tamor told Gabriel on the evening of the last day of the gala.

"What is it?"

She unwrapped a basket, revealing a multicolored, one-foot-high cake. "Are you ready for a picnic?"

"Absolutely," he said with a smile.

* * * * *

Michael and Yofiel strolled through the streets of Kanah the next day and stopped at their favorite café. Michael retrieved a little white box from his pocket and placed it on a table in front of her.

"This represents our adventure," he said.

"What is this?" she asked. She opened the box. "Oh, beautiful, Michael—a gold locket in the shape of the fruit from the Tree of Life. Thank you."

"Open the locket."

"Oh, a pink diamond floating inside."

"You did say pink is your favorite color."

She smiled.

About Author

Kevin Spinks was born in Jackson, Mississippi in the United States, raised in Columbus, Georgia, and now lives in sunny Jacksonville, Florida close to the beach with his lovely wife, Sandra. He's an award winning author who enjoys making memories with family and friends by visiting exotic and interesting places on the planet. He's a graduate engineer of the George Institute of Technology and also earned a business degree at the University of North Florida and an MBA degree from Nova Southeastern University. He worked in the military defense industry making fighting vehicles and in the commercial industry making airplanes. He became an engineer like his dad who worked in airports, but his love for God and books came from his mom who would always take him and his three sisters to church and to the library. He rode dirt bikes as a kid and later with his two sons. He enjoys reading, working out, and volunteering with his church for community projects including hurricane disaster relief. When his sons were young, he would tell them imaginative bedtime stories like his dad before him. So it's no surprise that this story is about heavenly and demonic creatures in the unseen realm of make-believe places.

You may contact Kevin through his website: www.kevinspinks.com.

ACKNOWLEDGMENTS

The joy of writing your first book and thinking you're done is short-lived when you discover something referred to in the industry as "the rewrite." I thank my editor, Carol Gaskin (Editorial Alchemy), for teaching me how to write when I already thought I was good at it. She could have sent me packing, but instead demonstrated incredible patience and skill in reviewing the pile of words to help turn them into a recognizable story. It's like when a skilled artisan chisels away at a block of wood to reveal a thing of beauty. I brought the wood and she uncovered any beauty that it may have contained. I took her suggestions and revised the novel again and again, so any errors in the first edition are purely my own.

Melana Cassell graciously edited the second edition of the book since I made many changes after publishing the first edition. She saved me more work than she'll ever know for authors are often blind to their own writing mistakes. Thank you so much sweet sister!

Kim and Jovana and their team at Deranged Doctor Design (DDD) did a superb job on the book cover. I described young archangel Michael and they brought him to life and made him dazzle. Thank you!

Finally, thanks to my lovely wife Sandra who patiently endured my seclusion as I typed away for endless hours and then would suddenly appear to ask tons of questions to get her thoughts and ideas on the scenes and characters.

www.ingramcontent.com/pod-product-compliance
Lightning Source LLC
LaVergne TN
LVHW041113080826
845145LV00007B/1797

9781737446002